CRITICAL PR.

RUTH AXTELL
MORREN
LILAC SPRING

"*Lilac Spring* blooms with heartfelt yearning and genuine
conflict as Cherish and Silas seek God's will for their
lives. Fascinating details about nineteenth-century
shipbuilding are planted here and there, bringing an
historical feel to this faith-filled romance."
—Liz Curtis Higgs, bestselling author of *Grace in Thine Eyes*

"Morren's engrossing style is sure to please her readers as
well as win over new fans. This pleasing saga has likable
characters and just enough tension to
satisfy gentle romance enthusiasts."
—*Library Journal*

WILD ROSE

Selected as a *Booklist* Top 10 Christian Novel for 2005

"The charm of the story lies in Morren's ability to portray
real passion between her characters. *Wild Rose* is not so
much a romance as an old-fashioned love story."
—*Booklist*

"A beautiful, believable love relationship… Richly defined
characters and settings enhance this meaningful novel."
—*Romantic Times BOOKclub*

"An uplifting and spiritual tale of small town life in
turn-of-the-century New England. *Wild Rose* is a
gentle, but poignant offering from Ms. Morren and
proves that she is an author to watch in the coming
months. This is a book you will not want to miss!"
—*Romance Reviews Today*

WINTER IS PAST

"Inspires readers toward a deeper trust in the transforming power of God.... [Readers] will find in *Winter Is Past* a novel not to be put down and a new favorite author."
—*Christian Retailing*

"Ruth Axtell Morren writes with skill, sensitivity and great heart about the things that matter most....
Make room on your keeper shelf for a new favorite."
—Susan Wiggs, *New York Times* bestselling author

"Faith journeys are so realistic, all readers can benefit from the story. Highly recommended."
—CBA *Marketplace*

RUTH AXTELL
MORREN

Dawn in My Heart

Steeple
Hill®

Published by Steeple Hill Books™

If you purchased this book without a cover you should be aware that this book is stolen property. It was reported as "unsold and destroyed" to the publisher, and neither the author nor the publisher has received any payment for this "stripped book."

STEEPLE HILL BOOKS

Steeple
Hill®

ISBN-13: 978-0-373-78567-4
ISBN-10: 0-373-78567-4

DAWN IN MY HEART

Copyright © 2006 by Ruth Axtell

All rights reserved. Except for use in any review, the reproduction or utilization of this work in whole or in part in any form by any electronic, mechanical or other means, now known or hereafter invented, including xerography, photocopying and recording, or in any information storage or retrieval system, is forbidden without the written permission of the editorial office, Steeple Hill Books, 233 Broadway, New York, NY 10279 U.S.A.

This book is a work of fiction. The names, characters, incidents and places are the products of the author's imagination, and are not to be construed as real. While the author was inspired in part by actual events, none of the characters in the book is based on an actual person. Any resemblance to persons living or dead is entirely coincidental and unintentional.

This edition published by arrangement with Steeple Hill Books.

® and TM are trademarks of Steeple Hill Books, used under license. Trademarks indicated with ® are registered in the United States Patent and Trademark Office, the Canadian Trade Marks Office and in other countries.

www.SteepleHill.com

Printed in U.S.A.

For Mora,

Without you,
I'd still be waiting around, hoping to be published…
Without me, you'd be…

Well, God knows…

Here's to obedience and discipleship.

Chapter One

✧

London, 1814

Tertius Pembroke, Fourth Earl of Skylar, observed his future bride across the drawing room.

"She's a comely lass, isn't she?" his father, the Marquess of Caulfield, asked in the false hearty tone Sky recognized as the striving-to-please one when he wasn't at all sure his news would be well received.

When Tertius said nothing, his father went on. "Look at that porcelain skin, those exquisite arms, the dainty turn of her ankle." He was positively gushing now.

Sky surveyed Lady Gillian Edwards, determined to find some fault with his father's choice. He took a critical appraisal, from the crown of her brunette curls cut in the latest short fashion to the tips of her silver slippers.

What he found in between was in no way displeasing. Pale skin delightfully tinged pink at the cheeks bespoke untouched innocence. A pleasant tinkling sound reached his ear when she laughed at what the young dandy beside her was saying.

Comely indeed, he thought, noting the even white teeth.

"A true English rose," his father added.

A low-cut evening gown revealed a creamy bosom. There was nothing inordinately immodest about the fashionable neckline, just enough to whet a man's appetite. A silver ribbon cinched in the high-waisted white gown.

"Well, haven't you anything to say?" his father demanded. "Didn't I tell you I'd picked the best for you?"

"So you did." At that moment, the young lady's glance strayed to him. The two stared at each other across the room. He weighing, judging. She caught in midsmile, a smile that slowly died as it wasn't returned, and she stood transfixed, as if uncertain what to do next.

Then the moment passed. His father nudged him on the elbow. "Come, Tertius. I told the duchess we would be here this evening to present you to her daughter."

Skylar made no reply, having become resigned if not wholly convinced of his duty to marry and produce an heir. He'd made it clear to his father earlier that he would commit to nothing until he'd seen the young lady.

"Duchess." Bending over her hand, his father greeted the stately woman seated near her standing daughter at the opposite end of the drawing room. "Delighted to see you. As always, you are looking more splendid than all the ladies present."

His father's eloquence grated on Sky's nerves. He, in turn, bowed over the duchess's gloved hand.

"Lord Skylar, my youngest son. It has been long since you last met, nigh on ten years, I believe."

"Lord Skylar." The Duchess of Burnham gave Tertius the barest nod while directing her comments to his father. "I remember. He was making his mark here in London." The elegant, middle-aged woman appraised him. "You are much changed, my lord."

Sky knew the words were *not* a compliment. "The tropics," he replied. "They either kill you or leave you a wrecked shell as you see me now." He gave a thin smile, having learned it was better to preempt an intended insult by stating it plainly. That usually gained one a temporary advantage.

"You have my deepest condolences on your brother's demise," the duchess said in the silence.

Skylar inclined his head a fraction to acknowledge her remark. He took time to observe his future mother-in-law. She was perhaps in her late forties or early fifties, her beauty skillfully maintained with the aid of cleverly applied cosmetics, her honey-hued hair not revealing any gray.

He gave his attention to her daughter. Lady Gillian was petite, brunette to her mother's fair hair and, not quite as slim but shapelier than her mother, dressed in white muslin adorned with silver ribbons. Up close she presented even more distinctly the picture of youthful innocence than she had from across the room. Her pink cheeks contrasted prettily with her dark hair. Her neck, slim and pale, led the eye downward to the creamy expanse of shoulder exposed by the wide scalloped neckline.

She did indeed appear to be of superior quality. Trust his father to choose well. As the marquess had described her, she was "exquisitely fashioned, in good health, untouched."

In short, all the endowments required in a wife of a peer of the realm.

His father beamed at him. "What do you think, Sky, isn't Lady Gillian a pretty lass?"

"She'll do," he said, wanting as always to put a damper on his father's perpetual good humor.

He hadn't noticed the color of Lady Gillian's eyes until that moment, but as she turned their dark-lashed focus on him, he was struck by their pale green. Wintergreen, he thought, taking in their icy hue, rimmed by a dark spruce. She looked as cold as an icehouse, he thought, comparing her to the warm, honey-toned women of the Indies, with their open nature and easy embraces.

Knowing it was up to him to initiate the act of courtship, he asked her, "May I entreat you to take a turn about the room?"

She gave a slight bow of her head. Like mother, like daughter, he thought, comparing her condescension with the duchess's.

He held out his arm and she placed her hand around it, barely resting her weight upon it. Slowly they promenaded the long, guest-filled drawing room, as his father's voice trailed after them. "See there, what a handsome pair they make." He could be speaking of a matched set of bays. "I knew they would be agreeable to the arrangement."

Sky led Lady Gillian about the room as the tinkling strains of Telemann vied with the babble of voices in the background.

The top of her head scarcely reached his shoulder. She was looking away from him, and he realized she hadn't looked at him since that first straight-on stare.

He had no clue how to court a young lady of the ton. He hadn't even done so back in his days as a young buck in London society, preferring the company of tavern wenches. And now it had been at least a half dozen years since he'd said anything meaningful to a young chit barely out of the schoolroom.

He cleared his throat. "Is this your first season?"

"No, my lord," she replied, not deigning to turn toward him.

"Your second?" he asked blandly.

The deep-fringed eyes stared up at him. "It's my *third*." The tone dared him to make anything of the fact.

Something about her haughtiness impelled him to bait her. "Hanging out for a title?"

"Putting off the state of matrimony as long as possible."

He raised an eyebrow. "I thought a young lady's sole ambition was to make a match approved by society?"

"If there were a worthy candidate, I might have changed my mind." When he continued studying her, she said, "It appears you have avoided the state longer than I. How old are you? Forty? And still not wed?"

"I'm sure the duchess has made you aware of my five-and-thirty years," he said, irritated that he felt the barb.

"Painfully," came the acid reply.

Wondering at her animosity, he said, "I have not 'avoided' the state, as you misjudge. In my case, there was no undue hurry. I was not in search of a fortune or anyone's good name to improve the Caulfield line. That responsibility rested upon my elder brother's shoulders. I could take a more leisurely approach to matrimony. A young lady hasn't that luxury. Her bloom quickly fades and soon she is what the gossips term 'on the shelf.'"

"I can assure you, my lord, I am far from on the shelf!" The hue of her cheeks deepened. "I have had plenty of offers, but I, too, could afford to wait. Just as you, I have no need of someone else's title or fortune."

"It appears we are well suited then. We should be grateful for our parents' having taken the trouble of the selection of partner out of our hands."

When she made no reply, he mused, "Three seasons… Aren't you concerned the gossips would have commented on you by now?"

She flashed him a look of anger. "I had no need to be! My mother has been very particular of whom she has allowed to pay court to me. When your father approached her, she viewed your suit favorably."

"How fortunate for me."

"As my mother has pointed out, apart from our difference in age, we are social equals in every way."

She feigned a cool facade, but contained some fire in her, he thought in grudging admiration. Beneath that exquisite bosom beat a proud little heart—perhaps as proud as his own. At least he wouldn't have to worry about diluting his bloodline with inferior stock. "We should suit admirably by all conventional wisdom," he concluded.

Her dark eyebrows drew together in a slight frown. "As to that, I have no opinion. I trust, as is customary, we shall each go our own way once we are wed."

"Do you?" he murmured. "That depends," he added softly.

She disengaged her hand from his arm and turned to face him. "Lord Skylar, I think we should be clear on this point. I have agreed to this betrothal because, as my mother has so sensibly explained to me, you are Lord Caulfield's heir, which means I stand to become the Marchioness of Caulfield someday. Apart from your advanced age, you possess all the qualities suitable for a good match." She gave him the same kind of appraising look her mother had. "In short, my lord, *you'll do.*"

Ah. Comprehension dawned. He had offended the chit and now she was striking back. She had spirit, and he liked that. Better than a simpering deb.

He smiled at her. "And did your mother further explain that, together, we need to produce one healthy male heir— a feat my dear, departed brother Edmund, for all his other accomplishments, was not able to achieve. What think you? Shall we manage it?"

She seemed unfazed. "It remains to be seen."

"I would say, rather, it remains to be done."

Her color rose to her already rosy cheeks until it suffused her whole face and neck at this direct reference to their marital duties. Tertius was almost sorry he had spoken so quickly, but he needn't have worried. She rallied admirably.

"You, my lord, are disgusting." With that pronouncement, she wheeled away from him and marched back toward her mother.

The next morning, Gillian paced back and forth in her bedroom. Her opinions about the insufferable man she had been introduced to the evening before had not changed overnight. Each time she thought of his words "she'll do!" she was outraged afresh.

"Mother, he's ghastly! You can't make me marry him."

Gillian stopped in front of the chaise where her mother lounged in her embroidered silk dressing gown.

She shuddered at the memory of Lord Skylar's supercilious way of looking down at her from his great height while he pronounced some shocking statement in that lazy drawl. And that last ungentlemanly remark! Oh, it didn't bear thinking on!

"Don't speak nonsense," her mother replied, examining her buffed nails in the morning light. "Lord Skylar is the best catch of the season now that he's inherited his brother's title."

"Well, let someone else have him…if they can stomach his company," she added under her breath as she resumed her pacing. She shook her head at the sprigged muslin her maid held out to her.

"He's positively gothic. He reminds me of some creepy villain with those black eyes and hair and those gaunt cheeks. When he looks at me, I feel as if he sees right past me."

"It's a pity Lord Skylar doesn't have his brother's looks," her mother conceded, "but he's just got over a terrible fever. Who knows what malady a person can pick up in the Indies? But after he's been in London a few weeks, he'll put on some weight and be in the pink of health, just in time for the wedding, you'll see."

"I doubt his manners will improve on further acquaintance." Gillian stopped long enough to remove her dressing gown and allow the maid to help her into the jaconet morning dress in pale green with the rows of pink ribbons along the hem.

"Oh, come, he was perfectly amiable to me."

"He might have behaved so with you, but with me, he was most provoking."

"Then you must exert yourself to be extra charming," her mother replied.

"It will take every ounce of my resolve, which I confess isn't any too strong at this moment," she added, tapping her foot impatiently as the maid laced up her gown.

"The fact remains, it's time you were wed. Don't forget you'll soon be twenty-one and that bloom will fade."

She glared at her mother. Had she and Lord Skylar been consulting together? Gillian went to her dressing table and studied herself in the glass as her maid brushed out her hair. She'd always been considered pretty. More than pretty. Maybe it was her nose, not aquiline but a trifle pert, or her eyes, not a deep emerald green, but that washed-out shade she wished in vain leaned a trifle more toward blue.

She'd always thought her coloring good. Now she wondered if her cheeks weren't too red.

As her maid arranged her hair into ringlets around her forehead and temples, Gillian looked at her in the glass. "Maybe we should try it away from the face today," she suggested, pulling the side curls back.

"Lord Skylar's is the kind of offer we've been holding out for," her mother reminded her from the chaise.

"*You've* been holding out for," Gillian corrected.

"Many a young girl has fared much worse in a choice of husband. You should be thanking your lucky stars old Lord Caulfield saw fit to approach us with this offer. As I said, you need to be married before you're any older. It's time you began setting up your own household."

Her mother came to stand beside the maid.

"What do you think?" Gillian asked her mother.

The Duchess of Burnham smoothed back an escaping

curl before nodding her approval. "It is simple, as is befitting a young lady."

As the maid stepped away, Gillian's mother placed a hand on her shoulder, her tone gentling. "You'll soon see the advantages of being a matron over a debutante. You'll have a freedom to come and go that you haven't heretofore known." She smiled. "If someday you meet a gentleman more to your taste, with your sensibilities…" She shrugged. "With a little discretion, you can enjoy the kind of romantic love you foolishly dream of now."

Gillian's further protests were stilled by her mother's words. She shivered. Why did it seem her life was ending before it had scarcely begun? Would she never have that fulfillment she read about in romantic novels—that she'd scarcely tasted before it had been snatched from her? Would the only avenue that remained to her be to hope for some furtive alliance sometime in the distant future? She considered the ladies she read about in the society news. Lady Melbourne and her daughter-in-law, Lady Caroline, women who were known for their lovers, and she wondered sadly if that was the only future left to her.

She thought of the pimply faced dandies that had surrounded her at every dance since her come-out and compared them to the ideal she'd been dreaming about and waiting for for so many years. A handsome, manly officer coming back to claim her as his own.

She sighed, dispelling the futile dream. Yes, she was ready for marriage. She needed a change. Too many years spent waiting…waiting for someone she was now resigned would never appear.

Her mother patted her hand as if reading her mind.

"What you need to think about is your wedding trousseau. We shall begin making purchases immediately. I shall have Mme. Rouget stop by and measure you for your wedding gown. How fortunate for Wellington's victory. Think of all the Paris fashions now available.

"Come, let us look at the spring edition of *La Belle Assemblée*. It's full of all the latest French gowns and bonnets. Since our glorious army has driven Napoleon off the Continent, everything has a military flair." Her mother held out the magazine to her. "Look at this riding habit with the frogged neck and epaulets.

"You must have half-a-dozen new ball gowns at least. You'll no longer be limited to white muslin but can be much more daring in your selections."

The thought was enticing. Gillian moved closer to her mother to look at the colored illustrations.

"You'll need a whole new wardrobe as the Countess of Skylar. Think of the estates you'll be mistress over. I imagine Lord Skylar will be purchasing his own residence in town and not expect you to live with Lord Caulfield, although his mansion on Park Lane is quite stupendous."

As her mother talked on, flipping through the pages of the magazine, Gillian managed to forget her initial encounter with the cold, rude Lord Skylar and focus on the advantages of life as a young society matron.

The rest didn't bear thinking on. Her mother wanted her married by the end of the year. A good six months away. There was plenty of time to enjoy being betrothed to one of the most illustrious names in the ton without dwelling too much on the wedding night.

* * *

"What the deuce were you thinking of, Tertius?" His father paced the confines of Sky's dressing room as Sky finished his toilette. "From what the duchess tells me, the girl is balking at the marriage. Don't you know how to woo a lady? Who were you living among, a bunch of wild savages in the Indies?"

Sky opened his eyes and glanced at Nigel, his valet, who was shaving him. "No, there was your usual small, tight coterie of the well-bred. I wouldn't call them all savages, would you, Nigel?" He arched an eyebrow at his valet as the man wiped his jaw clean and handed him a glass.

"No, sir," the black man answered, holding out a starched muslin square of cloth for his approval.

Sky lifted his chin as the man wrapped it around his neck and began the intricate work of folding it.

"Well, whatever they were, you're back among the civilized and grateful you should be. You at last have a purpose in life, thanks to poor Edmund's demise."

Tertius frowned at his father's waistcoat. "You know, I never liked puce on you. It makes you look bilious."

His father looked down at his middle, momentarily distracted. "No? Weston himself made it up for me." He walked to Sky's full-length mirror and stood in front of it, his head tilted to one side, his hands pulling the waistcoat straight. He moved his body this way and that before turning back to Sky. "The color of my waistcoat is neither here nor there. To get back to the point, all I want is for you to exert yourself, make yourself tolerably agreeable to a lovely young lady of irreproachable pedigree—"

Tertius snorted. "Who has been thrust upon me as soon

as I set foot on British soil, my newly inherited title not even having a chance to settle on me."

His father sputtered. "That's gratitude! I find you a perfectly suitable young lady to wed. I've already lost one son. I'll not let the other go without issue. You're five-and-thirty, Tertius. You look closer to the grave than Edmund ever did."

"I said I'd marry the chit," Tertius returned in an even voice. "What more do you want?"

"A little cooperation. You appeared long after Edmund's funeral," Caulfield retorted. "You come back surly and disagreeable and looking like a victim of typhus. You can't make me believe it was such a sacrifice for you to pull yourself away from the Indies. It certainly hasn't done anything for you."

"Oh, I don't know." His cravat finished, Sky stood and eyed it in the glass. "I had quite a comfortable life on my sugar plantation."

His father harrumphed. "Tending a plantation in the backwater of the kingdom, a job any good steward could do?"

Tertius's glance crossed Nigel's before his valet began silently putting away the morning's toilet articles.

"Well, what do you think, Father? Has Nigel mastered the *trone d'amour?*" He turned for his father to inspect the white neck cloth.

His father stepped closer and peered at his neck. "Not bad. Nigel, is it?" For the first time since entering his rooms, his father gave his attention to the manservant. "Got him in the Indies?"

"It would appear so," Sky replied.

"Don't be impertinent. Almost everyone these days in London has a blackamoor footman—but this is the first time I've seen one for a valet. Did it take you long to train him?"

"Nigel was an amazingly quick study," Tertius drawled. "From the cane fields to the intricacies of folding white linen, in what? Six months, Nigel?"

His valet's muddy green eyes met his. "Yes, sir, that would be about the time."

"What a fine specimen," his father remarked, as he took a turn around the West Indian. "Look at that brawn. He'd make a fine boxer. He reminds me of Cribb. I saw him spar it out with Tom Molineaux back in "10." Lord Caulfield stood in front of Nigel and eyed the breadth of his chest. "Your man makes 'the Black Diamond' look like a dwarf. Sure you wouldn't want to put him in the ring?"

"He's played Apollo for me at an evening's festivities, but I haven't as yet had him take up pugilism. It's an idea…" Sky mused.

"Apollo? Why not Atlas?" Caulfield asked, continuing to admire the valet's physique. "I imagine he looked splendid draped in a white toga."

"Splendid indeed. I chose Apollo because of the loftiness of his thoughts. Atlas represents brute strength, and I believe Nigel has a bit more than that in his skull, eh?" he asked his valet with a smile before turning to shrug on the coat Nigel held out to him. He took his watch and fobs from him, along with a pocket-handkerchief.

"Thank you. You may go," he told Nigel.

Lord Caulfield waited until the servant had left the room carrying an armful of linen. "Now, back to your affianced. You must make yourself agreeable. Take her out for a nice ride in Hyde Park. There are a dozen victory celebrations planned with Wellington's arrival. The first thing you can do is meet her at Almack's tonight and pay her court."

Tertius stopped listening to his father's instructions. Instead he thought about the young lady's angry tone and frosty green eyes. He admitted how deliberately unflattering his remarks had been. She'd had a right to take offense. He had nothing against her personally. If he was easily irritated, it wasn't due to Lady Gillian Edwards.

"Very well, Father, I shall see her tonight and endeavor to 'woo' her as you so quaintly put it."

Tertius scanned the company assembled in Almack's ballroom. Things hadn't changed much in his ten-year absence, he concluded as he took in the assortment of muslin-clad young ladies, most in white bedecked with pastel ribbons and flowers, standing amidst the gilt columns, their mamas and chaperones closely in attendance. The young misses simpered at the young gentlemen hovering around them. His attention went to the dancers and he finally spotted Lady Gillian. She was in the middle of executing a *tour de main* with her partner in the quadrille.

"She's a dandy little filly," his longtime friend, Lord Delaney, opined, quizzing her through his glass.

"She's accomplished in the quadrille, at any rate," observed Tertius dryly.

"From what I hear, she'll bring you ten thousand per annum. It makes little difference, in that light, I suppose, how well she dances," Lane added with a chuckle.

"She strikes me as a bit lively." Tertius narrowed his eyes, watching Lady Gillian laugh and bat her eyelashes at her dance partner.

"A tremendous flirt," Delaney informed him.

Tertius's frowned deepened.

"But no one has ever been able to take the least liberties with her," his friend added hastily, "on account of the dragon lady."

Tertius raised an eyebrow in inquiry.

Delaney nodded across the room. "Miss Templeton. See the dark-haired lady with the pursed lips?"

"The one who looks as if she's swallowed sour wine?"

"The very one. That's Lady Gillian's companion. She appeared soon after her first season, and she hasn't let Lady Gillian out of her sight since then."

Tertius felt a twinge of pity for the young lady if that disagreeable-looking lady was her watchdog. Miss Templeton looked like the typical spinster past her prime. "Let me guess, she's probably a distant relation living out some cheerless existence on too little."

"Yes, who knows where the Duchess of Burnham found her, but she never hesitates to tell anyone willing to listen how she is accustomed to better things. I believe she's a third cousin to the late Duke."

It crossed Tertius's mind to wonder how Lady Gillian would behave once her bodyguard were removed.

"Lord Skylar!" a lady exclaimed. "When did you arrive back in town?"

"Lady Jersey." Tertius bowed over her kid-encased hand. "The prodigal has returned, as you can see."

"My, yes." She stood at arm's length, surveying him. "It has been years that you've been away."

"A decade, to be precise."

"A decade!" Her eyes opened wide. "You were a young

man about town then, quite a rake as I recall. So, you have come from making your fortune in the Indies, I presume?"

He sketched another brief bow. "That was the purpose."

"Dear Lord Caulfield was at his wits' end, I recall." She peered at him more closely. "I don't know how that climate across the Atlantic agreed with you. You're awfully brown and thin."

He shrugged. "The sun is to blame for the one and a plaguey fever for the other."

She patted his hand. "London will soon put you to rights."

"One can but hope."

"Well, I trust you will find some pleasant amusement here tonight. Still unmarried?"

He nodded. "A state shortly to be remedied."

Lady Jersey, smiling delightedly, asked, "Is that what brought you here tonight? What think you of our pretty young ladies? There will surely be one to catch your eye."

"One already has."

"Oh, I'm all aflutter with curiosity. Tell me who it is, and I shall arrange an introduction."

Things had certainly not changed at Almack's. "In point of fact, my dear Lady Jersey, the introductions have already been effected. Our two families came to an understanding ere I set foot on British soil. It but remains for the betrothal to be announced."

Her mouth formed a small circle of astonishment. "Oh, my. When is the good news to be made known?"

"Within the week, I'm certain. Apropos of it, I would crave your indulgence on something touching this engagement."

"Oh, yes, tell me." Her eyes lit up in anticipation that she would be privy to some inside information.

"Since the young lady and I are already promised to each other, I would like to ask your permission to dance the waltz with her."

Her mouth formed another O as she blinked at him. "Oh, dear Lord Skylar, we do so frown on the waltz. There's been a mania for it ever since the Czar danced it here earlier this month. We could hardly refuse *him* permission. But we don't encourage it. I know it is danced all over the Continent, and at private dances in town, but we have always tried to maintain a certain standard of propriety at Almack's. We've only just introduced the quadrille this season. We are the upholders of the highest decorum for the young ladies who are presented every season, you understand."

"I understand," he interjected smoothly when it was apparent she would continue in this vein. He smiled his most charming smile. "But seeing how my betrothal to *Lady Gillian Edwards* will shortly be announced, I can see no harm in indulging us in this one dance."

"Lady Gillian?" Her eyes grew wide at this piece of information.

"Yes, though I know you can be trusted to be discreet about the betrothal until it is officially announced."

"Oh, of course. You can trust absolutely to my silence."

Knowing it would be all over town before another day had passed, he pressed his advantage. "So, my lady, will you favor me with this request?"

She pursed her lips and made a few sounds of debating with herself. Finally she drew herself up. "Very well, I suppose a waltz with Lady Gillian wouldn't be improper under these circumstances. But only one, mind you. There will be talk. I must go and explain to the other patronesses why I have given you my leave." She gave him a conspiratorial smile. "I shall even request that the orchestra play a waltz after this set."

He bowed.

By this time, Lady Gillian was standing along the wall, surrounded by a gaggle of overly refined young dandies, from what Sky could judge. He ambled over, Delaney at his side congratulating him on his smooth handling of Lady Jersey.

When Sky arrived behind her flock of admirers, he stood a good half-head above them, so he could observe Lady Gillian easily.

"Oh, Pinky, you mustn't be so naughty. You know he can't help who his tailor is," she remonstrated with the young man nearest her. The others chuckled.

One by one they fell silent as they noticed Sky's presence. He didn't look at any of them but approached Lady Gillian as a path opened up in front of him. He bowed over her hand. "My lady, would you honor me with this next waltz?"

Her mouth dropped open at his request before she snapped it shut. She removed her gloved hand from his in what struck him as a studied gesture. "I must decline as I have not as yet been given the nod from the patronesses to dance the waltz."

"But I have." Fixing his eye on the so-called Pinky, an effete-looking young man with too much pomade on his hair, Sky quelled him with a mere look as he opened his mouth to speak. Then he turned his attention back to Lady Gillian. With a deliberately imperious gesture, Sky held out his arm as the first strains of the waltz began. Silently she placed her gloved arm in his.

The two walked onto the dance floor, where Tertius took her in his arms and began to lead.

"However did you get permission from one of the patronesses? They are notoriously strict, you know."

The two glided smoothly over the dance floor. "I told Lady Jersey as you and I were to be leg-shackled, I could see nothing objectionable to a waltz. I think the value of the gossip I gave her overrode any hesitation on her part."

Although he had said this with a perfectly straight face, he could see the smile tugging at her mouth at this last piece of information. She had beautiful lips, he conceded, full and rosy. "Haven't you obtained the nod from them as yet?" he asked.

"Goodness, no. They dislike me. I think they consider me too forward."

"Are you?"

She flushed and turned her face away from him. "They are a bunch of old ladies who wield absolute power in their little kingdom." She shrugged. "They are entirely too full of their own importance. I have danced the waltz on many occasions at private balls."

"You dance well."

"Thank you, my lord." Gillian gave him a slight inclination of her head, to show the compliment pleased her. Her dislike lessened a fraction. She had been impressed by the way he had silenced all those silly young boys surrounding her. And he did dance smoothly. He was too austere for her taste, however. During the entire dance, she felt as if she were being observed through a quizzing glass.

As the music played, she wondered idly what it would take to get such a man to fall in love with her. She hadn't a clue, she admitted, observing his dark features. His hair and eyes were nearly black, the hair a trifle long, raked back against a high forehead, his skin unfashionably dark.

With no conscious thought, she compared him to another dark-haired gentleman she'd known. The likeness ended there. The two were nothing alike, either physically or in their character.

She pushed aside the memory and focused on her dance partner. She had never known a man so completely insensitive to her charms. Since her come-out, she was accustomed to receiving praise, if not always in speeches, then certainly in the flattering looks directed her way. Young gentlemen flocked around her to pay her court. They laughed at her sallies and wrote odes to her.

She couldn't imagine this man behaving in such a manner. His less-than-complimentary assessment of her still rankled. As the dance continued, the idea of contriving an infatuation on his part continued to grow. How would she go about it?

At that second his gaze met hers. She couldn't read anything in it but indifference, before it strayed beyond her. Once again, she felt her annoyance grow. He could at least have given her a smile.

In half a year, she would be wed to this stranger.

She shuddered inwardly as the full implications gripped her.

She blinked, erasing the image that filled her mind, and set her mind to thinking of the beautiful trousseau she would have and the new measure of independence that marriage would give her. No longer would Templeton dog her every footstep or frown in disapproval at the least action.

Life as the Countess of Skylar was a step upward, she reminded herself. She wouldn't think about the other aspects of it. Or about the colossal obstacle she'd have to surmount in order to arrive there.

As soon as the dance ended, Lord Skylar took her back to her companions. Miffed that he hadn't even expressed the desire to dance another set with her, she removed her hand from his as he bowed.

"I shall come by and collect you tomorrow afternoon for a drive around the park. Is three o'clock satisfactory?"

Did he think her acquiescence was to be taken for granted just because their two families had agreed on their betrothal? Did it imply she was not to be won? "I must check my engagement book," she told him haughtily.

His eyes narrowed. "As I am your intended, I believe I take precedence over any other engagements. I suggest you clear your calendar for my invitations."

She cocked an eyebrow. "Do you?"

"If you prefer we not see each other until our wedding day and bed a stranger that night, be so good as to inform me. I can find suitable occupation and companionship until then, I assure you."

"You are insulting!" she said through stiff lips.

He gave her a thin smile. "But nevertheless honest. Until tomorrow afternoon then?"

Leaving her no chance to reply, he turned and left.

Chapter Two

Lord Delaney approached Tertius as soon as he saw him alone.

"Well, how goes the courtship?"

Tertius hid a yawn behind his gloved hand. "Normal, I expect."

"I must say you make a fine couple." He cleared his throat. "You haven't taken it amiss your father's ordering you to marry and choosing your bride for you?"

Sky shrugged. "As long as my affianced has received the proper upbringing and is a virtuous young lady, the two of us should make out tolerably well together."

Lane smiled. "You can rest easy on that score. Lady Gillian is a diamond of the first water. Your father has chosen the best of the season's crop."

Sky's lip twisted. "I'm sure that was no hardship for him. Women are his specialty."

Delaney laughed. "Lord Caulfield is an expert in the field of beauty and wit." He rubbed his hands together. "Speaking of which, the evening is still young. What say we leave this establishment and find greener pastures?"

Sky raised an eyebrow at his friend. "What had you in mind?"

"Since you've been away from London so long, why don't we start by getting you reacquainted with some of the—er—delights of town?"

"The only delights I recall are waking up with my head about to split open like a ripe melon and going to my father like a young whelp, begging him to cover a debt of honor incurred the night before."

Lane chuckled. "London hasn't changed much, but I trust you have. You are a man of means. You don't have to go to your father anymore, do you, to cover your gambling debts?"

"That is one thing that has changed for the better. I also know how to hold my liquor," he added as the two headed out of the ballroom.

"I have the most delicious thing to show you."

"Yes? Whereabouts?"

"Drury Lane." He removed his watch. "We're in time for the second show. Come along. You shan't regret it."

Once seated in Lord Delaney's box at the theater, Sky observed that the earlier show had been a performance of *Richard the Third* with Kean. He would have preferred seeing the debut of the actor who was causing such a stir on the London stage to the farce being enacted now.

"See, what do you think?" his friend asked him, leaning forward in his seat.

Taking up his opera glasses, Tertius regarded the players on the stage. He lingered on a pretty actress before replying to Delaney. "The one playing the maidservant?"

"Isn't she divine? Look at that leg, that shapely calf!"

"Yes, she is the handsomest of the lot," he said, continuing to eye the young woman who was retorting to a male actor. As she swiveled around, he gave her a slap on the backside. The crowd roared with laughter.

"Handsome? She's beautiful. A goddess."

Tertius nodded. She was beautiful, even beneath her painted face and atrocious wig. He recognized the classical features. Suddenly she looked straight at him and acknowledged his scrutiny with a saucy wink before performing a pirouette away from his end of the stage. He could say the wink wasn't meant for him for all the attention she paid him after that. But he knew it was real. He had enough experience to know.

"I tell you," Lane waxed on, "I shall have her before another fortnight is out. She has been holding off, but she won't be able to resist me much longer. Everyone in town is vying for her affections. I have sent her flowers, candies, baubles. Yesterday, I sent her a pair of silver bracelets. I promised their duplicate in gold the day she allowed me to visit her after a show."

"Has she replied?"

"Not yet. But I expect to receive word any night."

"Well, let's hope your gifts are not in vain."

Lord Delaney's hopes were not dashed. Before the end of the last act, a young errand boy delivered a note to his box. He smiled slyly at Sky after reading it.

"We are requested the pleasure of Miss Spencer's company backstage after the performance."

When the actors had given their last curtain call, Tertius followed Delaney along the dim corridor, as they wended their way past actors, stagehands and props. At the dressing-room door, the stagehand knocked and called out, "Your visitors, Miss Spencer."

"Send them in."

"Those dulcet tones, music to my ears," Delaney murmured.

The small room was crammed with costumes and various other paraphernalia ranged along the walls. Sky shoved aside a silken garment to station himself by the door.

Miss Spencer swiveled about on the stool in front of her dressing table. Her amber locks tumbled behind her shoulders. She was draped loosely in an embroidered silk dressing gown.

"Good evening, Lord Delaney. Who is your friend?" she asked, her gaze lingering on Sky. He stared back at her until she gave him a coy smile with her carmine-red lips.

"This is the Earl of Skylar, lately arrived from the Indies. He was bowled over with your performance and threatened me with untold dire consequences if I didn't escort him to meet you."

"Indeed? We couldn't permit that." She held up a slim, white arm, allowing a pair of silver bracelets to fall from her wrist to her forearm.

"You flatter me with sporting so trifling a gift," Delaney responded with a bow. "May I say your performance was magnificent tonight?"

"You may," she answered, her focus on the worked bracelets. Suddenly she yawned, a large gaping yawn. "I'm famished. Would you care to escort me to dinner?"

Sky watched his friend's unfeigned delight and anticipation. As she motioned the two of them to have a seat on a damask settee, she rose slowly and made her way behind a dressing screen. Lane lounged on the settee while Sky remained where he stood. He listened to their conversation as he watched the silk robe being tossed onto the top of the screen.

When Miss Spencer reappeared, she looked like a proper English lady in a long-sleeved muslin dress. Delaney helped her on with her cloak and together they went out to Sky's carriage. At Miss Spencer's request, he gave his coachman directions to the Shakespeare.

Despite the late hour the chophouse was full when they arrived.

"All the theater crowd comes here," she told them, "but the owner always has a place for me." They followed a waiter to a snug table by the mullioned windows. Golden candlelight glowed in the reflection from its uneven surfaces. The room was redolent with the smell of grilling meats and tobacco smoke.

They were soon served thick steaks smothered in oyster sauce and pots of porter. Sky relished each savory bite. For weeks he hadn't been able to tolerate any but the blandest soups and broths during the last bout of fever. He shoved aside the memory, not wishing to dwell on the long, terrible ordeal, only relieved it was over.

Miss Spencer frequently waved to or called out greetings to fellow theatrical acquaintances.

When their main course had been cleared away, they

enjoyed an apple tart. The actress listened tolerantly to Lane's flattering remarks but mainly treated him with careless disdain.

"What brings your friend back from the Indies?" she asked Delaney with a sidelong glance at Sky.

"A death in the family," Sky replied before Lane could speak.

"Oh, dear, not close, I trust?"

Sky cracked a filbert and offered it to her. "A brother."

"The eldest," added Lane. "You see before you the new Earl of Skylar."

She took the nutmeat from Sky's palm. "I see a gentleman of few words but deep thought."

"And very deep pockets," Lane added with a laugh.

She joined in his laughter. "Tell me, how is the theater in the Indies?" she asked Sky directly this time.

He shrugged. "Not to be compared to London, by any means."

"Is there a chance for a working girl like me?" she asked.

"I think a girl of your talents would have a measure of success anywhere she chose to reside."

"A measure only?"

"That probably depends on the efforts she puts forth."

"I'm a very hardworking girl."

"I'm sure you are."

"My dear Miss Spencer," Lane said, bringing her attention back to himself. Sky watched his friend strive to engage her, wondering if this young woman was anything like the series of dancers his father had enjoyed over the years of Sky's youth. He hadn't been back long enough to know whom his father was currently involved with.

Sky had discovered long ago his sire was a very private man. He wondered if there was anyone privy to all his secrets.

Sky had hardly seen his father. When the marquess wasn't at the races, he was at the gaming table or at someone's house in the country round about London.

The three of them lingered over their table until two in the morning. When at last they rose, Sky gave instructions to his coachman to drop off Miss Spencer first at her residence. She gave him a very pointed look of open invitation, but he ignored it.

When she had left them, Lane closed his eyes and leaned his head back against the seat. "Have you ever seen such an exquisite complexion? And those eyes, they make you feel either you can conquer all or that you're the biggest imbecile she's ever come across."

Sky had to chuckle at that. "She is, after all, an actress."

"Ah, her talent!"

Sky hadn't actually seen her act, merely prance across the stage, but he didn't point this out to his enamored friend. He shifted against the squabs, feeling a vague discomfort. He had already begun to feel it in the restaurant, but now it grew stronger. The meal had obviously not agreed with him.

Just a bout of indigestion, nothing more. Probably bad oysters. He refused to think it could be anything else.

Certainly not a recurrence of the fever that had almost killed him.

"Pity you shall soon be leg-shackled, although I think Lady Gillian is a wonderful girl." Lane gave a deep sigh. "But I wouldn't want to miss the delights of a Miss Spencer." He grinned wickedly at Sky in the darkened coach interior. "Of course, after a suitable period, the proverbial honeymoon, you can always keep an eye out for another such morsel."

"Except for the fact I'm one of those who believes in the exclusivity of marriage."

"What? You mean keeping one's marriage vows?"

Sky pulled aside the curtain, not caring to enter into a discussion on his views of matrimony.

"Oh, come on, man, show me one London couple who keeps their vows after, say, five years of marriage."

"I daresay one would be hard-pressed," he admitted.

"Is this some West Indian custom you've picked up?"

Sky breathed in deeply, hoping that would ease the queasiness stirring in his stomach. "Let's just say I would want to know my heirs are my own."

Lane nodded. "Of course. But say after a time, once your lineage is secure…"

"There's a small matter of pride. If I can't satisfy my bride, I probably deserve to be cuckolded."

Delaney laughed. "If only more gentlemen held that viewpoint."

They fell silent as the carriage crossed Haymarket. Then Lane ventured once again, "What if, despite everything, your wife should stray?"

"Well, let us hope my marrying a young lady of high birth who knows little of the world will give me someone innocent enough to conform to my way of thinking."

Lord Skylar appeared at Lady Gillian's residence promptly at three o'clock the next afternoon. Gillian saw him descend from his curricle, hand his tiger the reins and give him some instructions, before striding toward the front steps. She sat ensconced in a comfortable chair at her bed-room window, having retired to her room with a book at half-past two and neglecting to mention to her mother that Lord Skylar would call.

Twenty minutes went by before she received a summons. During that time, she had paced and stopped in front of her full-length mirror a half-dozen times, wondering why her absence hadn't been noted sooner.

She smoothed down the jonquil-yellow lawn dress and re-adjusted the moss-green ribbon tied under the bodice, knowing the colors enhanced her complexion and dark hair. Giving herself one final look in the glass, with a quick rear-ranging of her curls, she left the confines of her room.

She could hear voices through the drawing room door. Quietly she opened it, wanting to observe before being ob-served.

Lord Skylar sat forward on the striped settee, with his hands upon a cane, directing himself to Templeton. He looked perfectly at ease chatting with her.

"I know precisely what you mean," he said to Gillian's companion in an understanding tone. Gillian stared from his benign demeanor to her tormentor's parched features, which reminded her of a desiccated fish. Templeton coughed and reddened, stammering something in reply. It was probably the first time someone had agreed with her on anything.

Her mother sat across from them, regarding Lord Skylar with an interested smile.

"Ah, there is Gillian at last," she declared, turning to her.

Lord Skylar rose in a leisurely fashion and gave her a slight bow. "Good afternoon, Lady Gillian."

He wore black, and she realized he was still in mourning

for his brother. His appearance continued to unnerve her, those dark looks deepened by the dark garments he wore.

She gave him a brief nod. "Good afternoon."

He waited until she had seated herself as far away from him as possible before taking his seat again.

"Lord Skylar has requested your company for a ride around the park. He was hopeful to find you at home today. I told him of course you would be available to him at any time. He has but to send round a note."

Gillian gave Lord Skylar a tight smile, conceding him the victory. At least he hadn't given her away. "Lord Skylar did mention paying a call this afternoon. It must have slipped my mind."

"Slipped your mind!" Templeton's disapproving tone intruded. "Good gracious, my lady. You have better manners than that. You owe Lord Skylar an apology."

"She owes me nothing. I have found her at home and that is all that is required," he drawled, returning Gillian's smile with one of his one.

"I believe a ride is a delightful idea. It will give the two of you the chance to get better acquainted with one another," put in her mother. "It is such a lovely afternoon."

"As you wish, Mama."

Lord Skylar rose again. "Then, as we have the duchess's permission, I suggest we depart." He approached her chair and held out an arm. "Shall we?"

As they were leaving the room, she turned toward her companion. "Aren't you coming with us, Templeton?"

Her mother answered for her. "No, my dear. Since you are taking a drive with your betrothed and his groom, you have no need of Templeton."

Gillian blinked at her mother. Before she could say anything, Lord Skylar led her out the door.

"Don't forget your parasol and shawl, my lady," Templeton called out.

Gillian was too amazed at her sudden freedom from Templeton to be aware of Lord Skylar handing her up into the close confines of the curricle. As he took the reins and whip from his tiger, she unfurled her parasol in the open carriage, aware all the while of how closely she sat beside him.

She watched his gloved hands as he maneuvered the curricle around the crowded square and was forced to concede he was a competent whip. He skirted the crested coaches parked in front of the stately residences while avoiding the oncoming vehicles clip-clopping toward them.

"You have a fine pair of grays," she commented once they were away from the crowded streets of Mayfair and approaching the green expanse of Hyde Park.

"I can take no credit. They were Edmund's. Not the pair that killed him," he added.

"I'm sorry. It must pain you to think about your brother…the suddenness of the accident."

"By the time I was informed, he was long dead and buried, but yes, it still came as a shock. I never expected him to go in quite that manner. An overturned coach…a broken neck… He was still in his prime and always had a strong constitution. I'd always expected him to live to his nineties."

"You must have looked up to him," she commented, wondering how it felt to suddenly inherit the place of an elder brother and heir. As an only child herself, she had always thought it would be nice to have a brother or sister, someone to turn to and confide in when there was no one else.

Lord Skylar glanced at her before fixing his attention back on the congestion in front of the park gates. "Everyone admired Edmund."

She glanced at his profile. The words were spoken as a statement of fact. Before she could comment further, she noticed they were passing the gates without turning in. She sat up. "Where are you taking me?" she demanded as they continued down Knightsbridge.

"Oh, to a little farmhouse in Kensington Village," he drawled, not taking his eyes off the crowded thoroughfare. "I thought I'd make love to you all afternoon and then return you to your mama in time for tea."

"Turn this vehicle around immediately!"

He grinned wickedly, sparing her only a glance, and she realized her mistake. She sat back and fumed. "That's not amusing."

"My apologies. You are easily repelled by any mention of the physical aspect of our relationship. It seems to bring out the worst in me. I ask your pardon."

Instead of replying to him, she craned her head around to take a last look at the park gates and gave a little sigh of regret.

"I hope you're not too disappointed with the change in plans. I have found the park choked with traffic. They've turned it into a veritable fairground since the victory," he said in disgust.

She turned back to settle in her seat. "I have scarcely seen the celebrations. Mother shares your opinion and deems it best to avoid the crowds."

When he made no comment but continued, focused on the road, Gillian fell silent, deciding to make the most of the outing. Tilting her head back, she breathed deeply of the warm June air, which was filled with the smells of vegetation from the park alongside and baked pastries from a nearby hawker selling meat pies. The sharp tang of leather from the curricle's seat reminded her of drives with her father.

She wished anew they could ride in the park, where her acquaintances might see her in this smart vehicle. It was well sprung and polished to a brilliant shine. Her hands caressed the supple leather seat. What a difference from riding in the closed landau with Templeton.

Suddenly, she laughed, looking upward past the leafy trees to the powder-blue sky and soft white clouds beyond.

Skylar gave her a brief look. "Enjoying yourself?"

"Freedom from my jailer."

"The redoubtable Miss Templeton?"

"The very one."

"If I had to select a companion to guard a young lady's virtue, I do believe I would have chosen Miss Templeton."

Gillian gave him a sidelong glance. "She has been my shadow for the last three years."

"Tell me," he asked, stepping up their speed as the traffic thinned, "are you in need of such an assiduous guard?"

Her smile disappeared and she looked away. "It is Mama's desire to protect me. That is why I was astonished she let me go on this ride without Templeton."

"Your mother trusts the contract drawn up between our solicitors. She knows the Pembrokes won't renege on an agreement once they've given their word. What transpires between now and the wedding date does not unduly concern her."

"Since you are going to behave with absolute propriety, I

suppose Mama's trust is not misplaced," she answered with a firmness she was far from feeling. When he gave her no such assurance, Gillian turned to study the scenery along the Kensington Road.

She decided she would enjoy her outing and not let Lord Skylar's unusual manner unsettle her. He was a gentleman, otherwise her mother would not have agreed to the match. She must believe that.

When they arrived in the village of Kensington on the outskirts of London, he took her to a small tea garden set in the middle of pastures where cows grazed peacefully. Gillian looked about her in delight at the quaint establishment surrounded by flowering gardens. Small round tables covered in pretty linen tablecloths were set up both in the main dining room and out in the gardens.

She readily agreed when he suggested they sit outside.

"Mmm." She inhaled the fragrance of moss roses, pinks and sweet pea growing in a profusion beside their table.

He helped her into a chair, and a waitress brought her a glass of lemonade and a pot of tea for him. Sky asked her to bring them a selection of their cream-filled pastries.

"What a charming place. I've never been here before." Gillian looked at the man seated across from her, against the backdrop of flowers, the drone of bees and the twitter of birds. "It's not the sort of place Mother would frequent." Nor you, she added silently.

"I'm glad it's still around. I have scarcely had a chance yet to explore all my old haunts. My mother would bring me here as a boy when I was home on holiday. I used to dream of the syllabub made with their cream."

She eyed him, finding it hard to imagine this austere

looking man clad in black ever being a little boy craving sweets.

"These look scrumptious," she said, preferring to turn her attention to the fruit tarts heaped with whipped cream the waitress set before them. She put one on her plate.

"The place is famous for its cream and butter," he explained, nodding to the cows grazing in the lawn beyond the garden. "I don't know how much longer it will be around. Everyone prefers Vauxhall, from what I hear."

Her eyes lit up. "How I'd love to go there!"

He raised an eyebrow. "You haven't been? In all your three seasons?"

"Mother thinks it vulgar. She believes it is only a place for the lower classes to go for their trysts."

He sat back, crossing his long legs, his fingers playing idly with a teaspoon. "Some would say the same thing of tea gardens. We have the place practically to ourselves. The lower classes must indeed all be at Vauxhall."

She looked around at the airy yet intimate surroundings. It did seem ideal as an out-of-the-way place to meet a sweetheart. Her thoughts went unbidden to other times, times she thought long dead and dormant, when she had been desperate for such a place. She turned her attention to the pastry in front of her. She was in a different position in life now. Older. Ready for a home of her own.

She took a bite of the warm tart and savored its buttery crust and rich custard hidden by the sweet strawberries and fresh cream atop it.

"You're not having any?" she asked with a glance at his empty plate.

He shook his head. "You go ahead."

"I should think you could use some of these pastries," she commented, remembering her mother's mention that he'd been ill.

"Are you of the opinion as most that I am in need of 'fattening up'?"

"You are quite thin. Is that just natural or—or…" She hesitated.

"Have I been ill?" he finished for her, taking a sip of his tea.

"Mother mentioned something of it."

He nodded. "Yes. I was ill." He did not elaborate. After a moment, he asked her, "Tell me, Lady Gillian, what do you expect from this marriage?"

She washed the taste of strawberries and cream from her mouth with a swallow of lemonade and set down her glass, wondering at the directness of the question.

When she didn't answer right away, he said, "Come, you agreed to this arrangement between our parents. Despite all their interests in our union, I don't believe your mother would force you against your will. You have seemed less than willing up to now."

"Well, that's due solely to your—your somewhat less than gentlemanly manner."

"I was somewhat caught by surprise by my father's announcement. I had no more stepped off the ship than he was insisting on my marriage. I beg your pardon if my manner has offended you. I was still adjusting to the notion of having my bride already picked out for me."

"You objected to the match?" she asked curiously. "You've reached your majority. Surely your father can't make you marry someone you don't know."

He leaned back in his chair and focused his gaze on a fat

bumblebee hovering over the stalks of blue delphinium. "After considering all his persuasive arguments, I had to concede his point. I am not getting any younger. Edmund's death taught us all that we can depart at any moment. Without an heir—" He shrugged. "Our estates are entailed. If I expire without leaving a male heir, all our lands pass to a cousin. The mere thought brings on an attack of gout to my poor sire."

"But wouldn't you want to choose your own wife?"

"I am afraid I have neither the inclination nor energy at this point in my life to sort through all the young ladies of marriageable age presently making their debut in society. The mere thought is both exhausting and excruciatingly tedious."

"You certainly don't believe in flattery," she replied, not sure whether she should be insulted or amused at his description of the Marriage Mart.

"Since most of the candidates would have been merely after my title and fortune, it makes things much simpler to select a young lady who is already possessed of these assets."

"But to marry a virtual stranger—" she began.

He gave her a humorless smile. "My father is a philanderer, an inveterate gambler and, above all, a lover of pleasure. Whatever my opinion may be of his way of life, I cannot fault his taste in women. He is a connoisseur of the fairer gender.

"When he promised I would be pleased with his choice, I could not but agree to have a look at you. He sang your praises. I can't say you displease me, fair Lady Gillian."

Her name sounded like a caress in the softly pronounced syllables, his dark eyes appraising her.

"Is he as good a judge of horseflesh?" she asked evenly, once again inclined to feel affronted.

He looked amused. "He's an excellent judge of horseflesh."

"Then I should be flattered."

He shrugged. "That's up to you. I'm merely telling you that my father has an eye for beauty and the finer things of life."

She squirmed, feeling he could see things she had revealed to no one. When she didn't answer right away, his tone gentled. "I have told you my reasons for agreeing to the match. Can you not confide something to me?"

Not ready to do any such thing, she persisted with the topic. "If you have such confidence in your father's opinion, why were you so ungracious the first evening we met?"

He raised a dark eyebrow in inquiry.

"Oh, come, my lord, you remember perfectly well how you behaved, looking me up and down as if I were a mare. Telling your father I'd do."

He smiled, his forefinger playing with the contours of his mouth. "That was not against you. My father and I, how shall I put it, don't like to concede the other a point scored. I would no more admit to him he is right than I would wear a spotted waistcoat."

Not quite mollified, but beginning to understand him better, she nodded.

"That still leaves why you acquiesced to your mother's choice." His soft tone intruded on her thoughts.

"I want a home of my own," she finally admitted, looking down at the doily under her glass.

"A home of your own," he answered, surprise edging the low timbre of his voice. "I would not consider you homeless."

"I want to be mistress of my own household."

"Well, you will have ample opportunity as the Countess of Skylar."

"It is what I have been trained to do. I know I would do it well." She felt her face warm as she spoke the next words. "I want to have children of my own and bring them up. You are right when you say I am tired of playing the debutante. I would like my life to serve some purpose."

"I think we will suit," he said finally. "I, too, want to run my father's estates and prove I can manage them well. I need a wife for that. A good one. I want a woman I can trust. She may play hostess for me whenever she wants. I want to devote my time to my estates and to taking my seat in Lords. I can grace whatever parties she chooses to give, but I don't intend to become caught up in the social whirl.

"I expect my wife to remain faithful to me, as I will to her."

She met his gaze. His dark eyes seemed to be probing her, willing her to confess any tendency toward waywardness. Would they ferret out her past secrets or only demand future fidelity?

She said nothing. He continued. "I will be frank with you, my lady. I have not led the life of a saint. I sowed my wild oats here in London before I was banished across the Atlantic." A faint smile tinged his lips, though his tone was bitter.

"In the Indies I dedicated myself to turning around a failing plantation. I have just ended a six-year relationship with a wealthy island widow. It was not a love union, merely a mutually agreeable arrangement. I left no illegitimate children behind.

"Forgive my frankness to your maidenly ears. I do not wish to offend your sensibilities, but I want to make it clear I ended any entanglements and fully intend to honor my wedding vows once I take them. I expect my future wife to do the same. Do you understand me?"

Her face had blanched at his unvarnished confessions. Did he expect the same of her? A complete disclosure of her past conduct?

Perhaps with his confession, he was making it clear the past was behind him and he would behave differently as a husband. Her heart lightened. The past didn't matter. She, too, intended to honor her wedding vows, despite her mother's advice, no matter how distasteful they seemed to her at the moment.

She swallowed. "Yes, I understand you. I, too, will—" she almost choked over the words "—honor our wedding vows."

He sat back, as if relieved some decision had been taken. "Good. I will tell my father to have the betrothal announced and the banns posted. We can discuss a date with your mother."

He raised his glass to hers. "Let us toast our future union."

She raised her glass slowly to his, keeping her eyes fixed on the two glasses, preferring not to meet Lord Skylar's penetrating dark gaze.

After that, as if deliberately seeking lighter topics of conversation, Lord Skylar took her for a stroll about the gardens. He spoke to her of the different plant life in the tropics. They drove back to London in the late afternoon. Gillian had long since put the serious part of their conversation out of her mind and focused on the enjoyment of the day. As they neared London once again, she felt a sense of regret that the outing would soon be over.

She enjoyed watching Lord Skylar's handling of the curricle, as she had her father. The two would have liked each other, she realized, and she felt a passing sadness that her father would not have the chance to meet her future husband.

Lord Skylar turned to her. "Would you like to take a

turn?" he asked offering her the reins. Her eyes widened. Most men were so proud of their skill with the ribbons and so protective of their precious vehicles and horses, they would never allow a female companion to try her hand. She smiled and nodded, taking the reins from him.

She had her own low phaeton with its pair of ponies, but it had been a while since she'd handled a pair of horses. She kept the horses at a steady pace, glad they were still on the outskirts of the city. Lord Skylar seemed in no hurry to have the reins back. As the streets became more congested, he finally took them back.

"You handle the ribbons well. Who taught you?"

"My father. We often rode together."

"Do you know anything of horseflesh?"

She nodded again, surprised anew.

"Maybe I'll take you to Tattersall's with me. I'm looking to buy my own horse now I'm back in England. Everything in our stables is either Father's or Edmund's."

Out of the corner of her eye, Gillian spied a movement on her side of the road. She craned her neck to see around the coach passing them at that moment.

A dog dashed into the street to avoid a man's whip. Without thinking, she grabbed Skylar's arm. "Stop the carriage!"

"What the—" he began, as his pair pranced at the sudden jerk to the reins. Not waiting to find out what she'd caused, Gillian jumped out of the curricle before it had come to a complete stop.

"Lady Gillian!" She heard his sharp command, but she paid it no heed. She dodged traffic and ran toward the dog. Just before a coach ran it over, Gillian lunged at the dog and grabbed its neck.

Hearing the neighing of horses almost on top of her, she dragged the dog back with her.

"What are you thinking of doing, old fellow?" she crooned into its ear as her hands patted his neck, afraid to let it go. "You could have gotten yourself killed. We couldn't have that. No indeed! There. You come back off the road with me." As she reached the edge of the street, she noticed the crowd around her. Astounded faces ringed her.

"Miss, are you all right? You almost got run over. If the coachman hadn't stopped in time—"

Not removing her hand from the dog, still feeling its trembling beneath her fingertips, she realized the full extent of the situation. Coming from behind the onlookers was Lord Skylar, his jaw set.

The crowd parted for him and he came straight to her.

"Are you hurt?"

She shook her head. Before he could say anything more, she turned to look for the man who had caused the commotion, as far as she was concerned. He stood behind a table, selling trinkets.

She marched toward him. "How dare you, sir! Taking a whip to a poor, defenseless dog. You should be whipped yourself."

The man looked at her in astonishment. "Why—why, that cur's been pestering me. It's a worthless stray. Ought to be taken out of its misery."

Her outrage knew no bounds. "I'll have you reported. I'll see you—" Before she could utter her threat, she felt Lord Skylar's hand on her arm.

"The lady is understandably distressed with the near miss she had. Her nerves are overset—"

She opened her mouth at Lord Skylar's cool tone. "My nerves! I'll show you nerves." Wrenching her arm from his grasp, she went in search of the dog. She found him cowering behind a stack of crates. "Come on, boy. Don't be afraid." She petted him, crouching down to his level once again. "We'll take you away from this place, from that awful brute…"

"She means no disrespect," she heard Skylar say to the vendor in a soothing tone. "Here, this should cover any damages. We'll take the cur away from here."

Then he was standing over her. "We'd better remove ourselves from the premises if we want to avoid a riot. The man's an unemployed soldier. He'll soon have the crowd on his side."

"Come on, boy," she coaxed the dog, her hand urging it forward. The dog was gazing at her with limpid brown eyes the color of topaz, and she fell in love with it.

She gave a last outraged glance at the man with the stall and only then noticed his missing leg, and the crutch he leaned against. She shuddered and turned in search of the curricle.

Lord Skylar pointed to where he had left it on the other side of the road, his tiger holding the reins. "We shall have to cross the street."

Gillian looked at him expectantly.

"What is it?"

She motioned to the dog. "Aren't you going to carry him? We mustn't risk his getting run over again."

She almost laughed at the expression on Lord Skylar's face as he looked down at the dog.

With a lengthy sigh, he finally stooped down and lifted the dog in his arms.

"Don't hurt him," she begged Lord Skylar.

"I hope you're addressing the dog and not me," he said dryly.

With a doubtful look at the curricle's immaculate interior, Skylar dumped the animal onto a rug on the floor. "We shall have to have the vehicle fumigated," Skylar told his tiger.

"Yes, sir," he answered, unable to aid his master as he held the horses.

After helping Gillian in, Lord Skylar climbed in, shoving the dog out of the way of his feet in the confined space. The dog whined pitifully.

"Be careful! He's been mistreated enough."

"I believe it's a she, not a he," he answered shortly as he took the reins from the groom and waited only long enough for the man to jump up in back before setting the carriage in motion.

He handed her his handkerchief with barely a glance. "You might want to wipe the dust from your face."

"Oh—" She took it from him, wondering that he'd even noticed her face in the entire fray. She scrubbed at her cheeks.

"Where are we going?" she asked as she watched him turn into the park gates.

"We can drop the mutt in the park. Either that or drive back to Kensington. Perhaps I could bribe a farmer to take it off our hands."

She twisted around in the tight space and glared at him. "We shall do no such thing. How do we know they will take care of it properly?" She laid her hand on his forearm, her outrage turning to entreaty.

"I would suggest, my lady, that you refrain from interfering with my driving a second time. If you did not cause an accident just now, or break your neck, I cannot guarantee your safety another time."

She removed her hand. "Didn't you see that man? What he was doing to this poor animal?"

"No, I was watching the traffic, a fact you can be thankful for. Otherwise, all three of us would probably have been thrown from the vehicle."

Finally conceding the folly of her jump, she said, "I'm sorry for the suddenness of leaving the curricle, but the man was whipping this poor dog, and he—she'd—run into the street. In another second she would have been run over by that closed carriage." Her voice broke at the thought of what might have happened. She sniffed into the large handkerchief, appalled at her reaction.

"Spare me from emotional women," Lord Skylar muttered.

"At least I'm not being heartless!"

"Excuse me. Next time I'll jump out alongside you with no thought for anyone else on the road."

She ignored his sarcasm. "This dog needs medical attention. Look at that wound." She bent over, noticing the gash from the whip. "Can't you take her home with you and have your stableman look at her?"

It was his turn to look at her in outrage. "*Home with me? That flea-ridden creature? For all we know, it's rabid."

She looked down at her knotted handkerchief. "I can't—that is, Mother wouldn't allow it into our house, not even into the stables. I—I've taken in some stray cats and keep them there, but Mama doesn't even know about them. I don't think I could keep a dog hidden for very long."

Lord Skylar remained silent, but after a moment she heard

him give another pained sigh. When she dared look around, she saw with relief that he'd turned around and was leaving the park. She said nothing but dabbed at her nose, being careful not to sniff audibly.

"My father's mastiffs will probably eat her for breakfast."

She glanced at him in alarm. "You mustn't let them! Can't you keep her apart from them?"

He said no more until he stopped in front of her house. She bent over one last time and petted the dog until Lord Skylar came around to her side of the carriage. She did not look at him as he helped her down.

"You're sure you're not hurt?" he asked curtly.

She nodded.

"You'd best change your dress before your mother sees you."

She glanced down at her light-colored muslin. Dust and dog prints stained it.

"She might have second thoughts of allowing you to go on another outing with me if she sees your dirty and disheveled condition from a simple turn in the park."

As he spoke, he took her arm and propelled her toward the front entrance. A footman opened the door before they reached it. Lord Skylar released her and stepped back. "Good afternoon, my lady."

She looked back at him and bit her lip. "You won't let the other dogs hurt it?"

"We'll muzzle them until they get used to this mongrel."

"You'll let me know how she gets on?"

"You'll hear from me." With a final tip of his hat, he turned and made his way back to the curricle.

Her attention went to the dog, whose chestnut head

peered out the side. She gave it an encouraging smile and wave. "I'll see you soon," she said, not at all sure she would be able to keep her promise.

Chapter Three

❧

Tertius lay on the narrow ledge. He dared not move or he'd fall over the edge. He couldn't see over it but felt instinctively the drop into the darkness had no end. Like the terror that gripped him, it was black and bottomless.

The tension in his muscles from keeping against the wall was dissipating his energy at a rapid rate.

A sudden spasm jerked him over the side. His heart in his throat, his body free-falled. He opened his mouth to scream but no sound came forth.

He awoke with a jerk into the dark room. Immobilized by fear that overwhelmed his reason, his every faculty, it took a moment to realize he was safe. It had been nothing but a dream.

Relief came in a slow wave that loosened his muscles, which were tight like twisted rope. As the reality of pillow and covers intruded on his consciousness, he relived the dream from the viewpoint of wakefulness. A sense of familiarity hovered over it.

As his breathing slowed and he listened to his heartbeat, he searched his memory. He'd been there before. As his thoughts cleared and sharpened from the deep sleep he'd been in, he remembered.

He'd dreamed of the ledge during his last fever.

The details finally faded, and he became aware of his actual surroundings—soft bed under him, hangings at each corner of the bedposts, pillow cushioning his head. As he took in each detail, he became conscious of something else present in the room.

The brief relief at waking evaporated as a new evil confronted him. He wasn't alone. His heart stepped up its pace again as the malignant presence at the end of the dark room made itself felt. It sat there, heavy and still, biding its time before it closed in on him.

He tried to call out but couldn't. Something gripped his throat and kept him mute. He tried moving his mouth, but it didn't respond to his commands.

Before all rational thought left him, the sensation receded, and at last he knew he was truly alone with the natural darkness. He remained paralyzed, voluntarily now, for several moments, his reason doubting what his senses told him.

As the darkness continued to feel normal, Tertius finally dared to move. Slowly, he drew back his bedcovers and felt for a candle. With shaking hands, he managed to light it.

The room was empty. His focus traveled to every reach of it. Everything appeared as he had left it when he'd extinguished his lamp last night. The long shadows of bedposts and hangings danced about in the candlelight, and he real-ized the hand that held the taper was still shaking, so he set it down.

He got back into his bed, propping up the pillows to rest against them. He wasn't a coward. He'd faced down plenty of dangers in his life. So why this blind panic in the face of an invisible danger? It was only a dream—it had to be. There was nothing in the room.

He wiped the sweat from the upper part of his lip.

He'd thought the dreams were finished when he'd gotten over his illness. Why were they coming again? And this lat-est phenomenon? It had been no dream; he'd been awake. What did it mean?

He was in England now. Somehow he'd thought nothing could follow him here.

Sky slept late the next morning. The bright sunshine made him laugh at his foolish terrors of the previous night. After a good breakfast, as he sat in his father's office going over papers given him by his father's solicitor, he was able to forget it completely.

A soft knock on the door interrupted his concentration.

"Yes?" he called out.

The butler opened the door. "Lady Althea has come to pay her respects. Would you like me to show her in? I have put her in the morning room."

Tertius swore under his breath. He had no desire to see his half sister. What did she want? He thought he'd never have to see her again once she reached her majority and left the family seat of her own accord.

"Very well," he finally said, as the butler stood awaiting

his decision. "Show her in here." Let her see he was busy and couldn't take time for a family reunion.

A few minutes later the young woman entered and stood by the door without moving farther into the room. The door closed softly behind her, and he was left facing the sibling he hadn't seen in over ten years.

She hadn't changed much, he noted, except for her unfashionable attire. She, too, was in mourning for their brother, Edmund.

"Hello, Tertius."

The very tenor of her voice exasperated him. It reminded him of some fearful servant, ready to cringe at its master's raised voice. It enraged him, since she'd never been mistreated by his family. On the contrary, she'd received every largesse.

He rose slowly from his desk and came toward her. "Hello, Althea. How've you been keeping?" he asked in an offhand tone as he motioned her to a chair.

She seated herself and loosened her bonnet strings. "Very well, thank you. I only just heard you had returned or I would have been by earlier."

"No hurry. I won't be going anywhere soon."

"I'm sorry about Edmund. It was a tragic loss."

He inclined his head a fraction to acknowledge the condolence. "Still shaming the family name with those Methodist practices?" he couldn't help asking as he flicked a speck of lint off the leg of his pantaloons, pretending a carelessness he was far from feeling.

He watched the color creep over her cheeks. Her hair, the same burnished gold he remembered, was no longer in two pigtails, but pulled back into a tight chignon. No loose curls framed her face. Not for pious Althea. How dare she pretend such holiness when her roots were so tainted? Time and distance had not diminished the impotent rage he felt every time he thought about her origins.

"I am still at the mission," she said quietly. "I don't believe I am shaming the Pembrokes in any way. I never took the family name. There is no reason for anyone to connect me to your family."

"Yes, so Father told me," he drawled. "You go simply by 'Miss Althea Breton.' How noble of you to carry the burden of your illegitimacy so bravely on your small shoulders."

She smiled at him, a smile that struck him as resigned, and he felt renewed annoyance.

"I don't carry any burden except those the Lord gives me, and that usually has to do with people you don't know nor will ever chance to know."

He said nothing but sat beating a tattoo against his pant leg, awaiting the reason of her visit. Was she going to ask for some donation for her charitable work? Hadn't Father already been more than generous in his settlement on her?

"Your father sent a note letting me know of your return."

"*Our* father, don't you mean? Isn't that what he wants you to call him? As well as take your rightful place among us and let the world know your true parentage now that Mother is gone?"

She swallowed and looked down at her clasped hands. "I'm sorry, Tertius. I have no desire to hurt either you or your mother's memory. I usually still refer to Father as my guardian. I still think of him in that way," she added with a small smile.

"How nice of you to consider my mother's sensibilities," he sneered.

She ignored the gibe and instead asked, "Did you have a good journey back?"

"The seas were calm for the most part," he replied, a part of him regretting his lack of manners. What was the matter with him? It wasn't Althea's fault who her parents were. But he'd never been able to stop blaming her for having been so blatantly thrust under his mother's nose. The late marchioness had been forced to endure the presence of a child who so clearly was not a "ward," but the result of one of her husband's many indiscretions.

"Father said you had been ill, and that's why you couldn't come any sooner," Althea continued.

"Yes, that is so. But I'm fully recovered now."

"I'm glad. You—you look thin," she said in the soft, hesitant tone that never failed to irk him.

He shrugged. "So everyone tells me." He made a point of pulling out his watch and snapping it open, wanting above anything for this interview to be over. He felt out of sorts and ill-humored. It was the poor night he'd had that was making him behave so surly.

"I didn't mean to interrupt you at your work," she said at once. "I merely wanted to welcome you back and tell you how sorry I was about Edmund."

He felt another twinge of guilt at his incivility. He was quite some years older than she—at least a decade—so he hadn't had much contact with her growing up. But whenever he'd come home from school, he'd catch glimpses of her. His father seemed to keep her well hidden on the large estate.

She'd always been cowering behind somebody's apron, usually a housekeeper's or servant's, those shy eyes looking out at him, a thumb stuck in her mouth.

He studied her critically. Her black dress with its narrow white ruffle high at the neck made her look older than her twenty-three or twenty-four years.

"How old are you now, Althea?" he asked abruptly.

She looked surprised at the question. "Twenty-four," she answered softly.

Tertius hated that diffidence. It had always annoyed him and brought out the worst in him. "You look older," he lied. In truth, she still looked young; it was her clothing and hairstyle that added years.

She didn't seem affected by the implied insult. He preferred a more spirited person. An image of Lady Gillian rushing to save a stray flashed through his mind. Her passionate defense of the mangy mutt stirred something in him like nothing else had in a long time.

"You look older than I remember," she said with a gentle smile. "You were a dashing young man of five-and-twenty when you left, and I was an awkward girl of fourteen, fearfully in awe of you and Edmund both."

"I hardly remember you," he replied, unable to stop his digs.

"I doubt you would. You were a young gentleman about town and I was away at school by then."

She stood and began retying her bonnet. He stood as well and waited for her to put her gloves back on.

He didn't thank her for coming. The words stuck in his throat. No matter how much his rational mind told him to treat her with courtesy, his gestures wouldn't follow suit.

"I'll show you out," he said.

"There's no need to accompany me. I'll see myself out."

"As you wish." He accompanied her only to the door of the office, where the two stood a moment.

Her clear gray eyes regarded him. He read compassion in them, and he wanted to tell her he didn't need her pity. Who was she—a poor, penniless, illegitimate half sister—to pity him?

Why then did he feel she had something to offer him? That she knew something of his fear and near panic of the night before? Of his feelings of inadequacy in filling Edmund's shoes?

"Tertius," she began.

"What is it?" he asked, not bothering to hide the impatience in his tone.

She reached a hand out to him but let it drop before touching him, and he realized he had braced himself for the contact. "I also wanted to...to let you know, if you ever need anything, you can come to me. You don't seem fully recovered. I hope your new responsibilities won't be too much of a strain—"

"You don't think me capable of assuming the duties of the new Earl of Skylar?" he asked, and then could have kicked himself for revealing his own weakness. It was the fault of that soft, sympathetic tone of hers.

"Of course I do! But as I said, you've been ill. Take it slowly and don't let the opinions of others control you."

He regained his calm tone. "My dear sister, your solicitude overwhelms me. However, you needn't concern yourself. I am perfectly capable of managing my affairs. And as I told you, I am completely recovered."

She merely nodded. "You needn't treat me as a sister if

you'd rather not. I understand. Just think of me as a trusted childhood friend who would do anything in her power to help you if you should ever need me."

She no longer struck him as a timorous inferior. Her tone had gained strength, as if she were supremely confident of her ability to help him.

What could she possibly help him with? "Thank you, dear Althea," he replied, managing a thin smile. "I shall remember that whenever I am in need."

She looked down, as if disappointed but not surprised at the condescension in his tone. "Goodbye then. I always pray for you."

"I'm sure you have many more deserving souls worthy of your petitions."

She made no reply as she exited the door. He shut it behind her and returned to his desk, but found it hard to resume his work. Drat her intrusion!

He didn't want to have the past tormenting him. He'd achieved an emotional distance from his father and was certainly not going to let a half sibling he hardly saw, let alone hardly knew, upset the careful balance.

He was on the threshold of beginning something new. He would prove to society that he was fully capable of filling his brother's shoes. With a lovely young wife at his side, and offspring soon to follow, there was absolutely nothing he need fear.

A few afternoons later Gillian entered the drawing room for tea. Once again she found Lord Skylar calmly seated with her mother and Templeton, one of her mother's fine Sevres cups and saucers balanced upon his knee.

"Yes," he told them, "she is of a very old pedigree, a direct descendant of a spaniel of my great-grandfather's on our Hertfordshire estate. She'll make a great companion for Lady Gillian." He reached down to stroke the dog's neck. "A very docile creature, I assure you."

Gillian could only stare at the "creature" in question. The rescued dog, chestnut coat shiny and clean, sat at Lord Skylar's booted feet. At that moment, it caught sight of Gillian. Immediately it jumped up, almost knocking over the edge of a silver tray on the table before Lord Skylar.

"Sit!" Lord Skylar's tone was more effective than a whip. The dog and owner stared at each other a few seconds—seconds in which Gillian's hand went to her throat and she held her breath, fearful of her mother's reaction. Her mother leaned forward in her chair as soon as the dog had moved, itching to have it removed from the room, no doubt.

Gillian could feel her whole body willing the dog to obey Lord Skylar. The seconds dragged on until finally the dog whined and, with a longing look toward Gillian, sat back down before Lord Skylar.

He smiled at the animal—a smile that broke the austerity of his features—and reached across the table for a biscuit. Breaking off a piece, he held it out to the dog, who gobbled it up eagerly.

"Good girl," Lord Skylar told the dog, giving her neck another rubbing.

"Good afternoon, Lady Gillian," he said, only then turning his attention to Gillian. "If you'd like to greet your new pet, she is eager to slather you with gratitude for your timely rescue."

Gillian needed no other prompting. She was at the dog's

side in an instant, kneeling beside her and receiving its wet greeting. "Hello, there," she said, not knowing what to call the animal, so she continued petting it and crooning over it.

She looked up at Lord Skylar with a wide smile. She hadn't heard anything from him since the afternoon outing and lived in terror that he'd inform her the dog had been found a home out in the country somewhere. He gave her a brief smile and turned his attention back to her mother.

"I am in the midst of a training program since the dog arrived from our estate. She was given a bit of a freer rein out in the country. We'll have her well behaved for the drawing room in no time." Again his glance crossed Gillian's and she saw the glint in his eye. She looked over at her mother, and she detected nothing but alarm in her eyes. Good, she thought in relief. At least her mother didn't see the mockery in Lord Skylar's eyes.

"Well, I don't know…" she began in dubious tones, her hand playing nervously with the gold chain about her neck. "We've never had any animals in the house."

"Every fine lady has a drawing room pet. Most are lap dogs that do nothing but yap at the guests and nip at their heels. This one is a real dog. She'll be a good companion for your daughter when she goes out walking."

"I don't know…" her mother repeated. "She has Templeton."

Gillian and Lord Skylar both glanced at the woman in question, and Gillian was hard-pressed not to burst out laughing.

"I assure you, Miss Templeton," Lord Skylar said smoothly, "you will feel safer with a well-behaved watchdog between the two of you. You'll fear no cutpurses or pickpockets. With the parks so crowded with riffraff during the festivities, you need a fearless animal with you."

Templeton smiled, her rouged cheeks bright. "Oh, yes! I am so grateful for your thoughtfulness. The streets are an absolute peril nowadays for a lady."

"Templeton!" her mother said sharply. Then she cleared her throat and turned back to Lord Skylar. "As I said, we're not at all sure we can keep…her. We're not accustomed to pets in the house. Perhaps in the mews…?" she suggested in a faltering voice.

"Oh, Mama, look at her! She's so clean. And look how quietly she sits. Mayn't I try her in the house?"

Lord Skylar ignored Gillian's spirited tone. "I have received my invitation to Prinny's grand fete for the Duke of Wellington. My father and I would like to request the pleasure of your company that night. We would be honored to escort you and Lady Gillian."

"Indeed. The Regent's fete?"

Gillian watched her mother's dignified features. Not by a hint did she give away the fact that they had not as yet received their invitation, and that her mother looked assiduously through the pile of mail each day for the coveted invitation.

"Yes, on the twenty-first," replied Sky smoothly. He took another sip of tea. "I hear Nash is working furiously to complete the special hall at Carlton House in time. I'm afraid it will be frightfully crowded, but I thought as a memorable historical event, it would interest Lady Gillian." He glanced her way again. "Something to tell her grandchildren. The day she curtsied before Wellington."

"Yes, most assuredly," her mother agreed. "We shall be happy to have your escort."

"Thank you, my lady." He set the delicate porcelain cup and saucer down. "I would beg leave to take Lady Gillian with me for a turn about the square to acquaint her with her new pet. I can go over some of the commands I've taught the dog."

He stood. "We shall be merely down below, in plain view, if Miss Templeton should care to sit here and observe us." He moved to the window and pushed aside the curtain.

"Very well, but don't keep her long."

Down in the square below, Lord Skylar relinquished the dog's leash to Gillian as they walked beneath the linden trees. She took it eagerly. "She's beautiful. What did you do to get her coat so shiny?"

"I gave her to a groom and told him to make sure to rid it of any fleas. I presume he bathed it, deloused it and fed it."

"And your father's dogs, how did they behave?"

"Apparently they have accepted her."

She looked down shyly. "I don't know how to thank you." She giggled, remembering her mother's losing battle before Lord Skylar's smooth, invincible logic. "I never thought I'd see the day Mama would agree to an indoor pet."

"She hasn't exactly agreed yet," he corrected her.

"She will. After dangling the prince's dinner in front of her," she added with a sly glance at him. "I would call that a masterful stroke."

He shrugged. "You were invited."

"Not *yet,* we haven't been."

He raised an eyebrow.

"I'm sure we shall receive an invitation," she added quickly. "We have gone to all the major receptions there since Prinny became regent. But I believe since Papa passed away, the royal summonses are slower in arriving. Mama begins to fidget as the time draws closer."

"I am glad, then, to be able to relieve her mind."

"I have never met the Duke of Wellington," Gillian marveled. "I can hardly wait to meet such a brave man. He has saved England and much of the Continent."

"Have you been following the campaigns closely?" he asked, slanting her a curious look.

She could feel the color rising in her cheeks. "Yes, just as everyone else in England has." Not caring to delve into the topic too deeply, she returned to the previous matter. "To think Mama has agreed to an abandoned stray from the streets!"

Taking the change of topic in stride, he said, "This dog is of good stock."

"Oh, yes, the finest," she said, laughter bubbling up. "If you are to be believed, she can probably trace her lineage back to Charles the First's favorite pooch."

"I may have exaggerated the facts to your mother, but I didn't altogether lie. This dog has some illustrious spaniel blood. If it has been, er, tainted along the way with some lesser-known varieties, that doesn't take away from the fact that she's *almost* purebred."

"'Almost'—that won't convince Mother."

"Then let us hope she believed my story."

She laughed again. After a moment, she turned to him. "You can be very charming and believable when you want to be. Do you only do it when you wish to obtain something from someone?"

"That usually is the case."

"I think you could get almost anything you wanted if you set your mind to it."

"Do you?" he asked noncommittally.

"Don't you set your mind to it very often?" she asked, remembering his ungracious behavior when they'd first been introduced.

"It is wearing, I'll admit. And so often not worth the trouble, wouldn't you agree? Or are you yet so young that you haven't suffered any disillusion?"

She remained silent, preferring to concentrate on holding the dog in check on its leash.

But Lord Skylar was not finished with the thought. "I still find it hard to believe you have remained free these years in London. There is no young gentleman who has stolen your heart? No drawerfuls of avowals of everlasting love and no keepsakes—a lock of hair, a monogrammed handkerchief…?"

"No, there is nothing!" she answered a little too warmly.

"A young lady with your attributes?" he asked in disbelief. "Your mother hasn't kept you *that* locked up. And Templeton, no matter how forbidding she might be, wouldn't put off a true suitor—"

"My father would have wanted me to wait for someone—" She stopped.

"Yes?" he prompted when she didn't continue. "Someone like…?"

"Like you," she said on a moment's inspiration. Maybe if she flattered his vanity, he would be satisfied and let the subject drop.

He chuckled. "Wealth and a title—have there been a dearth of good candidates fulfilling those requirements these last three seasons?"

"Well, with the war on, you know, so many young men have gone off to Spain."

"But not elder sons."

She could feel his keen eyes on her. "Well, there was no one," she repeated. "Why haven't *you* married all those years out there in the Indies?" she asked, turning to him. "I can't believe there were no suitable candidates out there."

He prodded at a fallen leaf with his walking stick. "Perhaps I didn't like what I saw of matrimony."

"What do you mean?" she asked puzzled.

"Matrimony among our class seems to be a hypocritical arrangement between two individuals who agree to turn a blind eye to the other's dalliances. Forgive the bluntness, but so often it is only one of the partners who gets to enjoy the pleasures of extramarital affairs, while the other is forced to suffer in silence."

For someone who had never been married, he spoke as if he were acquainted firsthand with that kind of pain. It was not in the tone of voice, which had retained its airy, slightly amused quality as if he were commenting on a light romantic comedy. But the words themselves were, as he had said, blunt, and certainly improper to be speaking to a young, unmarried lady.

"I know many things go on in society," she began slowly. "I believe my parents were happily married, however unfashionable that might appear," she said, wanting to believe it, despite her mother's cynical words of advice. Could she have cheated on dear Papa? No. Gillian wouldn't give credence to the idea.

Lord Skylar swung his walking stick to and fro along the gravel path. "That is indeed a feat, if indeed improbable."

"I could never consider such a thing of Papa! I know he was faithful to my mother," she stated with finality.

"Well, for the sake of your memories, I hope you are right." He smiled, a smile that had a hint of tenderness in it. "So, you see why I have retained my bachelorhood. Besides, I had an elder brother to fulfill the duties of heir. He, alas, died childless."

Gillian turned to her new pet, tiring of the topic of marriage and fidelity. "What shall we name her?" she asked with a tug on the leash.

"We?"

"Well, you are part owner, you know."

"I haven't the foggiest. I'll allow you the honor."

Suddenly the animal in question spied a squirrel scampering up a thick trunk. She dashed toward it, yanking the leash out of Gillian's hands.

"Heel!" Lord Skylar's sharp command brought the dog to an immediate halt, though she whined in protest, her nose sniffing forward. Sky picked up the leash.

"Good girl," he told the dog, bending down to pet her and offering her a biscuit from his pocket. He then rose and took over the leash. The dog strained toward the tree where she'd spied the squirrel. It was no longer in sight.

"I'm sorry, dear," Gillian spoke to her pet. "But you'll never catch it now. It's gone up the tree," she explained, petting the animal's neck.

They resumed their walk. "You'd do best to train her early.

Keep a firm hand on her and reward her when she obeys," Lord Skylar advised.

He gave her a wry look. "You'll probably mother her to death, indulge her every whim, and end up with a spoiled, ill-behaved mutt on your hands."

She merely laughed at him. She was beginning to suspect he had a rather tender heart behind that detached demeanor. Perhaps he wouldn't make such an awful husband.

Tertius walked along the streets of Mayfair after he'd escorted Gillian and her new pet back home. The day was a splendid summer one. He passed the shops on Bond Street. The sidewalks were filled with shoppers. He stopped to glance in at a window or two, but his mind was distracted. He kept thinking of his impending marriage. It no longer seemed a burdensome task.

In less than a fortnight he'd gone from outrage at his father's preposterous announcement that Tertius must not only marry posthaste but that the bride was already picked out, to a sense of anticipation at his forthcoming nuptials.

The chit was getting to him, he realized, looking at the latest satirical prints in Ackermann's bow window. He continued his walk, wondering when this shift had occurred. His mind kept going to the afternoon of their outing, her smudged face turned up to him in entreaty, seeking his help and protection for a poor, starved creature.

He shook his head, still finding it hard to believe how easily she had bent him to her wishes.

Or had his feelings begun to change even earlier in the day, when she'd looked down at her plate in the tea garden and shyly told him how much she wanted a home and children of her own?

He tried to rationalize his feelings. It was reasonable to expect him to be married at his age, with his new position. Lady Gillian was not only a very appealing young lady, but she fulfilled all the requisites of wealth and lineage to be joined to the Caulfield line.

If the amiability between the two of them continued to grow, there should be no reason for their marriage not to succeed.

Another inner voice warned him that undoubtedly his parents' marriage had started out this way. At one time they must have had a regard for each other. He knew his mother had loved his father until the marquess had destroyed that love with his repeated infidelities.

Tertius turned left onto Piccadilly, telling himself it was too pleasant a day for such pessimistic thoughts. He reached Sackville Street and headed for Gray's, where his family was accustomed to buying their jewelry.

He looked at various pieces until finding what he wanted.

Yes, the emerald pendant and earrings would look lovely against Lady Gillian's pale skin. He also chose a set of wedding bands, telling the jeweler the bride would be in later for a fitting. At the last minute, a gold ring mounted with a diamond and ruby caught his eye. He purchased it as well.

Telling the jeweler to have the other things delivered later, he tucked the jeweler's box with the ruby and diamond ring into a pocket and left the store. He would present the ring to Lady Gillian at the Regent's fete.

A feeling of pride filled him as he thought of the ring gracing her slim hand.

Chapter Four

❧

Tertius picked Gillian up in his curricle the next afternoon and took her to Tattersall's at Hyde Park Corner.

A large crowd was congregated around the tall column at the entrance of the brick building.

"Oh, it must be the day of settling racing bets," Gillian exclaimed. She hadn't been here since her father had died. He'd taken her along whenever he'd won a race. She looked up the column at the statue of the fox atop it and remembered the excitement of those days.

Tertius commented, "Maybe the crowds will stay out here and give us a chance to look at the horses inside in some modicum of peace."

He gave the reins to his tiger with instructions to tool around the park for about an hour and handed down Gillian. They walked into the courtyard of the three-story building that boasted the best horse auction in London.

"I should think your father's stables already contain the best cattle in town," Gillian said as they eyed the horses being paraded on the stone and gravel walkways in the courtyard.

"He has a fine stable," he conceded. "So did Edmund."

"But you want your own animal." She looked at him in understanding as she petted the neck of a fine bay. He felt gratified that he didn't have to explain to her. "Here in town Mother lets me take out my small phaeton hitched to a pair of ponies. Occasionally, I ride my mare in the park with my groom."

"We should have ample opportunity for riding once we leave London," he promised her.

"Will that be soon…after the…wedding?" Her voice faltered, and he realized the idea of being married to him was still daunting to her.

"Actually, it would be nice to tour some of the estates before the wedding—for the hunting season. You and your mother—and Templeton—" he grinned "—could be my guests."

She smiled in relief. "That would be delightful. Where are your family's estates?"

"Oh, the main one is in Hertfordshire—a monstrous thing. There's another up near Leicester, another down in Dorset and there's even a very gothic property way up in the West Riding in Yorkshire. I haven't been there since I was a child. I daresay we shall have to visit them all once we're married. Who knows when my father has last been to them, except for the family seat in Hertfordshire, of course."

"Well, I shall enjoy touring them all!" she said, her eyes shining in delight. "May we entertain at each?"

"Entertain away. As long as I have a few good hunting and fishing companions, I can always manage to avoid the rest of the company if they prove too tedious." As he was speaking, they walked around the animals being walked about the courtyard.

"What do you think of this one?" he asked Gillian of the black horse snorting and pawing the ground.

The groom holding the animal spoke up before giving Gillian a chance to reply. "Oh, he's a high-spirited fellow, but you'll get sixteen miles an hour outta 'im once you've got 'im well broken in…"

"He's not broken in?" Gillian asked.

As the groom continued listing the selling points to Gillian, Sky walked around the animal. He bent down and examined his knees and fetlocks, then went to his hindquarters. When he felt the animal's hock and cannon, the horse fidgeted.

"You take it easy," the groom spoke to the horse.

Straightening, Sky asked the groom, "Has he ever thrown a splint?"

"Naw, me lord, never!"

Sky touched Gillian on the arm. "Come, let's see what they have in the stables."

"But guvner, this one here's the finest you'll see today. He'll be up on the block soon."

They left the man talking and entered the stalls.

"You didn't like him?" Gillian asked curiously.

"The groom was lying about him. That horse has clearly had some injury near his hind cannon."

They ignored the hunters and matched pairs and concentrated on the riding horses. Gillian liked a high-stepping bay mare. Sky kept going back to a gray gelding.

"He's a beauty," agreed Gillian, smoothing down his forelock. "Aren't you?" she asked, directing herself to the horse.

"We'll see how he performs," Sky said, watching her fondness for the horse. She had an affinity for animals, and the tenderness in her manner drew him. Her skin was so soft he craved to reach out his forefinger and touch her cheek, but he didn't know how she would react. Her embarrassment over his mention of their wedding told him she wasn't ready to face the physical aspects of marriage. It was understandable. She was a young lady, probably as innocent as a babe. He'd have to be patient and initiate her into the ways of a man with a maid gradually.

"Shall we stay for the auction?" he asked.

She turned to him with an eager smile. "Oh, yes. I haven't been to one since Papa passed away. Will you bid for this one today?"

He shook his head. "Likely not. There's still time. I just came to look around today."

"You must have been quite a whip in your London days," she said in a teasing voice as they continued along the dim, straw-strewn passages of the building.

He smiled. "Yes, I was a member of all the clubs…the Four-in-One, the Jockey, the Whip… Edmund and I would compete against each other. Our favorite pastime was bribing the jarvey of the stage to let us have a go at the reins. We'd start out at the White Horse and ride neck-or-nothing between London and Salt Hill.

"We'd come roaring into the inn, our horses in a lather,

all of us caked in mud, our poor rooftop passengers hanging on for dear life. It's a wonder we didn't break our necks. Father would be livid when he'd find out. But Edmund would just laugh and tell him it was nothing he hadn't done himself when he was young, and Father would have to admit the truth of that." Sky sobered, remembering his brother's end.

"I never thought it would be a coaching accident that would get my brother."

"Were you and Edmund close?" she asked softly.

"We were only a year apart."

"Do you miss him?"

"Not anymore. I hadn't seen him in over a decade."

"Why didn't you come back to London in all those years?"

He shrugged. "There was nothing for me here once my mother passed away."

Before she could ask him anything more personal, he said instead, "Enough about me. Tell me instead how a young lady would ever have been inside a place like Tattersall's. I imagined you with the typical upbringing."

She gave him a saucy smile. "What is that, may I ask?"

"Oh, a French governess until you were about twelve, then off to Miss Something-or-Other's fine establishment on the outskirts of London. You'd see your parents on the rare occasion until your come-out…."

She laughed. "How did you know? And what about you? Your boyhood, let's see…" She put her finger up to her lips, pondering. "Eton, then Cambridge, probably sent down a few times."

"You can't imagine how many," he replied dryly. "I probably wouldn't have graduated if not for a young lad

I met in my last year at Eton—a brilliant fellow. Latin declensions rolled off his tongue with the ease of a Roman orator."

"So, you were a lazy scholar."

"I never believed in exerting myself over anything until—"

"Until?" she prompted.

He shrugged. "Until I made a bargain with Father. In exchange for his paying off my last gambling debt, I would go out to the Indies and take over a failing plantation. I told him I'd turn it around and make it yield a profit."

"Did you?" she asked.

"Not at first. It took a few years longer than I'd anticipated."

They walked back into the sunshine of the stone courtyard in time for the auction. Gillian became wrapped up in the bidding. When the black horse went for a hundred pounds, Sky shook his head and looked at the young buyer in disgust. "He wants a showy mount and doesn't bother to look further than its appearance."

After the auction, Sky returned Gillian to her house. Before helping her down from the carriage, he removed the small jeweler's box from his pocket. "I got you this the other day. I was going to give it to you at the Prince's fete, but now seems the best time."

Her eyes widened in delight as she reached for the box he held out to her. "What is it?"

He smiled at her childish enthusiasm. "Why don't you open it and see? If you don't like it, you can pick out something yourself."

She bowed her head over the velvet box and, with a flick,

undid the tiny clasp. Inside lay the diamond-and-ruby ring. The ruby shone brightly against the white satin cloth.

He heard her sharp intake of breath. "It's beautiful!"

"May I?" Before she could move away, he took the box from her hands and removed the ring. He held it out to her. "Would you like me to try it on you?"

"Oh yes!" She removed her glove and held out her hand.

He took the pale, slim hand in his darker one and slipped the ring onto her finger. The gesture made him think of the marriage ceremony and the finality of that moment when he'd slip the wedding band on her finger. It would signal the beginning of their life together.

The ring fit perfectly and looked nice on her. Maybe it was a good omen.

"Thank you…it's lovely."

"Not more so than its owner."

The smile on her face grew, lighting her pale green eyes and parting her rosy lips.

He strained to lean forward and kiss them, but he held himself back.

Next time, Jilly-girl, he promised, liking the sound of the nickname that popped into his head. He would taste of them the next time they met.

Gillian glanced across the carriage to her mother. They had spent most of the day on their coiffures and dresses, and by eight in the evening, they sat in a queue of carriages that inched along the cobbled street. They had finally left Bond Street and now stood at the top of St. James's Street.

She chanced a look out the open carriage window to see how many coaches were lined down the street behind them.

The interior was hot and stuffy so they had been forced to keep the windows down, to the displeasure of her mother.

She could see why. As soon as she did so, the crowds packed along the sides of the streets began ogling her.

"Hey, ducky, you're a comely thing."

"Come, lean out farther, so we can see that pretty frock."

"Look at those pearls."

"Are the flowers in your hair real?"

"Gillian, put your head in immediately!" her mother said.

"Who's in there with you, love?" a female bystander demanded. "Is it Lady Bessborough?"

"I think it's Lady Hertford," her companion decided. "The prince's favorite."

"No," decided a poorly dressed man who had the effrontery to press his head into the coach window. "This lady's not fat enough!"

Gillian had pulled her head back in as the soon as the man approached. Now, she imitated her mother who sat in icy silence until the man removed his head from the window.

"The line of carriages seems endless. I can't see how far down Bond Street it stretches, but there are certainly many more coaches than when we first arrived."

"That is why I insisted we leave early. Remember at last year's fete for poor King Louis?"

Gillian was thrown back in her seat as the coach suddenly lurched forward. It only traveled a few yards before stopping again.

"They should have guards to control these crowds," her mother complained.

Gillian didn't reply, having heard the same lament several times already.

She and her mother had eventually received their invitation from the Prince Regent. Whether Lord Skylar had expedited it or whether they would have received it anyway, she had no way of knowing. In any case, they were on their way to Carlton House to greet the great Duke of Wellington.

An hour later, their bodies damp with perspiration, they arrived at the gates of the Prince's official residence. The wide, colonnaded portico was lit with dozens of torches. At long last their carriage came to the front and they were handed down onto the red-carpeted steps and ushered into the high-ceilinged entry hall.

Gillian glanced ahead at the long line of guests inching past the dark red porphyry marble columns. She didn't see Lord Skylar's dark head in the crowd, but countless guests had already headed into the rooms beyond. Once they had received their invitations, he had told them he would meet them at the fete.

She had been through these rooms before on other state occasions, but she knew the Prince was always carrying out renovations, so there would doubtless be new things to see. She was also curious to see how the Prince would outdo himself to welcome home the returning hero, after his splendid celebrations the month before to honor the Austrian, Russian and Prussian royalty.

Gillian and her mother moved with the line of guests through the Blue Velvet Room, the Rose Satin Drawing Room, the new Gothic Dining Room, the Golden Drawing Room, and the long Conservatory—each room a brilliant display of gilded cornices, elaborately painted doors, frescoed ceilings, thick French carpets matching the colors of the walls and furnishings. The finest Dutch and French works of art from the Continent, old masters and new, decorated the walls.

Gillian was struck again with wonder at the luxury of the palace. In the giant ballroom, the guests filed past the Prince Regent, his corpulent body dressed in a magnificent, medal-laden uniform. Beside him stood the smaller Arthur Wellesley, the First Duke of Wellington, his slim body erect.

Gillian curtsied deeply to the Regent.

"What a pretty thing you've become, Lady Gillian," he told her gallantly.

"Thank you, Your Royal Highness," she replied demurely, knowing that was all that was expected of her. She followed her mother to greet the Duke.

He bowed his head over her hand.

"Congratulations on your many victories, Your Grace. I…read about each one in the *Courier* and *Gazette,*" she told him shyly, wishing she could express her admiration for all he had done for his country. How his men must adore the thin-faced commander with the deep-set dark eyes and brows. His dark hair was beginning to gray. His uniform, a splendid red with a dark sash and high, braided collar added to his regal bearing.

"Thank you, my lady," he answered quietly. "If every soldier has such a beautiful and loyal follower at home, that must be a reason they were so brave and stalwart on the battlefield."

She smiled, feeling the tears smart in her eyes. With a final squeeze of her hands, he let hers go and turned to the next guest.

She followed her mother blindly for a few moments, remembering the Duke's words. It was as if he knew the deepest secrets of her heart. Secrets buried so deep, no one on earth knew of them.

They continued through the crush of people out into the gardens. The architect, John Nash, had specially designed a muslin-draped corridor leading to an immense hall with an umbrella-shaped ceiling. In the center was a temple wreathed in masses of flowers. From it emanated the sounds of orchestra music. More covered walks led in all directions out from the hall. Gillian could see supper tables laid out in the different tents leading from them. The muslin walls of these corridors were painted with battle scenes. Gillian looked curiously at one of the titles, *The Overthrow of Tyranny by the Allied Powers.*

Her mother was talking with acquaintances.

"Hello, Lady Gillian." Cubby Eaton greeted her, the sickly sweet scent of his toilette water identifying him before she turned to see him. "You look absolutely ravishing this evening."

"Thank you, Cubby," she replied. "I would say you look rather dashing yourself." He wore a dark coat, but his waistcoat was yellow satin embroidered in shades of blue and green. His cravat was so wide and stiff it pushed his shirt points into his cheeks. His chestnut hair floated in stiff and shiny waves away from his forehead, its spicy pomade reaching her nostrils as he bent over her gloved hand.

"Had a chance to greet the Iron Duke yet?" he asked.

"Yes! Wasn't he dashing?"

"Perfectly so. I could just see him wielding that sword in battle." Cubby took a stance and thrust forth an imaginary sword.

"Who else is here tonight?" she asked.

"Oh, the usual. The pointed absence of Princess Caroline, poor dear, amusing herself with one of her lovers at Kensington, no doubt. There's talk of her going abroad now that Paris is liberated."

He looked around the room through his quizzing glass. "The Queen is here, of course, to support her son…all the royal highnesses…Princess Charlotte, looking well despite her heartbreak over that handsome hussar, Captain Hesse." He glanced around as if looking for the person in question. "Ever since she met the dashing Prince Augustus in King Frederick's suite last month, I think the bloom is returning to her cheek."

"I think it was heartless of the Regent to forbid her to see Captain Hesse," Gillian insisted. "And to break open her desk and take all her letters from him. It was shockingly cruel."

"Well, you can't be a mere seventeen and expect to have liberty in matters of the heart. You must wait until you are married at least," he said with a twitter.

Just then Gillian saw Lord Skylar approaching. She smiled, looking at the contrast between Cubby and him. Short and tall, round and gaunt, gaudy and somber.

"Good evening, Lady Gillian," he said, and bowed. "I am glad to see you made it in one piece to this sad press of humanity. You look lovely."

Sky found he meant what he said. His future bride looked exquisite in a sheer white muslin dress over satin. A silver tissue wrap covered her shoulders. It looked liked gossamer. Silvery blue ribbons accented her dress and hair. A simple wreath of tiny flowers decorated her hair, in contrast to the mass of diamonds in the room. All the pawn-shops of London must have been emptied that afternoon to supply the ladies—and gentlemen—he realized, eyeing with distaste the large diamond stickpin in Cubby Eaton's cravat.

"Were you caught up in the line of coaches?" Gillian asked.

"I had my driver drop me off about a block away rather than swelter inside."

"Mama would never have permitted that, although we were quite wilted by the time we arrived."

"You look as fresh as a newly opened lily at dawn."

She warmed under the praise. To regain her composure, she asked him, "Have you been to Carlton House before?"

He glanced around the surroundings. "Yes, but it has undergone quite a transformation since I was last here."

She laughed. "I think it has gone from Oriental to Greek to French in the years you've been away. Now, it's clearly 'military mania,' as Lady Bessborough would say."

"Shall we go in to supper?" he asked, offering her his arm.

"Yes, certainly. Cubby, would you like to join us?"

"My dear, I couldn't deny myself the pleasure."

It was a long dinner, with over a hundred hot dishes served, from roast larks to roast beef, with truffles appearing in almost every dish.

It was difficult to make conversation except to one's immediate neighbors. Her mother sat on one side, Cubby on her other. Lord Skylar sat across from her. He conversed with a duke on one side and a marquess on the other.

Afterward there was dancing in the main structure to the music of two orchestras. Dozens of scarlet uniforms stood out amidst the dark blue evening jackets of the men and the pale colored gowns of the women. Gillian scrutinized each officer, hoping for another glimpse of the Duke, but in vain. There were far too many people.

When a Scottish reel ended and Lord Skylar led Gillian off the dance floor, the crowd momentarily prevented them from moving ahead. Gillian found herself standing in front of a Guards officer. She had studied enough uniforms to place this one.

The gilt badge pinned to his sash bore the distinctive eight-pointed silver star of the Order of the Garter and the double row of brass buttons set in pairs down the front of his jacket further identified him as an officer of the Second Foot Guards, otherwise known as the Coldstreams.

Licking dry lips, she lifted her eyes higher. Wide gold braid edged the dark blue facing of the scarlet jacket. Gold epaulets showed a pair of broad shoulders to advantage. The high, stiff collar framed smooth-shaven cheeks bronzed by the sun. Dark hair, almost blue-black, was combed carelessly back from a wide forehead.

And finally—how could she ever forget—those blue eyes, like lapis lazuli, in which a wicked hint of humor always lurked? They stared into hers now. For one, long second that blue gaze held hers.

Laughter was evident in them. No surprise, no shock. Only amusement, as if it had been only yesterday he'd bid her adieu and gone off to fight the French.

"Lady Gillian," he exclaimed. "Upon my word."

Feeling the floor slide beneath her, she tightened her hold imperceptibly on Lord Skylar's arm.

"Are you all right?" he asked solicitously.

"Yes," she managed.

Gerrit Hawkes turned to his companion, a beautiful lady whom Gillian recognized as a leading member of the ton, and said in a teasing voice, "This young lady was a mere slip of a girl out of the schoolroom when I last saw her."

As introductions were made, Gillian could only hope her features revealed nothing of the turmoil inside her. Why now? Why here? Why hadn't she heard anything of his arrival from France?

He was so devastatingly handsome. The three years on the battlefield had not aged him, merely toughened the youthful features into the rugged lines of manhood.

"Captain Gerrit Hawkes of the Coldstream Guards," he told Lord Skylar.

He'd been promoted from lieutenant to captain.

"Lately returned from Spain, I take it?" asked Skylar.

"Yes," the captain answered with a grin. "Via Paris."

"I congratulate you on your victories." Gillian heard Lord Skylar's voice somewhere above her to her left, but she had eyes only for Gerrit.

The captain inclined his head a fraction. "Thank you. The credit belongs to our commander."

"I heard he especially commended the Guards."

"Morale was rather low before he came. But the Coldstreams are well disciplined so he was able to depend on us in battle. When the tide began to turn after Albuera, we were there to witness it."

They chatted for a few minutes—an eternity to Gillian. How much longer could she endure standing?

"Well, I am sure we shall see each other again during the victory festivities," Skylar told him.

"I'm sure we shall, my lord." With laughter in his eyes, he bowed over Gillian's limp hand. "Au revoir, my lady."

As the crowd parted enough for them to continue on their way, Lord Skylar guided her forward. Looking straight ahead of her, seeing nothing, she kept walking where she was directed, her thoughts on only one thing. Gerrit was here. He was alive and he was back.

"Let me find you somewhere to sit and something to drink," Lord Skylar said as they reached a frescoed wall at the outer edges of the room.

They finally found an empty settee in a secluded corner of the Rose Satin Drawing Room.

Once she had a place to collapse, her urge to faint disappeared. Instead she found herself restless. "Are you sure you're quite all right?" he asked her again.

Turning away from his concerned gaze, she fanned her overheated cheeks with her ivory fan. "Just a little faint with the heat," she said.

He left her to go in search of some refreshment. She waited, hoping it would take him a long time before he returned.

How she wanted to go back outside to get a glimpse of Captain Gerrit Hawkes.

The only man she'd ever loved. The only one she ever *could* love.

She remembered his avowals to love her always in the few letters she'd received from him, which her mother had destroyed, but not before she'd memorized their contents.

Dearest Heart, you possess me body, mind and soul....

My life is in your hands. With one word you—and you alone—decide if I live or die....

I bid you adieu, most probably to die on the battlefield. I only pray it will be honorably. My last words will
be your name whispered on my dying lips....

It had been nearly three years since she had heard anything from him, although she'd followed the movements of
his company from the newspaper accounts. She'd known of
his first engagement in the Battle of Barrosa through to the
siege of Ciudad Rodrigo and Badajoz.

When he had been wounded at Salamanca, she'd despaired, having no way of knowing if he had recovered.
Through her close friend she had inquiries made and once
again rejoiced when she knew he had survived.

She devoured the accounts of the assault on San Sebas-
tian and the army's triumphal crossing into France and
march to Paris. She had agonized and prayed for his safety
until certain from the newspaper lists that he'd come out
unscathed.

He'd received his commission as a lieutenant and now he
was a captain in command of a company. He must have
been decorated for bravery in battle. Of course he had been!

"Here is some ratafia." Skylar handed her the glass and
seated himself at the other end of the settee. She was glad
of that, not knowing how she could bear it if he so much as
touched her hand tonight.

She sipped the sweet drink and remained silent, wondering how she would appear normal for the remainder of the
evening. It must be well after midnight. She feigned a yawn,
although the last thing she felt was sleepy.

"Tired?"

"Yes, frightfully."

He glanced at his pocket watch. "It's almost three. The festivities are still in full swing. I'm sure they will go on until dawn."

"They usually do."

"If you'd like, I'll fetch your mother and tell her you'd like to go home."

She debated, part of her wanting to leave, the other longing for another glimpse of the captain. "I don't think she'd want to leave. I shall be fine if I sit quietly for a bit."

He nodded.

Strains of music reached them, and the sound of guests, many of them walking through the room or standing in groups around it, but their own corner was solitary.

"You look beautiful tonight," he told her softly, a warm look in his dark eyes.

"Don't say that," she said more sharply than she'd intended.

He raised an eyebrow at her and she sat, caught by the question in his dark eyes. "Haven't you ever been paid a compliment before?" he asked.

She looked away. "It's not that. I…it's just…nothing. I must be tired. Maybe I should go home."

"As you wish," he said, rising and holding out his hand to her.

"Perhaps we could go riding tomorrow afternoon after you are rested from tonight's fete," he suggested, escorting her out to the main hall.

"All right," she replied absently.

"We can meet at the Stanhope gate of Hyde Park around five. Would that suit you?"

"Yes, fine," she replied, surveying the people around her, searching for that blue-black hair.

* * *

As dawn crept over the city, Gillian sat up in her bed, her knees drawn up under the covers. On one sat a gold locket snapped open. It was the only thing her mother hadn't found when she'd ransacked Gillian's room in search of any evidence of her clandestine meetings with the young gentleman from her dance class.

Gillian stroked the black lock of hair that lay on one side of the locket. Soft and silky.

She had truly felt for the young Princess Charlotte this past spring when her father, the Regent, had pried open her private desk and confiscated every letter, every memento exchanged with the handsome Captain Hesse.

Gillian, too, had been seventeen, when her mother had discovered her amorous correspondence with the twenty-one-year-old Gerrit. Every desk drawer had been ransacked, every letter burned in the grate.

By the following week, the duchess had engaged Miss Templeton as Gillian's companion. Her guard, she thought bitterly. Over the past three seasons, Gillian sometimes thought she would suffocate from the lady's presence. It was only now, betrothed to Lord Skylar, that Gillian was experiencing anything like the freedom she had known when her father was alive.

She looked at the ring on her finger. It looked lovely. But what was the price of wearing it? Marriage to a man she hadn't known a fortnight ago—when another who'd stolen her heart three years ago had returned on the scene?

Chapter Five

✤

Sky grimaced. The nausea was becoming worse in the rattling coach. It had started soon after he'd eaten that supper at the fete, but it had been faint enough to ignore.

But as the evening wore on, it had grown stronger, and it had been with a sense of relief that he'd summoned the coach for the duchess and her daughter.

Now Sky slumped across the seat of his own carriage, feeling with every bump of the wheels the desire to retch. He held on, knowing it was not far to his house.

He'd managed to hide his bouts of indisposition up to now, but they were becoming more severe. The fever couldn't be striking him again. No! He hit the seat with his fist in futile anger.

The coach stopped. He sat up, allowing the groom to let down the steps and open the door. Sky exited as if nothing was the matter and bade the man good-night as he held the front door open for him.

The candles in the candelabra had gone out, but they weren't needed. Already a gray light crept into the house.

Glad his father was away—Sky neither knew nor cared where—he staggered up to his room.

"Good evening, my lord," Nigel greeted him from the chair where he'd been dozing.

Sky collapsed on his bed.

Nigel hurried over to him. "Tired, my lord? What's the matter?" he asked more urgently when Sky said nothing but sat with his head between his knees.

"It's hitting me again," he answered finally through gritted teeth. "I can feel it."

Nigel touched his bowed forehead. "Your skin is warm."

He nodded assent. "Get me something—a basin. I don't know how long I can hold my meal down."

Nigel hurried to comply. Then he gently helped Sky remove his coat and waistcoat. He undid his cravat and let his shirt hang loose at the neck. As soon as he'd removed his boots, Sky lay on the bed, his legs curled up in an effort to mitigate the discomfort. Nigel threw a blanket over him.

He heard Nigel's soft tread across the room. He came back with a cold compress.

"You'll have…to…cancel my engagements tomorrow. Tell everyone…I—I've gone out of town." He couldn't think beyond the pain in his gut and between his temples. "Go. Leave me in peace."

Nigel leaned over him, his brown face inches from his. "It's her. She won't let you go."

"Don't speak idiocy," he mumbled, closing his eyes to those greenish-yellow irises looking at him with such certainty.

"She won't stop till she have you back in Kingston."

Sky groaned. "You think a human can make me this sick? What do you think, she's laced my food with arsenic all the way across the Atlantic?"

"She have her ways."

Sky cursed. "Get out. You can't help me anymore. Don't let anyone know anything. Say I'm out of town, say anything but that I'm ill. And don't, for pity's sake, call any doctors."

"Yes, sir. I'll leave the laudanum by your table."

A few minutes later the room was silent. Soon it would be fully light. Who knew how long he'd be laid low this time. One thing was certain, he would rely on no more physicians. If the illness hadn't killed him the last time, the physics they filled him with would have. The bleedings alone had probably cost him most of his strength.

Finally relief came as Sky heaved over his washbasin. After cleaning himself, he measured the laudanum drops into a glass of water Nigel had left, doubling his usual dosage, hoping for numbness from the pounding between his temples. Finally he climbed under the covers, seeking the blessed unconsciousness of sleep.

Gillian's mare stamped restively as she waited with her groom at the entrance to Hyde Park. She patted the horse's neck and whispered a few words to her. Then she flipped open her watch. They had been waiting three quarters of an hour and Lord Skylar had yet to appear. Had he forgotten his invitation? Or had he been too tired from the evening's exertions?

He hadn't struck her thus far as a gentleman who would forget an engagement, least of all with his fiancée!

Perhaps he was indisposed after last night. Although he insisted he was recovered from the illness that had hit him in the Indies, to Gillian he still looked like a man recuperating.

Yes, that must be it, she decided, feeling a momentary sympathy for him as she remembered his solicitude to her last night when he'd thought her fatigued.

Her groom coughed behind her. "My lady, hadn't we better return? The crowds are getting thick."

She debated a minute longer. She wasn't ready to go back yet. Since last night, a restlessness had seized her. Finally, she turned to her groom and said, "I shall go for a ride first."

"Very well, my lady." Together the two entered the park and headed for the Ladies' Mile.

As they were returning along the Row, she spotted Gerrit in the distance. He and a fellow officer were leaning over an open carriage, having a good time chatting with the ladies inside.

She pressed her lips together, determined to ride past him without acknowledging him. It hurt to the quick to admit how little she had meant to him. She had given him everything, and he had never even bothered to let her know he was back in town. Clearly he had forgotten her in the intervening years since their tearful goodbye.

Gillian skirted some other riders and was almost past the carriage, the laughter of its female occupants intermingling with the lower-timbered laughter of the officers—one she recognized so well. It was like a fresh wound, hearing it now, and knowing it was not meant for her.

"Lady Gillian!"

She looked up involuntarily and then wished she hadn't.

Gerrit looked splendid in his scarlet uniform and shako. He had one hand raised and his devastating smile reached into her very heart.

She gave a nod and kept on going.

Five minutes later she heard the muffled clip-clop of hoof-beats against the sandy path behind her. She kept riding.

"Good afternoon, Lady Gillian. What's your hurry?"

His black charger had pulled up alongside her mare with ease. His voice sounded amused.

"Good afternoon, Captain Hawkes. I am in no hurry. This is my usual gait."

"Care to go for a canter? I recall you used to be quite a good rider."

The challenge was unmistakable. Without a word, she veered from the crowded path and went off onto the grass. Gerrit's horse was right beside her. Only her groom, with a faint, "Lady Gillian!" was left several paces behind.

They rode across the vast parkland, under massive elms and plane trees and wide fields. Finally, after several moments, having reached almost the opposite side of the park and nearing the ring, they slowed their horses.

He tipped his hat to her with a smile. "You have improved."

"So have you."

He grinned, showing those devastatingly white teeth against bronzed skin. "It comes from marching anywhere from ten to twenty miles a day across all sorts of terrain in Spain and France."

"I read your name in the lists when you were wounded."

The amusement in those blue eyes deepened. "Were you concerned?"

She could not share his humor. "The only way I could discover if you had recovered was to have a maid talk with a maid at your household."

He sobered. "I'm sorry if I caused you worry."

Her smile was tight. "I wouldn't describe it precisely as 'worry.' More like agony of mind and soul."

He looked down at his gloved hands on the reins. "I'm sorry I didn't write you after I arrived on the Peninsula."

She waited.

He sighed, as if sensing the moment had arrived for explanations. Would he have ever given her any if she hadn't run into him at Carlton House?

"I didn't write you anymore after those first few times because, once I understood what I was really in for—between the summer fevers and the long sieges to capture Ciudad Rodrigo and Badajoz—I doubted very much if I'd ever be home again in one piece.

"My closest comrades didn't come home. Those who didn't die on the battlefield died of the putrid fever from their wounds. The few that are home are missing a limb or two. I didn't want you to be obligated to half a man."

"Oh, Gerrit, you know that wouldn't have mattered."

He gave her a smile that made her think no time had passed at all and he was still that wonderful dancing partner in her quadrille class. "To you it wouldn't, but to me it would have.

"You've grown very beautiful, Gillian," he said softly. The way he looked at her made her feel warm all over.

And then he had to ruin it all by saying with a smile, "I

hear congratulations are in order. The future Countess of Skylar, and someday the Marchioness of Caulfield. I stand in admiration."

"Doesn't it matter to you?" she blurted out before she could stop herself.

His blue eyes looked into hers with absolute understanding. "Of course it does, but what is that to the purpose? Your father and mother would never have countenanced a match between the two of us—I'm a third son, don't you recall? I had few prospects except to die a glorious death on the battlefield. I did you a service by not letting you hope.

"Look at you now, betrothed to one of the biggest titles and fortunes on the market. Every young lady envies you."

The words were a bitter consolation. Once again, as she had three years ago, she felt caught in a web not of her own making. Before, her mother had forbidden her to see Gerrit. Now, her mother had neatly tied up her future to the most eligible bachelor on the market.

"Come now," Gerrit told her, "cheer up. We can still be friends. Let's finish our ride before your groom takes you home."

When Tertius finally awoke, he shivered under the weight of the coverlets and his head felt as if a vise were pressing his temples together.

Thankful to be conscious at least, he made an effort to sit up.

Nigel was immediately at his side. He pressed him back down on the bed, feeling his forehead. "The fever is strong. You must stay put." He turned to pour some water from a pitcher and measured some drops into the glass. "Here, drink this. It's barley water." He held his head up enough for Tertius to take a few sips. The liquid felt good against his parched lips and mouth.

"I must get up. I have too much to do."

"You not be going anywhere today. Let others do what has to be done."

"Talk to Father's secretary," Tertius told him, lying back down on the bed, finding it too difficult to concentrate. "Tell him to cancel my engagements and send out the proper notes. You know what to say." Hadn't they just been down this road a scant few months ago?

"Yes, sir."

The new dose of laudanum was already taking effect. Suddenly nothing mattered but the oblivion of a drugged sleep. Tertius burrowed down, trying to get warm. He felt, rather than saw, Nigel rearrange the covers and put another coverlet over him.

Nigel made his way down to the ground floor. He knocked on the door he knew led to the study, although he had never been in that room himself except when Lord Skylar had shown him around the first day.

"Come in," a peremptory voice called out.

He entered quietly and went to the desk. Mr. Scott, Lord Caulfield's private secretary, watched him. "Yes, what do you want?"

"Lord Skylar wishes to inform you he will be unavailable for a few days," he said, hoping it would be only a few days. "He instructs you to cancel any of his appointments and send out the appropriate messages."

"Well, why doesn't he come and tell me himself?"

"He had to leave town on urgent business." He knew he wouldn't be able to keep the charade up before the rest of the servants, but perhaps the secretary could be made to believe Tertius wasn't in residence.

Mr. Scott stood and came around the desk. "You may inform your master I am not accustomed to taking my orders from a valet." His look said clearly that he didn't welcome Nigel's presence in the study.

Nigel took a step closer, not liking to use this weapon but finding no alternative. He stared down at the man, knowing he had probably never had a six-and-a-half-foot black man standing over him.

The man cleared his throat and retreated. "Very well, you may inform Lord Skylar I shall do as he asks."

Nigel bowed silently and left the library.

"Over my dead body," Mr. Scott added when the door had shut behind the black man. With that, the secretary turned back to his desk and straightened some papers, the hammering in his heart making it impossible for the moment to concentrate on anything else.

From the study, Nigel went down to the kitchen. He approached the cook, knowing the eyes of the kitchen maids followed him.

"Excuse me, Mrs. Jenkins. I would like to request some strong beef broth for the next few meals."

"What's a matter? Somethin' ailin' you?"

He hesitated, but knew he wouldn't be able to fool the other servants. "No, it be for Lord Skylar. A trifle indisposed."

"Too much to drink at the Prince's reception last night?"

"Precisely."

"Tsk-tsk. I hope he's not going back to his old ways. We was so hoping for him to settle down—have a family—now that poor Lord Edmund's gone." The cook shook her head with a sigh. "Very well, I'll send the broth up."

"Thank you, madam."

She turned away from him and noticed the scullery maid. "Stop that gawking and get to chopping them vegetables."

"Yes, ma'am." The girl closed her mouth and dragged her attention from Nigel. As he turned to leave the room, he glanced at the other kitchen maids. They hastily looked away and bent back to their tasks. All but a housemaid—he recognized her different rank by her black dress and starched white apron. She backed away a step as he passed by, but kept her gaze fixed on him.

As the door swung closed behind him, he took a deep breath, allowing a moment to release the emotions each step outside Lord Skylar's rooms occasioned him. He hated the feeling of being an oddity, which had gripped him since arriving in England. He might as well be in a freak show. The only other men of color he'd seen since coming to these shores had been an occasional footman dressed in ridiculous velvet knee breeches, coat and white powdered wig and gloves.

At least Lord Skylar no longer made a spectacle of him. He had learned over the years that the only times his master made sport of anyone was when he himself felt threatened.

Three nights later, Gillian sat with Templeton, smiling and chatting with the many beaus who stopped by her box to pay their respects during the performance. Her eye kept scanning the boxes opposite. During the last act of the first performance, she saw Captain Hawkes enter Lady Win-throp's box. She could see him conversing over the ladies' shoulders, see their smiles, and she burned with jealousy over what they found so amusing.

Lord Caulfield's box remained empty.

It had been three days since his missed engagement in the park and rumor had it he was out of town.

How dare he? How dare he make such a fool of her?

Her only consolation was in showing Captain Hawkes how sought-after she was by all the young gentlemen in their circle. When the lights were raised during the inter-mission, he acknowledged her with a smile and bow of his head.

Later, as she sat pretending to watch the performance, she heard a low voice behind her.

"You look ravishing."

Gerrit's low voice vibrated against her ear, sending a shiver through her.

"I dreamed of you many a night lying in my tent. I imag-ined you in my arms under the stars, our two bodies keep-ing each other warm."

Her glance darted to Templeton, but she seemed en-grossed in the comedy. Gillian didn't dare move.

The audience burst out in laughter and Gerrit took the moment of distraction to touch the spot behind her ear with his lips—the briefest, softest of touches. Surely no one saw it, but it burned Gillian's skin. How could she bear sitting there, pretending nothing was happening?

Did he mean it? Had he really thought of her in these three long years? Gillian longed to believe it.

"Ride with me in St. James's Park tomorrow afternoon.

We can view the pagoda. I'll find you there by the lake," he whispered.

She made no acknowledgment she even heard him, but her mind was already feverishly at work as to how she would arrange a visit to St. James's without Templeton. Perhaps if her mother thought she went with a friend?

How could she even be considering such a thing! She was betrothed. It was scandalous to think of meeting a man other than Lord Skylar. But what was the meaning of Lord Skylar's absence? How little he must think of her to leave with no word.

She mustn't contemplate meeting Gerrit. But she had to know what he really felt. Her gloved hands clutched her fan tightly.

"You are mine, Gillian. You and I both know it," Gerrit murmured against her ear. "Don't deny a returning soldier what you promised him so long ago...."

She drew in her breath. He hadn't forgotten! Hadn't she pledged her troth to this man long before she met Lord Skylar? Not in any public way, not in a legal document drawn up between his family and hers, but in secret, in the pledging of two hearts to become one.

Late the next morning as they were breakfasting, the Duchess of Burnham read from the *The Times:*

> "Lord Cabot Pembroke, the third Marquess of Caulfield, Second Earl of Bakersfield, announces the betrothal of his son, the Earl of Skylar to Lady Gillian Elizabeth Edwards, daughter of the late Duke of Burnham and his Dowager Duchess."

Gillian dropped her knife. The words sounded ominous, so coldly printed in a newspaper. They made the arrangement talked of by her mother permanent and unchangeable.

"I can't believe it!" she exclaimed.

Her mother looked up. "What don't you believe?"

"How could he?" The alarm grew in Gillian the more she thought of the announcement. She wanted to tell her mother she wasn't ready. Couldn't they wait a few more months?

"How could who what?" Her mother looked more and more perplexed.

"That man!"

Understanding finally dawned. "You mean that *gentleman*, Lord Skylar?" her mother corrected.

"I don't call a gentleman one who forgets an engagement with a lady and does not even send round a note of apology and then publishes news of our betrothal with not so much as a by-your-leave."

"What on earth are you talking about?" her mother asked. "When did Lord Skylar forget an engagement?"

"Lord Skylar kept me waiting almost an hour the other day at Hyde Park for our riding engagement and never appeared."

"Oh, dear. That's four days. He hasn't written?"

"No."

"I can't imagine what could have kept him. Perhaps he is ill." Her mother frowned, removing her reading glasses.

"I, too, thought he might be indisposed, but not even to send a note?"

"It is strange," her mother agreed. "I'm sure you'll receive something today."

"I was told at Lady Shrewsbury's ridotto that he was out of town. Can you believe that? And not a word!"

Her mother looked alarmed. "I'll make an inquiry through Lord Caulfield."

"You most certainly will not. I'll not go groveling for explanations to a man who doesn't even think enough of me to cancel an appointment." She got up from the table. "And now to publish news of our betrothal. It's too much!"

"I'm sure it was Lord Caulfield who was responsible for the announcement, not his son," her mother explained. "No doubt there's a very good explanation for all this. In any case, I'm glad about the announcement. This makes everything official.

"Now, we must set a date," the duchess continued, forgetting Gillian's outrage and getting down to the more important business of wedding plans. "I think a wedding during the Christmas season would be lovely. Lord Skylar would be out of mourning. I shall discuss it with Lord Caulfield."

Gillian was no longer listening. Her glance strayed to a society item in the copy of the *Morning Post* she'd been reading. It described the theatrical performance of the previous evening. The name "Captain Hawkes" caught her eye. *The much-decorated war hero, Captain Hawkes, was seen in Lady Winthrop's box....*

When her mother finally dropped the subject of the wedding date, Gillian sat back down and took a sip of tea to strengthen her resolve.

"Mama, I have invited Charlotte to go and view the construction of the pagoda at St. James's this afternoon. Might I drive the phaeton?"

Her mother turned to Templeton. "Can you accompany the girls?"

"Oh, Mama, we would be too crowded. The phaeton sits only two comfortably. Charlotte and I shall be fine."

"I would prefer you take Templeton with you. There are so many undesirables about in the parks these days."

"I can send a note over to see if Lord Skylar has returned. Perhaps he could meet us there," Gillian suggested on a sudden burst of inspiration.

"That's a splendid idea! But I still want Templeton to ride with you." Her mother went back to her newspaper.

Gillian stood up and excused herself, frustrated once again in her plans for seeing Gerrit.

As soon as she was alone in her room, guilt assailed her. How could she be behaving in such a way? She'd been ready to use Lord Skylar as an excuse to see another man. It brought back the time three years ago when she had concealed her meetings with Gerrit from her mother. How could she find herself in such a position again?

She remembered Lord Skylar's stipulation that one thing he required in a wife was her fidelity. She had given him her word.

Her heart pounded as she remembered the gravity of his tone. What would he think if he knew she was planning to meet her former lover?

She hid her face in her hands, too confused to know what to do.

She had to see Gerrit. Then she'd know what to do.

Just this one last time and then she would know.

One last time to determine what Gerrit really felt for her. She would tell him it was over. He had come back to reclaim her too late.

Was it too late?

If she were free, would he do the honorable thing this time?

A betrothal was a legally binding agreement. It was not easily broken.

No, even if Gerrit wanted to marry her, her mother would never countenance the match. The only course would be elopement.

The word filled her with terror. It conjured up tales of young girls brought back by a father or older brother in disgrace. But other couples had returned and been welcomed back into society after a period.

Hope sparked within her. But how to see Gerrit alone with Templeton following her around like a terrier?

Lord Caulfield pounded on his son's door and jerked it open before giving anyone a chance to answer it.

"What in thunderation is going on here? I get word from my secretary that your man is holding you hostage in here, away from all the other servants—" He stopped dead at the sight that greeted him.

The shadowy interior of the room was stuffy and had that closed, sickly sweet scent of medicine.

The oath died on his lips as he approached the bed. "What's wrong with him?" he asked the black man sharply.

Tertius cracked open an eye. Thankfully, his head no longer ached. He touched a temple tentatively, almost afraid the pain would return. "I would wish you good-morning or afternoon, Father, but I'm not quite sure which it is."

His father stood looking down at him. "It's afternoon," then as if realizing how ludicrous his reply was, he frowned.

"What's happened to you? How long have you been like this? I was told you were out of town—"

Tertius turned his head slowly toward Nigel, still afraid of experiencing pain. He arched an eyebrow at him. "How long has it been?"

"Five days," the man answered quietly.

Tertius turned back to his father. "You have your answer."

"Five days of what?"

"You tell him, Nigel. I find I am not quite up to it yet."

"Fever, vomiting, dysentery." He went down the list. "The same ailment that afflicted him in Kingston."

"Haven't you seen any specialists?" His father ignored Nigel and directed himself to Tertius.

"Every quack from Kingston to Bridgetown," he answered wearily. "I haven't yet given Harley Street the pleasure of diagnosing me."

"Well, what did they say in the Indies?"

He placed a hand over his eyes. "Let me recollect. Dyspepsia, inflammation of the bowels, brain fever, tropical malady…the list went on. Forgive me if all the medical jargon escapes me."

"And you've called no physician in now?" He turned furiously to Nigel. "What is the meaning of this? My son could have died!"

"I forbade him to," Tertius interrupted him with a feeble gesture. "Their only remedy is to bleed me. It leaves me even weaker than the fever."

His father turned away from the bed as if the sight of Tertius sickened him. "I cannot believe this. I thought you were well. You told me you were healed. Of all the calamities to befall this family…"

As his father fumed at the Fates, Tertius made an effort to sit up. Unwashed and unshaven, he knew he presented a spectacle. After the floor ceased to shift, he attempted to stand. Nigel came immediately to aid him.

"Hadn't you better stay abed?" his father called out in alarm.

"I've been prone for five days."

"There must be something the doctors can do. I'll send for my personal physician. He's one of the best—"

"I don't need any more physicians. All they can do besides bleed me to death is prescribe some worthless physics and elixirs." He held up a dark brown glass bottle. Suddenly, a wave of anger swept through him and he hurled the bottle toward the fireplace. Despite his weakness, he managed to make his target. The bottle cracked against the stone, its liquid contents spilling and immediately bursting into flames.

"I'd as lief drown myself in blue ruin," he said. "As you can see, the composition is the same. And it will be less dear."

His father approached him again. "You look at death's door." He looked him up and down, and Tertius felt the disgust in his voice. "First Edmund and now you. Can't I have one son who will outlive me? If anything happens to you, your cousin George will inherit and I shudder to think of that…."

"Lord Skylar will be well again for a spell." Nigel's soft tones startled them both.

"What's that?" Lord Caulfield frowned at the valet.

"Once the fever breaks, my lord recovers for a time…until the next bout."

Lord Caulfield looked from one to the other. "So, it's a recurring fever."

"It looks that way," Tertius spoke up before sitting back down. His legs felt like wet dish rags.

His father clutched his jaw in his hand and stared at the carpet. At last he spoke, as if coming to a decision. "There's only one thing to be done."

Tertius gripped the edges of his bed, bracing himself for what his father had in mind. Another exile?

"We shall move the wedding date up. The sooner you impregnate the chit, the better."

Tertius stared at his father. He hadn't expected that as a solution.

Why was he surprised?

To his father, he was only a vehicle for breeding. He wasn't, nor had ever been, this man's son in all the ways that mattered.

"Don't you see, Duchess, we must have them married as soon as possible. It's the only way." The marquess's eyes beseeched the duchess to understand the urgency of the situation.

"But if he's as ill as you say," she began cautiously, "why should my daughter—my only child—be saddled with a man who might leave her a widow before the honeymoon is even up?"

"Not just a widow. A *countess*—with a considerable fortune. If the worst should happen, she can always remarry. But I'm counting on my son to last long enough to father an heir.

"As you know, our estates are entailed. If Tertius should die without a son, everything goes to a ne'er-do-well cousin of mine. You have already experienced that in your own family," he added significantly. "Don't let such a disaster be repeated. All it needs is for Lady Gillian to bear a son. As mother to the future Marquess of Caulfield, your daughter will be in a very powerful position."

The duchess considered his words and slowly nodded as she came to the same conclusions as he.

"Very well," she said at last with a deep sigh. "I shall explain to her that we must move the date up. She won't like it. I don't know how much to tell her."

"Don't say anything of his fever. Why worry the girl? In my day we married whomever our parents chose."

"You are right. It would serve no purpose to worry her. We must hope for the best for your son's continued recovery."

"Of course. I leave things in your capable hands then." He rose and bowed.

Chapter Six

The next morning Gillian's mother paid a visit to her room. Gillian scurried to hide her two cats in her dressing room. Sophie, the new spaniel, lay quietly on her rug.

"Mama, what are doing about so early?" she asked her, tying the belt of her dressing gown more tightly around her waist.

Her mother eyed the dog with distaste as she sidestepped it widely and found a chair well away from it.

"I need to inform you of some changes in the wedding plans," her mother said calmly.

"What changes?" Gillian asked cautiously. The last thing she wanted to think about at the moment was her wedding. She hadn't been able to contrive meeting Gerrit at St. James's and her only hope lay in running into him again by accident.

"The marquess and I have decided there is no reason for

you and Lord Skylar to wait until the end of the year to wed. We decided it best if the two of you marry at the end of the summer. By then your dresses should be ready."

Gillian stared at her mother as if the woman had just told her to stand in front of a firing squad. "What did you say?"

"You heard me. The wedding date has been moved up."

A sudden, blind terror gripped her. It had been one thing to think of a wedding a good six months off—but to face marriage in a few short weeks?

But she could tell by her mother's tone that she was perfectly serious. Gillian gave a nervous laugh. "I can't possibly be married then. We've hardly started the preparations. Mother, be reasonable—"

"I am being perfectly reasonable. We may have to scale down our plans a trifle, but we'll still manage a perfectly acceptable celebration."

Gillian stood in one swift movement. "I haven't heard from the man in almost a week and now you're telling me I'm to be married at the end of the summer?" Her voice rose at the end of the sentence, and she knew she would have hysterics if she didn't get a hold of herself.

Her mother waved aside her objections. "Lord Caulfield explained to me that his son has been a trifle indisposed these last few days. But everything is fine with him now and he will soon be by to see you."

"But why didn't he send a note?" she asked, her mind working furiously. From not having to face Lord Skylar for several days to knowing she would soon be standing at the altar with him was too much of a shift.

"Oh, some confusion with his valet. The note was never delivered."

"I see." Gillian sank back down on her bed. What was she to do? "The end of the summer?" she repeated in a faltering voice. "It's preposterous. It's…so…so—" she searched for another excuse "—vulgar…as if we can't wait, like those couples who find themselves eloping to Gretna Green."

"Hardly. They are usually going against their parents' wishes. You have made a brilliant match. I would think you'd want to begin your married life sooner rather than later. Think of all you will enjoy as the new countess. Lord Caulfield is a widower. He will give you free rein as mistress of all his estates."

"But how can we possibly be ready? With all the victory celebrations, there's so much to do and see—"

"I should think by now the season would have palled for you *un petit peu*. There's no reason not to enjoy the remaining victory celebrations. But if you give it some consideration, I am sure you will come to the same conclusion as we have. It makes much more sense to be married sooner than later. It will give you and Lord Skylar a chance to tour all of the Caulfield estates before winter sets in. Your papa would have wanted to see you safely wed and this is an excellent match—"

The mention of dear Papa's name was too much. "Papa would *never* have forced me to wed against my wishes!" Whenever her mother needed to coerce her into accepting something unpalatable, she made it seem as if it were Papa's dearest wish.

"Your father entrusted your future to my care, and I've done my best to ensure you have the best imaginable one." Her mother's voice did not rise the least decibel, which caused Gillian to become more agitated.

She jumped up from her bed again and approached her mother. "Papa would never have chosen a stranger and thrust him at me and set a date without so much as a by-your-leave!" Her arms rose and tears stung her cheeks. "Was this Lord Skylar's idea? He's nothing but a—a cold, unfeeling brute. I won't have it! I refuse to marry him!"

Her mother stood and gave her a smart slap across the cheek. "Stop that bawling this instant. You shall marry whomever I choose *whenever* I say. Is that perfectly clear?"

Gillian stood staring at her mother, her hand cupping her stinging cheek. She sniffed and repeated, "Papa wouldn't treat me so. He wouldn't make me marry a complete stranger. I don't like Lord Skylar. I find him distasteful. I don't wish to marry anyone…not since—"

Before Gillian could stop herself, her mother finished for her, her eyes blazing, "Not since that penniless boy tried to woo you. He's back, do you know that?"

As Gillian shook her head in denial, her mother took a step closer to her. "You know he is, don't you? Don't you?"

"No!"

"You're lying! You've seen him, haven't you? Answer me!" As she raised her hand to slap Gillian again, Gillian raised her hands to cover her face.

"No! Yes! Only once!" She begged as her mother grabbed her by the hair.

"Where did you see him?"

"At the Prince's fete."

"Did you speak to him?"

She shook her head. "Only a few minutes. He merely greeted me."

Her mother let her go after looking into her eyes. Satisfied, she continued. "You almost ruined your reputation once for that worthless individual. Thanks to me, I discovered it in time and no harm was done. I will not have you jeopardizing this betrothal for some foolish infatuation you should have gotten over three years ago.

"I forbid you to see Captain Hawkes. Is that understood?"

At Gillian's reluctant nod, she stood. "Good. The sooner you're married and out of London, the better," her mother concluded, turning away from Gillian. "Your trousseau should be ready in a few weeks. We'll set your wedding date for the last week in August. It will be a smaller affair than I'd planned, but we should still have a nice crowd at St. James's church.

"We'll pay a call on the seamstress this afternoon and give her the news. Let us see if she can begin fitting your wedding gown."

Her mother continued with her plans as Gillian sank back on her bed, wondering how her life had so quickly gotten into such a coil in so short a time.

Late that afternoon she took her phaeton out to Hyde Park, hoping for a glimpse of Gerrit. Templeton was at her side. Her mother wouldn't let her out alone anymore, not since hearing of the captain's return.

The Row was clogged with the carriage company at that hour, which was what Gillian was hoping for—to see and be seen. She engaged in conversation with everyone she ran into, pretending a lightheartedness she was far from feeling, pretending she had all the time in the world. All to lull Templeton into thinking she had no other reason for being in the park.

They had only progressed halfway down the Row when she spied him. So handsome in his red uniform, riding atop his black charger, stopping to chat with the occupants of the many carriages that crawled along the path.

When he reached them, he tipped his shako to her and Templeton. "Good afternoon, my lady." He waited for an introduction to Templeton. Gillian complied, watching Templeton's face closely. She had never met Gerrit, having been hired by her mother after he'd left for the Peninsula.

"Good afternoon, Captain Hawkes. We are so proud of our heroes who fought so bravely under Wellington."

"Thank you, ma'am," he answered with a twinkle in his eye. "He is a brave commander, and we owe our victories to his fearless leadership." He turned to Gillian. "It is a beautiful afternoon…as was yesterday." His eyes were filled with meaning.

She thrilled at the look in them. "Yes, it is beautiful."

"There is a celebration being planned in Vauxhall the day after tomorrow. A band concert and fireworks in honor of the victory. I hope you will attend?" He directed his question to Templeton.

"Oh, my yes, we want to show our loyalty to our troops. What time is the event?" she asked, her hand at her breast.

"In the evening. But you must arrive early, or the carriage-way will be filled."

"In the evening?" Her voice was filled with doubt. "I don't know. I've heard Vauxhall is filled with cutpurses and…" Her voice faltered, not wanting to describe the types of women known to frequent the place.

"You will be perfectly safe in the central part. It is well lit. All the best ton frequent it. And with the proper escort…"

His glance strayed to Gillian as he said, "Perhaps Lord Skylar." Again his blue eyes were filled with mirth, and Gillian
wondered how he could say Lord Skylar's name as if it were
nothing to him.

"Oh, of course. We shall have to enlist his assistance,"
crowed Templeton, relieved to have arrived at a suitable arrangement. "We hope to see you there, Captain Hawkes."

"Au revoir, then." With another bow, he left them and
continued down the Row.

The following day, Gillian received a note and parcel from
Lord Skylar.

Dear Lady Gillian,
I beg your excuses for my absence of over a week. I
have been indisposed. I know there is no way to make
up for my disgraceful behavior, but I trust it will not
happen again. Please find with this note a token of my
sincere desire for your esteem.
    Yours,
    Skylar

His signature was a slanted black scrawl. She read through
the note and tossed it into her wastebasket. She tore open
the parcel and found another box from the jeweler. This one
was oblong. In it lay an emerald pendant and matching tear-
drop earrings.

Despite her resentment, she couldn't help gasping at the
sight of the sparkling jewelry. An unmarried girl didn't wear
such jewels. She would shine among all her friends. Lifting
the necklace from its satin bed, she held it up to the light,

observing the brilliant sparkles. She put it on carefully, then removed her own earrings and replaced them with the dangling green stones.

She was transformed from a young maiden into a sophisticated lady. She turned around slowly in the full-length mirror, imagining the satin wedding gown she had had fitted the day before, its train gracefully trailing several feet behind her, a sheer veil just covering her ringlets.

Then she remembered what would follow.

In a little over three weeks she would be married.

Lord Skylar had probably convinced her mother to move the date up. All because he needed to produce an heir. That was all he cared about.

He thought he could stand her up at the park then disappear for a week and send her a bauble to make up for his absence.

She unclasped the necklace and threw it into her jewelry case.

Well, he would see that it took more than a few jewels to make things right with her.

Nigel opened the door connecting his master's bedroom with the adjoining sitting room.

A parlor maid was dusting an armoire. He recognized her as the one who had stared at him in the kitchen. She stretched to reach the top carved scrollwork, revealing a pretty ankle in the process.

At that moment she half turned and noticed him. She dropped her feather duster and screamed.

He advanced toward her to reassure her he meant no harm.

"What are you standing there gawking for?" she demanded before he had taken more than two steps.

"I heard someone in here and came in to see who it was," he began.

"Well, you should knock or something," she said, picking up the duster.

"I'll do so next time," he promised.

"What are you grinning at?"

He wiped the smile off his face. "I'm sorry if I scared you."

"You didn't scare me!"

Her stern face finally broke into an unwilling smile as the two continued looking at each other. "You startled me. I'm not used to—"

When she stopped and color began to fill her face, he understood. "Not used to a black man standing in de same room staring at you?"

She looked down at the duster and toyed with the feathers. "No, I'm not." She looked up defiantly once she'd admitted it. "I've never been near one—not this near. You're very tall," she added.

"I be a man, like any other."

She nodded after considering a moment.

He cleared his throat as she began to say something.

"I'm sorry—" they both said at once. He gestured for her to continue.

"I wanted to ask if there was something I could do for you?" the maid asked.

"I wanted to see if someone could clean Lord Skylar's room a bit now that he be up. He's in his bath now, if perhaps there be someone who can come up and do his room."

She was brisk in her reply. "Certainly, I can make up his room right now. Why didn't you say so?" Without waiting for his reply, she marched past him into the master's suite.

"How is the master?" she asked, heading directly to the bed.

"He be better, though weak."

She threw open the bed curtains and stripped the bed. "Thank the good Lord. We were all worried about him downstairs." She eyed him across the bed as he helped her with a heavy cover. "We hadn't seen hide nor hair of him for some days and thought perhaps you had done something to him."

His eyes widened in alarm. "Me harm Lord Skylar? Why should I want to do dat? He rescued me from de cane fields. He gave me my freedom."

She looked at him over the bundle of dirty linen in her arms, as if seeing him for the first time. "You were a slave?"

"Yes."

"Did you come off a ship from Africa?" she asked in a low tone.

He shook his head. "My mother did. I was born on de island. My father was white…like you," he added deliberately, curious to see her reaction. The maid was a pretty thing, with pale, pink-tinged cheeks and reddish hair beneath her mobcap.

Her eyes widened at the comparison. "Never!"

"Oh, yes. He was her master."

Her eyes grew even larger. They were a pale blue. "That's wicked!"

"But it be de truth."

She nodded grimly. "It happens here, too, among the gentry and the servants."

"But there be some good masters. Lord Skylar is one such. He saw me in de cane fields one day and later won me from my owner in a throw of de dice." He grinned. "I was woken out of a deep sleep and told to get my things and go with dis white mon."

"My, my," she said in amazement. "And now here you are all the way in England."

The two smiled at each other, and Nigel felt the first real connection to another human being beside Lord Skylar since his arrival in England. "Yes, here I be in a new land, among new people."

Her smile disappeared. "None of us downstairs knew what to think about you. Mr. Scott, Lord Caulfield's secretary, filled us with scary tales of how you threatened him."

He had forgotten his encounter with the scrawny, unpleasant man. "I needed his cooperation, and he didn't seem at all willing."

"Well, you've made an enemy, I can tell you that much."

Nigel rubbed his chin. "I wonder if he ever did as I asked."

"What did you want with him?"

"To cancel Lord Skylar's engagements."

She gave a grim smile. "From Mr. Scott's tone, I would reckon he didn't do anything you asked of him. This place needs airing," she said decisively, setting down her bundle by the door and heading to a window.

She drew back the curtains and pushed the window open.

He went to the other window. "I can get dis one."

"Good. I shall fetch some clean linen and return immediately."

"I hope you tell those below stairs that I haven't done de master no harm." At that moment Lord Skylar called him from the other room. "You can even say you heard him speak."

She nodded. "I shall indeed. But I hope they can all soon see for themselves."

"He'll be getting up and dressed today, so I am sure you will all see him."

Already the room began to have a feel of life and not death. Nigel hoped things might truly take a turn for the better this time, but he knew it would take more than a good cleaning.

Though he still felt weak, Tertius was determined to let on to no one. He'd organized this party to Vauxhall Gardens for the masquerade and he was going to see it through to the end.

His party consisted of Delaney and two other friends from the old days. Gillian and Templeton and a couple of friends of Gillian's to even out the numbers. He'd even thought to include his father's secretary to escort Miss Templeton.

He watched the two now strolling along the tree-lined promenade. Seeing was a little difficult with only one eye. The other was covered with an eye patch. Coming from the West Indies, he thought it appropriate to don a pirate's costume to the Gardens.

He glanced at Gillian beside him. She was dressed in a medieval gown with conical headdress and trailing veil. He noticed the absence of the necklace on her graceful, low-cut neckline.

"Did you receive the gift I sent you?" he couldn't help asking when she said nothing about it.

"The necklace and earrings? Yes, I received them."

"Did they not find favor with you?"

"Oh, they were pretty enough," she said in a careless tone. "Thank you, my lord."

"Don't mention it," he answered mildly.

They were soon separated from the other couples. Skylar took Gillian to the Rural Downs to view the river. From there they toured the grottos and waterfalls and man-made caves. Sky noted that for someone who had never been to Vauxhall, Gillian was not showing her normal enthusiasm. She seemed unusually quiet.

"How is the dog?" he asked at one point.

"Sophie?"

"Is that what you call her?"

"Yes. She is settling in nicely. Mother seems resigned to her presence in the house. I must next get her accustomed to my two cats. She's a very docile animal, though, so I believe I shall succeed, although they are not so friendly."

"Your two cats don't inhabit the house?"

"Mother doesn't even know about them. They are in the mews, and I sneak them into the house every morning for a couple of hours."

"Your menagerie can have free rein in our home when we're married."

She turned away from him then, not even giving him a smile of thanks.

He observed her closely during the course of the evening. Something was wrong. At first he attributed it to pique at his disappearance of a few days, but now he believed it to be more deeply founded.

"Your mother informed you of the new date for our wedding?" he asked her, wondering if that might be the cause of her coolness toward him.

"Yes."

"Have you any objections?" he asked, still trying to feel her out.

"Would it matter if I did?"

Her tone was cold. The news must not have set well with her. "It would matter to me, but as to my father or your mother, I don't believe they will relent."

She turned to him. "And are you so powerless that you must do everything they say? Can't you stop it?"

"No, I'm not so powerless," he said, stung despite himself at her contemptuous tone. He wished he could tell her the truth. It was more than his father's prohibition, however. Pride held him back. Pride and reticence toward describing his own weak condition. "Let us say that in this case there are compelling reasons for moving up the wedding date."

"Such as?"

He shrugged. "I explained to you…I am five-and-thirty. Sometimes…" He hesitated. "Sometimes I think time is running out for me."

She gave a bitter laugh. "Sometimes I feel as if life has not even begun for me."

He stared at her, wondering at the remark in one so young. "You know you don't have to marry me if you don't wish to. I can tell my father it's off for good. All he has to do is find me another young lady of the ton," he ended dryly.

She did not respond for some minutes as they promenaded under the trees lit by thousands of little gaslights. It was a magical place. They should be strolling arm in arm as the many other couples around them were doing. Others had escaped down secluded alleyways and into the shadowy groves.

Finally she spoke in a voice so low he had to stoop to hear her. "I don't think it can be called off now. It has been published in the paper. The date has been set."

The reply was far from satisfactory. "None of those reasons is sufficient if you truly don't want to be married to me. You must let me know soon what your decision is."

She sighed but said nothing.

After a moment he said, "People will say we married in haste because you are in a family way. I suppose it doesn't matter what they say. You soon will be anyway."

"Must you forever bring that up?" she retorted, quickening her pace and walking ahead of him.

What kind of wife and helpmate would Lady Gillian make him if she already seemed to view anything physical with such distaste?

They headed back to the center of the gardens toward the gilded bandstand where a group of fiddlers was playing. They spotted Templeton ahead of them, walking with Mr. Scott.

"I'm surprised you included Templeton in our party," commented Gillian.

"I thought she needed an outing."

"You even provided her with an escort," she said in amusement.

Heartened at her first show of pleasure, he explained, "Scott is my father's secretary. A humorless sort. I thought he and Miss Templeton might cancel each other out. Either that or your companion can liven him up."

Gillian laughed and Sky was encouraged once again that things would sort themselves out between the two of them.

At that moment, an attendant handed Tertius a note. He frowned, wondering who would know he was here.

You are needed at your carriage. There has been an incident.
It was signed by the manager of the gardens.

Sky looked at Gillian.

"It seems I'm needed where I left the carriage. Let me escort you to Templeton, before I leave."

"I can do so, my lord," the attendant answered immediately.

"That won't be necessary," he replied.

"I can go with him," said Lady Gillian. "Templeton is right there within view."

"Very well," he agreed reluctantly. "I shan't be long."

As soon as he was out of sight down the main promenade, the attendant turned to her. "I was to take you to meet a gentleman."

Gillian's eyes widened and her heart began to beat. Gerrit! He had managed it after all.

Even as she knew what she was doing was wrong, and the consequences if she should be discovered, she was following the attendant quickly down the most secluded promenade denominated "Lover's Lane."

She gave a quick glimpse over her shoulder. Good, Templeton's back was still turned to her, and Lord Skylar was nowhere to be seen.

The attendant left her at a stone bench under the immense branches of a plane tree. As soon as he'd departed, a tall man dressed in a flowing burnoose, his head covered by a turban, the lower part of his face draped with a scarf, stepped out from behind the tree.

"Gerrit!" She would know those twinkling eyes anywhere.

"My dear Gillian," he said softly, pushing aside the scarf.

"What are you doing? Did you send that note to Lord Skylar?"

He chuckled, a low seductive sound. "Clever, wasn't it?"

"Dangerous," she admonished. "If anyone should see me here, I would be ruined."

"You already are."

She stared at him. What did he mean?

"I have ruined you for any other, just as you have ruined me for any other," he replied smoothly.

He took her hand and kissed the back of it.

"I told your companion I would be here, didn't I?"

"I don't think this is what she anticipated."

"Your Lord Skylar made it all the more convenient for me by providing her with an escort."

"We were just commenting on the fact," she replied. "How long have you been observing us?"

"Long enough to know when to interrupt your tête-à-tête with your lord." He touched her cheek. "Do you love him very much?"

"Of course not!" she replied immediately.

"I carried you with me in my heart into every campaign," he told her.

She gazed at him, wanting so much to believe him. "Mother has moved up the wedding date," she told him.

"You wound me with such news," he murmured, bending to kiss her cheek.

"I don't know what to do. If only there were some way…"

"To what?"

"To postpone things. I wish I didn't have to marry at all!" she burst out.

He hugged her tightly to him.

"You don't know how much I regret not carrying you off with me to Gretna Green back then."

"But you said the other day, you thought it was best this way."

"But each time I see you anew, I begin to regret the wasted years."

"I am betrothed. Lord Skylar says he still leaves the decision up to me, but Mother leaves me no choice. She says I am making a brilliant match. I cannot throw it all away for something that can never be." How much she wanted to hear him refute all her logic.

"But must we throw it all away?" he murmured, drawing her closer to him.

"What do you mean?" she faltered, hoping for what she knew was impossible.

"I mean, my dear naive darling, there are ways."

"What would you have me do? I can still refuse to marry Lord Skylar," she told him, straining to see his reaction in the shadows.

His voice vibrated against her cheek as he spoke in a low tone. "That would be a very unwise move."

"How do you mean?" she asked carefully.

"What would you do under such a cloud of scandal? If, on the other hand, you marry, that needn't mean you give up our friendship. I can arrange to meet you."

"So...you wouldn't marry me if I were free now?" she asked, drawing away from him.

He chuckled, holding her fast. "You wouldn't want me as a husband, believe me. I make a much better lover."

Those weren't the words she wanted to hear. "But you said you wished we had eloped..." Her voice trailed away.

"*Then.* I was a young boy. Now, I have aged too much and am far too cynical to make you any kind of husband."

Gently she pushed herself away from him, more disappointed at his words than she had imagined.

"It doesn't mean we can't manage to amuse ourselves. All the best ton does it."

"And if I don't want that?" she asked lightly, hiding the acute dismay she felt.

"You would be missing out on a vastly entertaining time. Your Lord Skylar looks to be a dull sort."

She eyed Gerrit with a sense of sorrow. What had she been hoping? For a last-minute reprieve? A knight in shining armor to carry her away and promise her true love?

He moved his lips toward hers, but she broke away. "No, I mustn't. I am betrothed. You mustn't contact me again this way."

He made no effort to detain her. Was she sorry? Had she expected him to? What would she have done if he had?

But he hadn't. She took herself to task sternly. No help lay for her in that quarter.

Her heart brimming with unfulfilled longing, she hurried back to the colonnaded center of the gardens. Glancing in every direction, she finally spotted Templeton seated at a box. Thankfully, Lord Skylar hadn't yet returned, but Lord Delaney and her friend Charlotte were joining Templeton at the box where they would all have supper.

Gillian smoothed down her hair and gown and adjusted her veil and cone hat, then slowed her steps to a stately walk as she neared the table.

When Tertius returned to the party, he looked serious.

"Where were you?" Delaney asked with a smile. "Leaving Lady Gillian all alone?"

"Oh, some foolish prank." He looked at Gillian as he explained, taking his seat across from her. "There was no one at the carriage when I finally got there. Were you all right? I'm sorry to have left you like that."

"I was fine. Think nothing of it," she answered hurriedly, glad Templeton's attention was engaged at the moment by Mr. Scott.

Later, when the two found themselves alone once again, Gillian turned to Lord Skylar. "You told me earlier that the decision to marry was up to me."

"Yes, I did. Have you come to a decision?" He was looking at her so intently it made her nervous and she lowered her eyes.

Licking dry lips, she finally replied, "I will marry you."

"Are you sure?"

She nodded, knowing there was no other way left for her. She wouldn't waste any more years waiting for something that was not to be.

Tertius spent at least three afternoons a week at Gentleman Jackson's boxing saloon or at Henry Angelo's fencing academy. He hoped the exercise would build up his strength. He realized he had lost a lot of his stamina since the last fever, and he had a long way to go to regain any measure of it back.

He was removing his coat and waistcoat at the academy, when a young gentleman approached him. He recognized him as the officer at the Regent's fete.

He nodded curtly at the black-haired man.

"Lord Skylar," the man said with a smile that had something insolent about it, "might I challenge you to a match?" He raised his foil in question.

Sky considered. He was accustomed to using one of the trainers. But an officer lately returned from Spain? The exercise would certainly be a rigorous test.

"Very well, Captain," he replied, handing his garments to Nigel and bending to remove his boots.

The two positioned themselves in their stocking feet and shirtsleeves on the long space reserved for fencing matches.

"En garde!"

They began their silent match, stepping forward and back with the rapidity of sandpipers on the sand. Thrust and parry, back and forth. For a time Sky was heartened, seeing he hadn't lost all his skill. He was even able to manage a riposte or two. But then he began to tire.

The young captain showed no signs of fatigue. He was like a barrage of artillery, strong and relentless. The slight smile that played along his sensual lips and around his deep blue eyes never wavered. Tertius had to fight to keep them from unnerving him.

The man seemed to be playing a game, and Sky couldn't fathom what it was. He didn't know him, hadn't ever seen him until that night at the Regent's—

Sky parried but was a split-second too late. Captain Hawkes's foil touched his breast. Sky recovered but had lost ground, his concentration distracted by his puzzlement.

He focused once more on the match. His muscles didn't respond as he wanted them to. They ached with the strain.

Finally the captain had him pinned against the wall.

"Touché, my lord," the captain said softly, that smile still hovering around his mouth.

How Sky would love to wipe it off his handsome face, but it was not to be this day, he admitted, giving the man a nod.

"What is it they say? A man's skill with the foil matches his skill as a lover?"

Sky narrowed his eyes at the man. What did he intend with the remark?

"My congratulations on your nuptials. You are a lucky man. Lady Gillian is exquisite."

The familiarity with which he said her name made Sky want to call the captain out.

"You know Lady Gillian?" he asked coldly.

Captain Hawkes held his foil upright and plucked at its tip. "We were thrown together as youngsters to learn the quadrille."

A group had gathered to watch the match and now they congratulated the captain.

"You must have gained a lot of practice over on the Peninsula against the Frogs," they told him, slapping him on the back.

"I relied more on Brown Bess," he answered, referring to his musket. "We seldom engage the enemy with bayonets. They usually run before then," he joked. As their laughter died down, he added more seriously, "It's a good thing, since they give us flank company officers nothing but sabers. Those curved blades make it dashedly difficult to kill a man. First you must slash his face to ribbons before any damage is done."

As they continued plying him with questions about the action he had seen, Sky took the towel Nigel handed him and wiped the sweat from his face.

He slipped back into the waistcoat and coat his valet handed him and combed his hair.

He barely glanced at himself in the glass, loathing the haggard man that looked back at him. His attention was caught by the captain's reflection in the glass. His head was thrown back in laughter at someone's jest, his shirt was open halfway to his waist, and his virility mocked Sky's own wasted frame.

"What I need is a drink," he told Nigel as he turned to leave the fencing academy.

Gillian was lying on her bed, stroking Sophie's glossy fur, when a maid knocked on her door.

"This parcel was delivered to you, miss," the girl told her with a curtsey.

Gillian sat up and took it from her. "Thank you."

She looked at it curiously. More jewels from Lord Skylar? She still felt uncomfortable since her evening at Vauxhall. When he'd returned, he had not seemed suspicious at all, only annoyed at being led on a wild-goose chase. She had promptly assured him that she had been well occupied; after all there was so much to see at the gardens.

Now she stared a moment at the parcel before opening it. Would another jewel add to her guilt? Finally she ripped the paper open and opened the box.

She gasped. Inside the tissue paper lay a tooled, red Moroccan leather dog collar. A folded piece of paper was tucked beneath it. She unfolded it and read:

I hope this collar finds more favor with Sophie than the emeralds did with you. Sky

No "Dear Gillian"; no "Your servant," or "Fondly" or any other sign of endearment. And he'd remembered her dog's new name.

She dropped the note and picked up the collar. It was beautiful. "Look at this, Sophie." She held it up against the dog's fur. "Aren't you going to look elegant? Better than any other dog around the square."

She undid the small buckle and put the collar around Sophie's neck. "Oh, Sophie, if you could see yourself." Gillian gave her dog a hug. "What a good girl you are."

She had been right about the dog's character. She was gentle and obedient. "I'm so glad you're mine now. Lord Skylar promised you could live with me wherever I go." Giving Sophie a hug, Gillian felt touched by Lord Skylar's gift, more so than by the jewels he'd given her.

The thought of them filled Gillian with a surge of remorse as she remembered her careless attitude toward his gifts. She would wear the necklace and earrings at the next opportunity, she decided.

Yesterday, the first of her new wardrobe had been delivered. Gillian walked over to her dressing room and pulled open her wardrobe. She fingered the satins and woolens, furs, sarcenet, and lawn of the new gowns, riding habits, cloaks and pelisses….

She stood there many moments, thinking of her future. She was sure she'd made the right decision in deciding to marry Lord Skylar. Any other girl would be overjoyed, but all she felt was fear and guilt. Sophie came and stood beside Gillian, and she petted the dog absently.

What did Lord Skylar offer her? Perhaps no grand passion or romantic fantasy, but he'd always treated her respectfully and kindly. Perhaps an affection would grow between them over the years and through their children. And in time, Gillian's feelings for Gerrit would disappear. Or, hopefully, be transferred to Lord Skylar, however unlikely that possibility seemed.

Yet, was it fair of her to give Lord Skylar nothing more than a mild affection, and an heir?

But he had never asked for anything more. He didn't strike her as a passionate man like Gerrit. All Lord Skylar seemed to require was fidelity and an heir.

Were these things enough for her?

She longed for warmth and affection and love.

Gerrit made clear he offered her none of these things.

He'd told her he had ruined her for any other man. Her conscience reminded her how true that was. She turned away from her wardrobe, too scared to dwell on the consequences of the reckless decision she had taken three years ago. In scarcely more than a fortnight she would be wed, and it remained to be seen if her new husband would have an inkling of what she had done three years ago.

She would make Lord Skylar a good wife, she promised her image in the mirror. The thought made her feel better, but would her future conduct be enough to erase her past?

Chapter Seven

A week later, Tertius attended a ball given by the duchess in honor of the nuptials. More than a hundred people crowded into the Burnham mansion.

His foreboding about the wedding had grown. He sensed all was not right with Gillian no matter how much she tried to convince him she was agreeable to the marriage.

He bowed over the duchess's hand then turned to Lady Gillian. His eyes focused immediately on the emeralds around her neck. "Good evening, my lady," he murmured as he bowed over her hand. "You look beautiful."

"Thank you, my lord."

He made no remark about the jewelry, but looked at her sharply before taking his place in the receiving line to greet the other guests. What had made her decide to finally wear his gift? Was it to mark the occasion of their first public appearance as a couple?

Later, after the two had danced a few sets, he asked her if she cared to take a turn about the gardens to cool off. She accepted and the two walked onto the quiet stone balcony.

When they stopped at the far end, away from other promenading couples, she fingered the emerald pendant hanging from her necklace. "Thank you for the necklace. It truly is beautiful."

"You didn't think so when I first sent it to you. What happened since then?"

She looked away. "Nothing. I always thought it beautiful."

"You were angry at me, then?"

"No—yes. It was because you didn't come riding that day, and I heard nothing from you afterward."

"I am sorry."

"Why didn't you keep your appointment with me that day? My mother said you were ill."

He didn't answer right away, not relishing the thought of getting into the whole sordid business of his fever. With a sigh, he said, "Let us say there was a breakdown in communication. I had instructed that a note be sent to you, but it seems it was never delivered. I take full responsibility for that lapse and have dealt with the matter so it should never occur again."

"You haven't answered my question. Were you ill?"

"No, I haven't, have I? I was indisposed. A few lingering effects of the long sea voyage taken so soon after the fever. Just a trifling thing."

"I would have understood if I'd known. But so many days of nothing but silence…I didn't know what to think."

"As I said, I'm sorry the note never reached you. As for the illness—" he shrugged, dismissing the topic "—a tedious subject."

Before she could contradict him, he said, "I have been thinking we could start our honeymoon journey at Bishop's Green in Hertfordshire."

"That is your family seat?"

"Yes, my dear." It was the first time he'd used a term of endearment to her and he did it deliberately to gauge her reaction. She made no acknowledgment of it that he could see.

"Who is its present mistress?" she asked.

"It has none. So you shall have that honor."

"What about your father?"

"Oh, he's rarely there. He prefers to spend his time in town or as a guest of the Regent in Brighton, playing the aging dandy."

She smiled. "I find him a sweet old man."

"Sweet? I wouldn't call him that." A vain, lecherous old scoundrel, he thought to himself. "At any rate, we can tour the estate at Bishop's Green. It is the closest of our estates to London—an easy journey for the first day." When she made no comment, he asked, "How is Sophie?"

"Wonderful. I'm sure she must have lived with a family at some time. She has adapted beautifully."

"No overturned furniture? Broken vases?"

She laughed. "Not a teacup."

They fell silent again.

His gaze wandered over her features, seeking something…some key to her thoughts. They had almost achieved their former camaraderie, yet he felt she still shied away from him. Her eyes had barely met his the entire evening.

"You've never called me by my given name," he said lightly.

She turned startled eyes to him before looking away again. "I don't feel I've known you very long."

"Are you waiting until we are wed?" he asked, amused.

Despite the semidarkness, he detected the color that rose in her cheeks.

"My name is Tertius, Gillian." Why was it so important all of a sudden that she say it? It was as if his name on her lips would mark her unequivocally as his.

"Ter-shus," she pronounced. Then she giggled nervously. "It sounds like a monk's name."

He chuckled in reply.

"Is this like a monk's kiss?" he asked.

Before he could question the wisdom of the move, he leaned his face toward hers.

"What—what are you going to do?" she asked, one hand going involuntarily to clutch her necklace.

"I'm going to kiss you," he whispered against her lips.

"You are?" she asked faintly. Her hand fell against his chest as if to stop him.

His gloved fingertips touched her chin lightly, guiding her face upward. He breathed in the scent of her perfume, soft and sweet like lily of the valley, suggesting femininity and innocence.

His lips touched hers, lightly, coolly, and he drew back after a few seconds, observing her once again from his height.

She hadn't moved. She looked a little stunned. Then she pressed her lips together as she looked off into the garden, and he had the impression that if she were alone she'd take out a lace handkerchief from her beaded reticule and discreetly wipe her lips.

He rocked back on his heels. His unplanned experiment had yielded no great surprises. Not a hint of desire had stirred her. He had no inclination to press her further at this time. In short, she was as interesting to kiss as a sponge.

He didn't understand how a person who showed such enthusiasm and spirit at other times could be so timorous when it came to the physical aspects of courtship.

What would his married life be like? he wondered dismally as he left the ball in the wee hours. Could he teach Gillian to enjoy the pleasures between a man and a woman, or would she stiffen every time he chose to come near?

Gillian's wedding trousseau kept growing. Her wedding gown now hung apart from all the other dresses, like a wedding cake towering above the other confections surrounding it. It was a magical creation of silk and satin and tulle edged in yards and yards of Belgian lace.

Her trunks were full of new things from underclothes and lacy nightgowns to slippers and half boots and bonnets for every sort of outing.

The excitement of so many new things helped keep any misgivings at bay. Now, on the eve of her wedding, she told herself sternly that she would survive it. She reassured herself as she remembered Lord Skylar's kiss. It hadn't felt at all unpleasant. Maybe she could grow to like it.

Her wedding night wouldn't be so very different. All she'd have to do was close her eyes and it would be over almost as quickly.

It couldn't be any worse than that last time.

Unfortunately, there was always that niggling worry. Would Lord Skylar be able to tell anything? She had no one to consult. She didn't dare ask her mother. In the old days she would have asked her maid, but her mother had long since dismissed Sally and replaced her with the dour-faced Martha. The two names said it all. Martha always looked disapproving, just like Templeton. Martha reminded Gillian of those schoolgirls who never misbehaved and would go running to the teacher the moment another girl did.

So who could advise her? No one. Where was her dear papa when she needed him most? A wave of despair swept through her. None of this would be happening if Papa had still been alive when she'd first met Gerrit. If her father had seen how much she loved Gerrit, he would have arranged for the two of them to be married. He'd never denied her anything.

But now she had no one to confide her terrible secret to. She'd have to pray and hope for the best. *Dear God, Don't let Lord Skylar find out. Don't let him know.*

She knew what she'd do, she determined after pacing her carpet. Act the way she'd acted the first time. Frightened, a little scream of pain—would it still hurt? Undoubtedly. So, that wouldn't be difficult, she thought with a grimace.

For truth be told, she was terrified of her wedding night. Lord Skylar—she couldn't bring herself to think of him by his Christian name—just standing there observing her, let alone—

No! She wouldn't even think of what awaited her.

On their wedding day, Tertius stood before his bride in the crowded cathedral. Despite the precipitate date, the church was packed with both families' many friends and relations.

When Gillian lifted her veil, her wide, frightened eyes swallowed up her whole face. She looked ready to faint. Tertius wondered if such had been the pallor of those aristos being led to the guillotine.

Her hand was cold when he placed the gold band on her finger.

He bent to kiss her for the second time in their acquaintance, and it was like kissing a marble statue, cold and lifeless. He replaced her veil, the fleeting image of covering a corpse's face flitting through his mind.

He took her arm and led her from the church, to begin their new life as one.

Tertius rested his head against the edge of the tub. For some inexplicable reason he was loathe to leave its warm cocoon. He should be counting the minutes impatiently before he could be with his new bride. Instead he was filled with an inexplicable sense of dread.

"Shall I bring you your towel?" Nigel's noiseless approach no longer startled him. Tertius merely opened his eyes and said, "I suppose so."

"Your bride be waiting, all prettied for you."

Tertius made no comment, submerging his head one last time in the warm water before standing and taking the soft towel handed to him by his valet.

As he was wrapping the towel around his waist, he caught sight of himself in the mirror opposite him and immediately averted his gaze. He'd always been thin but now he looked positively emaciated. He hadn't managed to gain back any of the weight lost during his fever in the Indies, and the latest bout had taken even more.

What was the matter with him? The frustrated question revolved for the hundredth time around his mind as he rubbed himself vigorously with the additional towel Nigel gave him. When it wasn't a fever, it was excruciating migraines like a vise at his temples, behind his eyes. Even the blandest foods disagreed with him. He was no doubt becoming dyspeptic, like his great-uncle Harry, who was forever popping peppermints into his mouth, a habit Tertius was beginning to develop of late.

It must be the wretched English climate with its fog and coal smoke, he told himself in reply—ignoring the glorious summer weather the city had enjoyed.

The wedding banquet had been rich and sumptuous, but he hadn't dared overindulge in either food or drink. Even so, he still felt a nervous flutter in his stomach.

He donned a silk nightshirt and dressing gown. At least they'd both be fully gowned. Just as well, he thought, though the thought gave him no pleasure. It wasn't what he was accustomed to. As he belted the dressing gown, again forced to notice the spareness of his waist, the sudden question popped into his head, *what would Edmund have done?*

He looked at himself in the mirror, startled for a second. It had been a long time since he'd stopped asking himself that. It was a question that had plagued him many times during those first few years out in the Indies as he struggled to prove himself on the failing plantation.

He felt the gooseflesh rise along his arms. Why the question now, on the eve of his wedding night? Edmund was dead, and he, Tertius, was alive. So, what did it matter what Edmund would have done?

As Nigel handed him his tortoiseshell comb, Tertius asked

him abruptly, "Do you believe the dead come back to haunt us or help us?" He tried to smile, as if the question were asked in jest.

"The dead be all around us," he answered seriously, his muddy green eyes as always shockingly light against his smooth brown skin.

"But it's not the dead to fear as much as the living," Nigel continued as he hung up the used towels.

"I agree with you there," he replied grimly. "Right now, the thought of bedding an innocent virgin stops me cold."

Nigel didn't smile in reply. "I wouldn't fear the new Lady Skylar as much as the old Angelique."

"Angelique and I parted on very good terms. I know you are used to females throwing hysterical fits when you break things off, but Angelique was a mature, intelligent woman who knew the conditions of our...friendship."

Nigel shook his head, pity in his eyes. "Angelique be not so sweet at your goodbye as you think. She put a curse on you, as sure as I'm the son of Rose. Everything you touch start to go against you—family, riches, gaming, health. You'll see." He looked at him significantly. "It's the voodoo. It make everything turn against you. You might think you're free of Angelique, but she have you."

Tertius gave a grunt of laughter though he didn't feel at all like laughing. "I'm miles from her."

"It doesn't matter how far you go from her. She has you like this." Nigel clamped his large brown hand around Tertius's wrist, his nails pink with the pressure. "She can make you dance as if you right dar with her."

Tertius shook him off with another laugh. "You're a fine one to talk to on the eve of one's wedding night."

Nigel stared into Tertius's eyes, his expression serious. "I don't speak like this to spoil your evening but to warn you. You must have someone with more power than she to ward off dis curse."

Tertius turned away from him. "Thanks for your warnings, but I think they are unnecessary. I shall bid you good-evening before your mumbo jumbo begins to make sense. I'm off to produce an heir. Wish me luck," he quipped, eyeing his man from the doorway of the dressing room. "You go on to bed. I shan't need you any further tonight."

Tertius entered his bedroom. He was used to the superstitious practices of the Indies, but he knew it had no power over a European.

It was true he had begun to tire of his six-year relationship with the Creole woman, Angelique, and was almost relieved when his father's summons came. It served as a convenient way to end things with his mistress.

Why or when his restlessness with Angelique had begun he didn't exactly know. She was the perfect mistress. A widow, wealthy in her own right, old enough to lead an independent life and know how to please a man, why had Tertius begun to feel constricted—almost oppressed—in his last year or so in Jamaica?

Angelique was beautiful, intelligent, a renowned hostess, and an independent woman successfully running a plantation of her own.

Why had he felt she had encroached into every area of his life, from becoming his hostess to probing into his business affairs?

Tertius prowled his room. As he'd told Nigel, Angelique

had taken the news of his departure with amazingly good grace. Better than he'd expected after their longstanding relationship. She'd even hosted a large farewell party for him.

Tertius brushed aside Nigel's ghoulish warnings. He had more important things on his agenda tonight. How to please one surely nervous and uncertain young maiden.

Despite his mocking tone to Nigel, Tertius felt queerly hesitant tonight of all nights. He didn't understand exactly why. Did it make so much difference that this was to be the first time he would make love to a woman—his wife—in a joining sanctioned by God? Did a wedding ceremony make so much difference? He twisted the new wedding band around his finger. The matching band was now around a small, slim finger of a young woman sitting in the next room. He glanced toward the connecting door. His life was no longer independent after this night. It would be shared with another body and mind.

With this ring I thee wed… He remembered the vows he'd taken today. *With this body I thee worship…*

As he knocked on the door to his bride's chamber, he found that he very much wanted to please his new wife tonight. He wanted to start their marriage off on the right note. He felt, despite their not having known each other more than a few weeks, there was hope for a solid partnership between the two of them.

"Come in," he heard her voice say.

Taking a deep breath to still his own sudden nerves, he opened the door.

The room was softly lit. A quick glance told him her maid had gone. They were alone.

He entered silently, closing the door behind him.

"Hello, Gillian," he said.

She stood in the center of the room, her dark hair cascading down her shoulders, the shorter curls framing her face.

He drew in his breath. She wore a beautiful ivory silken gown and robe, both edged in a wide swath of lace.

He approached her, almost afraid of her fragility. Would she bolt as soon as he touched her?

His father had certainly chosen well, he had to concede. His bride was beautiful. He reached out his hand and brushed the back of it across her pale cheek. Although she didn't move, he sensed her stiffen. Were all brides this scared, he wondered? He hadn't ever thought much about this night, assuming everything would go naturally. But now he realized he was facing an entirely different element than he'd ever faced. This was an innocent young lady, brought up to know nothing about the facts of life, a woman unlike the countless women he'd known, as a young man about town in London and later as a wealthy planter in the tropics.

He drew out a breath, feeling a sudden compassion—a most unexpected sentiment to be experiencing on his wedding night. He felt an urge to protect this delicate young creature put into his care, to reassure her that everything was going to be all right. He valued her purity and innocence. That was the main reason he had agreed to this marriage, wasn't it? He wanted a woman whose moral integrity he could trust to be the one to bear his children and carry his name.

He watched her convulsive swallow and decided to lead her over to a settee, ignoring the wide bed that seemed to call too much attention to itself all of a sudden.

"It was a tiring day for you, was it not?" he asked gently, rubbing his thumb over her cold hand.

She licked her lips and nodded. He realized then how she was experiencing more than maidenly nerves. She was absolutely terrified. He was going to have to be very patient.

"We'll leave sometime tomorrow on our honeymoon trip," he told her. "The carriage is all ready. It's a short drive to Bishop's Green. I think you'll like the estate. I grew up there. Parts of it are quite ancient, though many wings have been added over the centuries...." He began to describe his family seat.

As he spoke, he eased back against the sofa and told himself the evening was young.

Tertius drew himself away from Gillian. He was silent a few seconds, staring at his bride in disbelief, his mind rebelling at the evidence his body confronted. His wife's eyes were shut, her head averted as if she found him and the whole act she'd just submitted to distasteful or—or— His disquiet grew as he considered the possibility that her reluctance came not from maidenly fear but fear of discovery.

"They've sold me used goods." His words, considering the chaos in his mind, came out sounding calm.

Her eyes flew open, and the two stared at each other.

"You've done this before." As her head immediately began to shake mutely back and forth against the pillow, he repeated, "You're no shy, innocent virgin."

Before she had a chance to utter a denial, he pushed himself off her in one swift movement and stood, his nightshirt falling into place. When she said nothing, but pulled the bed covers up to her neck, his calm demeanor collapsed.

"Answer me!"

Her eyes only grew wider, her denials more vehement. That only increased his anger. "All that time you made me think you were nervous out of ignorance. You knew all along what was coming, didn't you?"

He eyed her in disgust. She was sitting up, her knees drawn up under the covers, her eyes round circles of fear. If she had been terrified before, she didn't know what fear was. He leaned over her and grabbed her, dragging her off the bed, her feet stumbling under her.

She whimpered, "Don't hurt me! Please, don't hurt me! Please!" She struggled against him, her nightdress tripping her.

He shook her by the arms, determined to get at the truth. Her head flipped back and forth like a rag doll's as she cried out her denials.

"Who was it?" he demanded, feeling his own face aflame with rage at the thought of being made a fool of. "How many have there been before me? Answer me!" He swore at her, but she only cried out for him to stop, that she didn't know what he was talking about.

"What an act you put on, pretending such prudery with me! You didn't even like me to hold your hand, did you? What a fool I've been."

"No, that isn't true! I swear! I don't know what you're talking about!" she sobbed.

"You didn't want to receive a kiss of mine, while all along you've been making free with your favors! Have you had all the young bucks that cluster around you? That pimply faced Cubby?" He gave a bitter laugh. "And here I thought you were scared of a real man, that you had to surround yourself with those effeminate dandies—"

"Please let me go. I don't know what you mean. You're frightening me," she cried, trying to pull away from him.

He pushed her away from him, realizing in that instant how close he was to hitting her, and he'd never hit a woman in his life. She collapsed against the bed but he felt no pity.

She'd made a complete fool of him. She and her mother and doubtless his own father, too.

Oh, this was rich. There had been a whole conspiracy waiting for him as soon as he'd stepped off the ship and he'd fallen for it, utterly and completely.

He experienced raw, blinding fury in that moment. The more he looked at his wife's huddled body on the edge of the bed, the more he heard her pathetic weeping, the more he simply wanted to put his hands around her pale, slim neck—a neck he'd found so attractive only moments before—and throttle it. Press it until he squeezed all the life from it.

He had to do something. Without thinking he grabbed the first thing in his vision—a chair—and threw it against her dressing table. All the crystal bottles went flying off. He heard Gillian's scream like a distant noise in the background, hardly making an impression past the thundering in his head.

He took another item—a stool this time—and flung it across the room. Whatever item of furniture he came across, he picked it up and threw it away from him, until he came to a large wardrobe, which stood immovable. He banged his own head against it in futile rage, beginning to feel hot, angry tears squeeze through his eyelids.

No! He wouldn't give in to them.

A knock sounded on the bedroom door. "Is everything

all right?" came Nigel's muffled voice through the connecting door.

"Leave us!" he shouted.

His rage momentarily dissipated—but by no means spent—he turned back to Gillian. Her hands covered her mouth and she drew away from him in absolute terror as he advanced.

"Never fear, I have no desire to touch you ever again." He felt his power as he stood over her. A power that was meaningless in light of what she had done to him.

"What I want is the truth. If you don't wish me to throw you out into the streets tonight with nothing but your night rail, you'd better tell me how many men you've bedded in your *three full seasons*. How many were there? Who arranged things? Your mother? Was she your procuress?"

He could feel the anger rising in him again at the thought. "You and she planned this, didn't you? Holding out until the two of you snagged a title, didn't you? You harlot!"

She shook her head, the tears falling silently down her cheeks. The sight only made him want to strangle her anew, to snuff that scared look off her face.

"No one," she kept crying out. "There's been no one!"

He took her arm and made her stand again. "Then you shall force me to escort you outside. I won't have a molly under my roof, taking my family name, sleeping in my mother's bed!" The last thought brought such revulsion, he stopped in midstride.

"No!" she screamed in terror. "Don't, please don't throw me outside! I have nowhere to go." Her cries were pitiful but he remained unmoved, sickened by the thought of whom he had brought to his mother's marriage bed.

"Then tell me who has enjoyed what was to have been my sole privilege." His voice was icily glacial now. He meant to have the full truth, if he had to drag her through the streets of Mayfair back to her mother's house.

"I—no one—"

He took her closer to the door.

"No, please," she implored him. When he opened the door, she stopped him with her hand.

"I'll tell you," she whispered at last. Her dark hair was plastered against her wet cheeks, but her vulnerability only disgusted him now. What he had found fragile beauty at the beginning of the evening he looked at as tawdry, soiled goods now.

"I'm waiting."

She closed her eyes. "It was only one man. Only once…" she whispered.

The tears slipped down her cheeks. Suddenly he let her go, unable to bear the touch of her anymore.

He realized a part of him had wished he had been mistaken. But the evidence hadn't lied. He had been sold used goods.

He left her then, unfeeling to her sobs.

"What are you going to do?"

Her scared cries reached him as he shut the door between them.

Chapter Eight

✣

Tertius entered his own silent bedroom, his bed neat and made.

His thoughts revolved around and around his brief courtship, trying to find clues but coming up empty. Everything he'd seen of Gillian had bespoken innocence and purity and ignorance of the world, all the qualities he'd desired in a wife.

He walked over to a decanter of brandy and poured himself a drink, watching his trembling hand in disgust. He couldn't even drink—it would upset his stomach.

Nevertheless, he downed the fiery liquid, needing something to calm his inner rage.

What a colossal fool she had made of him.

He had to think.

What was he going to do?

He refused to live under the same roof with that woman in the room next to his.

Divorce.

As soon as his mind had formed the word, he revolted from its ugliness. Divorce was only sought in the most extreme cases of flagrant adultery. It brought nothing but scandal and disgrace in its wake. He wouldn't dishonor his family name or title in such a fashion. He thought of the family motto: *domat omnia virtus*—virtue conquers everything.

He poured himself another tumbler of brandy.

It was enough the private shame his wife had brought him. He wouldn't let her do further damage to his name.

That left only separation for him and his wife.

He wasn't going to let her stay in London, that was certain. If she hadn't remained chaste as a girl, she certainly wouldn't scruple to cuckold him as his wife.

So, banishment. But where?

All their trunks were loaded onto the chaise-and-four for departure in the morning. He glanced toward the windows. It would soon be light. He had to come to a decision before then. He wouldn't let her remain under this roof one more night, defiling his mother's bed.

They were going to set out for Hertfordshire, but his mind balked at letting her go to his family seat. No, he would banish her to a remote estate. He thought of their many properties and came at last to the most isolated.

Yes, the one in Yorkshire. He would have her sent there. If he never had to see her traitorous little face again, it would be too soon.

He sat down and penned a letter, and then as dawn was arriving, he went to Nigel's room.

The man was instantly awake at his touch. He sat up in his narrow cot, eyeing Tertius with concern. "What is it? I heard such a ruckus before—"

"Never mind that. I want you to unload my trunk from the coach this morning. Then give this letter to Lady Gillian—" he wouldn't call her by his name anymore "—and instruct the coachman that he is to take her to our farther estate in the West Riding. Penuel Hall in Spaldgate beyond Leeds. Her maid will accompany her." He thought of something. "Wait—no, not her maid. Get someone who doesn't know her." He thought of the various housemaids. "Tell that girl, Katie, she's to be her new lady's maid."

"But, my lord, what about you?"

"I shan't be accompanying her. Inform me when she has left. Then you and I shall set out on the horses. I'm not sure where we'll be headed or for how long. Do you have that?"

The man nodded, his look clearly wanting to ask more.

"Good. I'm going to catch a few hours' sleep and then we'll leave." He turned away from Nigel and headed out.

"My lord—"

"Don't." He held up a hand, staving off any questions. "This is between my—between Lady Gillian and myself." He left the man's room and returned to his bedroom.

Once there, he measured out some drops of laudanum into a glass, knowing he must get some sleep if he was to be in any shape for a hard ride later in the morning.

Gillian only managed to make it back to the bed after Tertius left her room. She sat there for she didn't know how long, her mind and body numb.

How had he detected her secret? Despite all her efforts,

he had known. She brought her hand up to her mouth, unwilling to recall those moments. Despair engulfed her.

She didn't know what she was going to do—or what he was going to do to her. She only knew she wanted to die.

If there were something she could drink at that moment to end her life, she would do so. If she could fall into a sleep never to awaken, she would do so.

But there was nothing within her reach.

She stared at the rubble in her room. She daren't walk near her dressing table for fear of cutting her feet on the broken glass.

How could she have ever thought Lord Skylar a cool, reserved man? The man was a monster. She truly believed he would have killed her. She didn't know what had stopped him, but he had been like a wild beast. She'd never seen a man behave as he had. Her own father had never treated her mother so.

At the thought of her father, feeling began to flow back into her, and tears welled up and spilled from her eyes once again.

Oh, Papa, Papa, where was he when she most needed him?

Suddenly she felt the need to wash herself, to rid herself of every vestige of tonight's shame. She crossed to her pitcher of water. Unmindful of how cold it was, she scrubbed and scrubbed herself, her tears mixing with the water.

She didn't think she'd ever feel clean again.

Early the next morning, she was awakened after a too-short, too-light sleep by sounds in her room. She started up, frightened that Lord Skylar had returned. But it was only a maid, bending over, clearing up the mess by her dressing table.

"Good morning, miss. I didn't mean to wake you."

"Who are you?" she asked groggily, her eyes barely able to open, her head pounding. "Where's Martha?"

"I'm Katie." She stood and bobbed a curtsy. "Beggin' your pardon, my lady, I'm to be your new maid."

"What do you mean?" Gillian put a hand to her aching head, wondering if she were still asleep.

"I was told to pack my bags and be ready to travel north as soon as you were up and dressed. Would you like me to bring you something hot to drink?"

"You're...coming with us?" she faltered, still disoriented.

"I'm to accompany you." The maid felt in her apron pocket. "If you please, my lady, I was to give you this. I'm sure it explains everything."

Gillian took the sealed white notepaper suspiciously. What did it mean? She looked at the maid, who quickly bobbed another curtsy and stammered her excuses. "I'll be right back with a nice cup o' tea."

When she'd gone, Gillian opened the letter.

My lady,
I am sending you away to one of our estates. You will have no communication with anyone here in London. You have brought enough shame and dishonor to my family name to last a lifetime.

Do not even think of contacting your lover. If I discover you have, I will drag you through divorce court and publicly humiliate you the way you have done privately to me. Furthermore, I will leave you penniless. Then you will see how quickly your lover's ardor will cool.

I myself will handle all correspondence with your mother, so you needn't look for succor from that quarter. I will make it abundantly clear to her what consequences the two of you will reap if she tries to aid or abet you in any way.

You will have your material needs amply seen to, thus you are in no need of any private income.

I rue the day I ever heard your name, Gillian Edwards, or saw your deceptive face. I will be content if I never lay eyes on it again.

Tertius

Gillian fell back against the bed. So she was to be banished. What was to become of her? Once again, silent tears ran down her cheeks. How had all this happened in the space of an evening?

All she'd done was obey her mother and marry the man she'd picked out for her. Why was she to be punished for the rest of her life for one mistake made three years ago as an ignorant young girl?

After that she moved like an automaton, obediently drinking the cup of tea and eating the dry toast Katie brought her, allowing the maid to help her on with her traveling outfit.

It wasn't until she was on the sidewalk before the carriage that she remembered her pets.

She turned to Katie. "Sophie and the cats. Where are they?" Her voice rose on the last words.

"I don't know, my lady. I wasn't given any instructions concerning them."

A sudden hysterical fear possessed her. Where was she going? What was to become of her? She was truly and utterly alone for the first time in her life. As that fact sank in, she knew a depth of fear that threatened to overwhelm her if she didn't get herself under control.

Taking several deep breaths to tamp down the tremors beginning to possess her limbs, she caught hold of her last remaining reserves of self-possession.

Then she drew herself up and addressed the maid in her most imperious tone. "I'm giving you instructions now. Go and see my pets brought to my traveling coach with enough provisions for the journey. I shall not board this carriage until they are with me."

The young maid looked alarmed for a moment. Then as if taking a decision, she merely bobbed her head once more and left to locate Gillian's two cats and one dog.

A fortnight later, Tertius returned from one of his country estates to London.

That night he dressed for the theater. After a light dinner—he had little appetite these days—he headed out. He gave instructions for his coachman to take him to Drury Lane. When he arrived, he glanced with indifference at the playbill. A tragedy with Kean to begin with then a farce as the second show. He scanned the names of the actors.

Good. Miss Laurette Spencer was in the farce.

The theater boxes were only half filled, most important families having left town since the royal visitors had left. The pit was filled with the usual rowdy crowd.

Tertius let himself be taken in by the dark drama. It suited his mood perfectly. Kean's riveting performance reflected his own agony of mind.

During the intermission, Tertius gave an attendant a note with a coin, with instructions to deliver it backstage.

Before the end of the farce, he received his reply. Miss Spencer would see him in her dressing room immediately after the show.

Tertius hadn't heard from his friend Delaney lately and had no idea how things stood between him and the actress. He would soon find out. He knew it wasn't unusual for this type of woman to take more than one lover at a time.

When he knocked on her door—it seemed a lifetime since the last time he had stood there—once again he heard her voice bidding him to come in.

He closed the door softly behind him. There she sat as the last time at her dressing table. She hadn't yet removed her costume, a boy's outfit this time, revealing the outline of her shapely legs.

She swiveled around to greet him. "Good evening, my lord. To what do I owe this visit?"

He entered further into the small room and indicated the settee Delaney had occupied last time. "May I?"

"By all means. May I offer you a drink?"

"No, thank you." He removed his gloves and placed them over his silver-topped walking stick. "Your performance this evening was…delightful," he said after a second's consideration.

She gave a playful bow of her head. "Thank you, Lord Skylar."

"You remember me."

"I remember you very well." Her look was significant.

After a moment, she added, "I've often looked for you in the boxes, but with no success. Did you find the shows at Covent Garden more entertaining?"

"I haven't been to the theater lately."

"I read about your nuptials. They were unexpected. I think many people were surprised at how swiftly the wedding took place."

"I didn't come here this evening to speak of my marriage."

"I'm glad to hear it," she said, with a small smile playing around her lips.

He clutched the cane head. "I came here to talk about a business proposition—an amorous one."

She rose, smoothing down her shirt and trousers and giving him full view of her assets. "I'm all attention."

"I'm willing to give you whatever you require in return for your *exclusive* attentions. What are your requirements?"

She came and sat beside him, all seductiveness gone, her tone businesslike. "A flat in Mayfair with sufficient servants to staff it, a coach and driver, and an allowance of—" she pursed her lips, considering "—one hundred quid a month, plus credit at a dressmaker's of my choosing…in addition to your gifts, of course." Here she allowed herself a smile, and he knew she meant jewelry.

"You don't come cheap," he said lightly.

"I guarantee full satisfaction."

"You sound supremely confident."

"I know what I'm capable of. I also promise exclusiveness and discretion."

"I require those qualities."

She eased back on the sofa back. "So, are we agreed?"

"We are agreed. I'll open an account for you at the bank for you to draw on tomorrow." He stood. "Are you available tonight?"

She stood as well. "Do I have your word as a gentleman?"

He gave her a curt nod. "You have my word."

When he left her in the wee hours of the morning, he still didn't feel like returning home. He had his coachman drive him to a tavern in the vicinity.

During his fortnight away, he had forced himself to drink steadily. It usually ended up making him sick, but he considered the few hours of numbness more than made up for any unpleasant side effects.

Tonight was no exception. He took a fresh glass every time the waitress came around with a tray. He lost heavily at the gaming tables, but he had become accustomed to that as well in the last fortnight.

As dawn approached he went down to the basement and watched the end of a cockfight. The two roosters were a bloody mess by then, missing eyes and feathers but determined to fight it out to the bitter end.

By then, Tertius's stomach was beginning to revolt. He got up and looked for the exit, feeling the need for some air. He found a back entrance that led out into an alley. Empty kegs were standing there. He wove around them, a part of his mind wondering why he subjected himself to this.

He turned into another alley, needing only to gulp fresh air. Unfortunately, what he breathed in was fetid and putrid, the combined stench of rotten vegetables and human and animal waste.

He groped in the dark, knowing he should just get to the

main street and find his coach and return home. But the thought of its closed, dark interior and the bumpy ride home only filled him with a greater nausea.

If only he could find some relief.

It was then he heard the footsteps behind him. Before he could unsheathe the sword from his cane, he was attacked from behind.

"What've we got here, 'enry?" asked one man.

"A swell," answered the other, the greed evident in his voice.

As the two men spoke, they were busy, one holding Sky by the arms, the other landing his fist in his gut. As Sky doubled over with the pain, his arms pinioned behind him, the second one began feeling for his purse.

"It's empty!" The man swore and threw the wallet away into the darkness. Next he found Sky's watch and ripped it off his waistcoat.

"See if he's got any jewels."

"He's got nothin' on," the man said in disgust. "What kinda dandy is 'e?"

"See if he's got a ring."

Sky clenched his hands, regretting that he'd worn his family crest.

The man soon found it and pulled it roughly off his finger.

Before they left him, the man gave him a good swing at the jaw and another in the stomach. "That's to show you not to be wastin' our time." With that they were off, disappearing down the alley as Sky collapsed onto the slimy ground.

Loathing filled him as he struggled to his feet. There was a time when he had been able to defend himself against common street thieves. How many times in the Indies had he gone about on his own at night, his lightning reflexes ready to spring upon anyone foolish enough to think they could rob him?

These days he couldn't even hold his liquor.

Slowly, he found his way back out onto the street and located his coach. The coachman was nowhere to be seen, still inside the tavern drinking, waiting for Sky to summon him. Well, he hadn't the energy or inclination to reenter the pub.

With fingers that scarcely obeyed him, Tertius struggled to open the door of the carriage and heaved himself inside, where he collapsed against the squabs.

When he awoke, he was being lowered into his own bed by Nigel.

"Where…wha—" he mumbled groggily.

"It's all right," murmured Nigel. "Jenkins called me down to help bring you up. He found you asleep in de coach. It looks like you been set upon by thieves. You took a beating to your face."

Tertius touched his jaw gingerly and winced, the details of the evening falling into place. "Yes, there were two as I recall." He let his head fall back onto his pillow. "Foolish of me not to hear them. Too far gone, I suppose."

"You shouldn't a gone out alone."

Tertius closed his eyes wearily, the pounding in his temples beginning afresh. "I must be getting old, not to be able to fight off a couple of ruffians. Need to go to Jackson's Saloon and train…"

"It's her," Nigel's voice cut through his meanderings.

He opened his eyes. "Her?"

"I told you she wouldn't like your leaving."

He snorted. "So, we're back to that again. Now she's sending some cutpurses to attack me."

"It's part of de curse."

"Stuff and nonsense. That's for you superstitious Africans."

"There be power in those curses."

"I wonder how my face will look tomorrow," mused Tertius. "Will I have to cancel my engagements at the gambling halls?"

"I know a man who left his woman and a week later he was dead," continued Nigel as if Tertius hadn't spoken. "He was killed by a machete swung at him in de cane field."

Tertius listened, fascinated despite his skepticism.

"Another was cheating on his woman and she had a curse put on him. He got a slow, wasting disease."

Tertius grinned weakly. "So, everyone must be falling left and right on the islands if all it takes is speaking some incantation over someone. A wonder anyone is left...."

"Some are strong enough to resist de black magic if de curse not powerful enough. But most people find protection."

Sky quirked an eyebrow and was immediately sorry as he felt the pain.

Nigel approached him with a cold, wet cloth, which he laid along his bruised jaw.

"What about you, Nigel? Aren't you scared you've looked at someone the wrong way and you might drop dead tomorrow?"

Nigel eyed him solemnly. "You laugh about something deadly. I be protected." He dug inside his collar and pulled out a little pouch on a leather thong. "It be made up special for me. It wards off de evil and sends it back. Whatever was wished on me will strike the one who sent it…or one of his loved ones."

Despite Tertius's desire to laugh at the absurdity of what he was hearing, he felt a shiver of fear course through him.

"I know a man who put a curse on another. His witch discovered it and had it returned to de sender. De first man's only son be eaten by a shark."

Tertius felt sickened by the tale. He closed his eyes and turned away from his valet. "Leave me. I must get some sleep."

Afterward, once he was alone and the room was still, Tertius opened his eyes. He had known he wouldn't sleep.

Every night it was similar. He would awake from a bad dream and the terror would begin. His mouth dry, his body in a sweat, his heart palpitating, he would feel powerless to fight the onslaught of pure, blind panic. And his valet's words would begin to have a semblance of truth.

Either that or he was going mad.

He didn't understand it. Even in the wild days of his youth, he had never experienced these kinds of effects from drinking. He'd never been a fearful man. He'd done a multitude of wild stunts in his youth, and faced down plenty of dangers in the Indies both from man and beast.

Why this sense of absolute fear?

And always that sense of oppression. He had already begun to have a vague sense of it in the Indies, but since he'd returned it had grown stronger, pushing him down, making him feel that none of his efforts would avail.

His mind was playing tricks on him, he kept insisting to

himself. But in the still darkness of his room, it was difficult to retain his rationality.

The only help these days came in the form of his laudanum.

With a groan, his body aching where he had been punched, he sat up on the side of his bed and reached for the bottle.

A few days later, as soon as the swelling along his jaw was down, Sky was back at the gaming tables. One of his acquaintances from his pre-Indies days lounged back in his chair.

"I heard they're trying a new treatment on old Farmer George."

Another fellow across the table grinned. "Indeed? Are they still hoping to bring our sovereign back? I shouldn't think the Regent would be too keen on that."

"To think the old king had his first spell when he was only twenty. I believe it started as a stomach disorder."

Tertius glanced sharply at the speaker, a man he'd known in his London days. The man, a youth then, had grown paunchy, his hair thinning.

"They say his spells are always preceded by a dream. And now it seems he'll never get out of his last one."

The first speaker fingered a rouleau in the little wooden dish at his side. "They say his physicians have ordered a new cure." He gave a wicked grin. "They call it the 'salutory fear' regimen. They keep him tied in sheets, a handkerchief stuffed in his mouth."

"A straitjacket, I believe they call it," another speaker added.

"I know a few people I'd like to prescribe that treatment to."

"In my immediate family." They all chuckled.

"What's the matter, Sky? You don't look so good."

"Nothing a shot of brandy can't fix," he said, signaling to the passing waiter.

As he took a sip of the liquid, trying to forget the conversation he'd heard, he saw his father enter the card room. He hadn't seen him since his wedding, a day he'd prefer to obliterate from his memory.

His father glanced his way and stopped in midsentence with the gentleman he was walking with. Sky almost laughed at the stupefaction on his face. Instead, he merely lifted his tumbler a fraction and saluted his sire.

Lord Caulfield recovered quickly, Sky had to admit. He walked calmly over to his son.

"Good evening, Sky. Back in town?"

"Yes, for the time being."

Later that night, when Sky finally returned home, he found his father waiting for him. He signaled him into the library and turned to pour himself a drink.

"I walk into Brooks's this evening and whom do I see? My newly married son, who is presumably on his honeymoon somewhere in Cornwall or Kent by now.

"Instead of hearing tidings of the news I'm expecting, I hear stories of his drinking and gaming." His father faced him. "I've heard you've taken up with Miss Spencer, otherwise known as the Little Lad, for her fame in boy's togs. Rumor has it you've set her up magnificently in our own neighborhood. Soon she'll be seen at the best parties." His father looked at him in absolute displeasure. "By heavens, Sky, have you no shame? Not even I treated your mother this way."

A pulse began to beat in his temple at the mention of his mother, but he managed to say evenly, "I wouldn't bring Mother into this if I were you."

His father had the grace to look away. "Whatever I did away from your mother, I did with the utmost discretion. I never flaunted my affairs."

Sky snorted and reached for the decanter. "Yes, I suppose bringing the evidence of one of your affairs to live under our roof was being discreet to the utmost."

"The poor girl had nowhere to go. Her parents were killed in the Terror. She would have starved to death in France if I hadn't taken Althea in."

Sky had stopped listening.

"Anyway, this is not about me, it's about you. You're not a young lad of twenty anymore, Tertius. You're a grown man. I expected you to come home mature, ready to take over from me. I'm getting tired. I need you fit for visiting all the estates. Look at you. You're nothing but a self-indulgent, dissipated profligate just like you were when I sent you off to the Indies."

Tertius hardly heard his father's drone. It was too familiar from over a decade ago. He thought he'd forgotten what it was like in all that time, but the cadence was the same. It was funny how all the years in between seemed to count for nothing with his father. The fact of turning a profit on a plantation every year, despite hurricanes, slave unrest and a variety of other issues had gone unnoticed by his father. It shouldn't have surprised Sky.

"…I thought those years in the Indies would be the making of you. You had me fooled for a while there. But I see how wrong I was. You're a wastrel, Sky. You're not half the man Edmund was—"

Sky took another sip of the liquid, glad of the warmth it gave him. He didn't care how much he cast up his accounts later; it was worth it for its numbing effect now.

"What have you done to that lovely young wife of yours? I chose the best I could find, the cream of the crop."

Tertius smiled thinly. "We didn't suit."

"What kind of nonsense is that—'didn't suit'? Marriages are arranged every day between families, and the parties don't go around after a few days saying 'they didn't suit.'" His father stood in front of him, his eyes demanding an answer.

"Since you insist on an explanation, let us say your lily-white maiden of the ton lacked one vital article."

Father and son looked long at each other until Tertius knew his father understood. He saw him age visibly before his eyes. It wasn't that anything changed; it was that Tertius noticed for the first time the sagging cheeks beneath the powder and rouge. At least his father had finally stopped wearing a wig, but he hadn't discontinued to powder his thinning locks. Sky realized how soon he himself would begin to look like that—not that he resembled his father physically in any way, but soon the skin would begin to lose its firmness and the hair its fullness.

"I'm sorry," his father said at last, his voice sad and weary. "I thought I'd chosen well. Diamond of the first water…all that. I've known the duchess for years and the girl's father before that. How could it be? I can't believe it."

Sky turned away, his anger toward his father evaporated. "Well, believe it or not, as you will. It means nothing to me." He set his glass down and left the library.

Instead of heading up to his room, he headed back out.

It was a warm night, and he decided to walk to a hack stand, his own coachman already having put the coach away.

He felt relief that he'd evaded Nigel, who'd taken to accompanying him on his nightly rounds.

He would be more careful this night, Sky told himself, gripping his walking stick. He could go and visit Laurette. He was certainly paying her enough. But somehow he wasn't in the mood. Instead he told the jarvey to let him off in Covent Garden. He knew a couple of good taverns in that neighborhood.

A few hours later he exited a pub, his legs unsteady. He was good and thoroughly drunk, as he'd intended. All cautions forgotten, he staggered in the streets, trying to get his bearings. As he turned down one street, he saw a light at one end, and a crowd gathered. He headed that way. Light, that was what he needed. He'd be safe from cutthroats in the light.

His mind focused on that fact and he concentrated on putting one foot in front of the other.

When he arrived at the gathering, he could have wept for disappointment. It was nothing but a street meeting. Some fool was standing on a block proclaiming the Savior and describing the horrors of hell for those who refused the invitation. The flames from a few torches surrounding the man gave substance to his graphic illustrations. Tertius watched the flickering shadows against the brick walls and on the faces of the poor fools, their faces upturned, taking in the vivid descriptions.

Tertius turned away.

No one could save him now. He remembered those years

of catechism as a young lad. How little those lessons served him now. What was it? Fragments of a verse came to him, "The Lord is my shepherd, I shall not want…"

What a joke. Hadn't he wanted? Look where it had got him.

Suddenly he was forced to turn into another dark alley and fall to his knees to retch.

These days he couldn't hold down his liquor as in his youth, or much else, for that matter. Everything disagreed with him. His guts were in a continual turmoil; he'd end his days facedown in a gutter. What an ignominious way to go, he thought, wiping his mouth at last on his neck cloth, unable to do anything about the vile, acid taste in his mouth.

He staggered to his feet and made his way back out to the street. When he finally arrived at his home, Nigel, after scolding him for being out alone, helped him into bed, although Sky tried to shake him off.

"A pity my dear wife doesn't know what a losing bargain she got for a husband. Never mind, soon she'll be a dowager countess, her worries past…." He doubled over in pain as Nigel finished pulling off his boots.

His father was right. He was no Edmund. The word he'd been running from since his fateful wedding night stared him in the face now.

Failure.

The word rang in his mind like a gong. He was nothing but a fraud and failure.

You're not half the man Edmund was and never will be. How could he ever have thought to fill his brother's shoes? What audacity.

He couldn't even manage a respectable marriage. He couldn't hold his head up in English society. In his thirty-five years he'd only managed a mediocre success in an insignificant society a thousand miles across the sea. What a colossal conceit to think his puny success would hold any account here in his homeland.

Chapter Nine

February 1815

Tertius woke up in Laurette's bed with a blinding headache, and he knew the fever was upon him full force once again. For six months he'd played a danse macabre with it as it attacked in small skirmishes, just enough to let him know it still held sway.

But now he knew he was in for a siege.

He groaned as he rolled over in the soft feather bed.

He touched Laurette's bare shoulder. There was no response.

He shook her harder, but he knew from experience she was a deep sleeper.

"Laurette!" He winced in pain as he spoke her name sharply.

She moaned but didn't waken.

Shaking her more roughly and continuing to call her name, he finally succeeded in semi-awakening her.

"Wha—what is it?" she asked, struggling to form the words.

"I need for you to bring Nigel—my valet—to me," he managed to say.

Consciousness penetrated. As she took in his appearance, understanding gradually sank in. She shoved her tangled hair from her face and frowned at him.

"What is it? Are you unwell?"

"You could say that," he replied. Until now, he had managed to hide his intervals of indisposition from her.

She slipped her hand from the covers and felt his forehead. Immediately she withdrew it and sat away from him. "You're burning up."

She rose from the bed and put on a wrapper. "You've got to get out of here. How long have you been ill?"

As she spoke, she twisted her hair into a knot and searched her wardrobe for a gown.

"Call my man. He'll know what to do," Tertius said quietly. If he'd felt a little less ill, he'd have found the situation amusing. "It's not the plague, my dear, so I wouldn't concern myself unduly."

She stopped in midstride, her frown deepening. "How do you know? Have you had this before?"

He nodded wearily, closing his eyes against the pain behind them.

"Why on earth did you come here last night if you knew you were going to be sick? I can't afford to fall ill. I have a performance tonight."

"Send for Nigel," he repeated, at the end of his strength.

"Yes…yes! I will!" She finally began to understand what he'd been telling her. He sank back against the pillows as she left the room in her dressing gown to send a serving boy with the message.

By the time Nigel arrived, Tertius's body was racked with chills.

He could hear Nigel talking with Laurette, but he hardly cared what they said or what was being done to him.

"I don't understand it. He was fine last evening. How long will it last?" Laurette's tone became more strident.

Nigel's tone, soft, came through the fog. "We never know how long it last. He come through every time, but his body grow feeble." As he spoke, he lifted Sky to a sitting position and pulled the nightshirt off him.

Tertius struggled to assist his valet as he dressed him. How he hated this helplessness, but he felt so weak.

"What about me? What am I supposed to do now? How long is he going to be ill?" Tertius could hear the note of panic in her tone as he walked across the room leaning heavily on Nigel.

"How am I supposed to pay my bills? Will I still be able to draw on the bank?"

"I don't know, madam. You'll have to speak to his secretary."

She grabbed Sky's arm as he was being propelled out the door. "You must continue our arrangement. Do you understand me? You can't leave me stranded like this!"

Tertius nodded wearily. "I'll see to it. You have nothing to worry about."

After that, he knew nothing more but bumping along in the coach and being carried to his own bed by Nigel.

Nigel wearily replaced the wet cloth over his master's forehead.

He was at his wits' end. Since they'd arrived in England, his master had been steadily deteriorating. Now Nigel truly doubted Sky's chance of recovery. He'd done everything he knew to do.

He stood and stretched, then walked to the window. The day was another inhospitable one, the clouds low and gray, pressing on a man's soul.

Never in his life had he been so lonely…or so cold. It was cold that seeped down into the bones and didn't let go.

On his native island, there was always the laughter of adults and children, no matter how heavy the toil. There was warmth and light, bright sunshine and crimson flowers.

The only person to even look at him like a human being since he'd come to London, besides his master, had been that maidservant with her sharp blue eyes, but she had long since left, taken away with the new mistress.

Since then, life had been growing steadily grayer and colder.

He knew what he'd do if he were still on the island.

For a while he thought he'd succeeded here in London. Through another black-skinned footman at another great house, Nigel had at last found a woman who knew the arts of white magic.

He'd gone to see the large woman, her gray hair braided tightly against her scalp in narrow rows. She'd smoked her thick brown cigar silently, reading the ashes as they'd grown longer on its fat end, and confirmed what he already knew in his heart.

"Your master indeed be cursed." Her brown eyes, their whites yellowed, looked into his, making him feel she could read everything in his soul. "It be a powerful curse. He near death now, ain't he?"

Nigel nodded reluctantly.

"It be a woman. A woman done it to him. She very angry with him. See him dead before she see him with another woman."

The witch heaved her heavy body up from the cane chair and moved about her small, cluttered room, collecting things here and there.

Nigel went home with a list of instructions and a bagful of ingredients.

He'd followed it all to the letter—the special baths, the water perfumed with fragrant oils as he'd chanted incantations over his master's wasted frame. He'd put the protective amulet around his neck; he'd burned incenses around his bed, all to ward off the evil attack from across the ocean, all away from the eyes of the other servants.

Lord Caulfield had done his part, summoning the best physicians he knew to prick and prod at his only son's body. Nigel had come to dread the sound of the clink of metal tweezers against metal dish as the physician picked up those leeches, their bodies wet and glistening like wedges of raw beef liver, and set them against Sky's skin, their bodies growing fat as they sucked out his master's life blood.

But all to no avail.

Lord Skylar was weaker than he'd ever seen him.

"Nigel?" His master's hoarse whisper came to him.

Nigel was immediately at his bedside. "Yes, my lord, what is it?"

"I'm going to die, am I not?"

"No, no you're not," he replied automatically, although it was getting harder to sound convincing.

"It's too powerful for me, no matter how much I fight it," Sky continued as if Nigel hadn't spoken. "What was it Job's wife told him—'Curse God and die'? That's what I ought to do, oughtn't I?"

Nigel shushed him and adjusted the covers around his thin frame.

Sky moved his fingers against his neck and felt the string around it. He grinned weakly at Nigel. "Don't tell me…it's some shark's tooth or tiger's claw to ward off evil. I hate to disappoint you, my dear fellow, but I'm afraid it's no good."

He had tired of talking, Nigel could see.

"I'm taking you home, my lord."

Skylar raised his eyebrows a fraction, not bothering to open his eyes. "Home? I thought I was home."

"This isn't your home."

"You mean back to the island?"

"Home is where your wife is."

Sky turned his face away on the pillow. "I have no wife."

"You have a young, pretty wife who been badly treated."

"The young, pretty thing you are referring to is a harlot."

"Nevertheless, I'm taking you home," announced Nigel.

Gillian laid her knife and fork parallel to each other at the edge of the blueware plate.

The rabbit pie had been a bit bland. Perhaps a touch of curry added to the sauce? She would speak to the cook about it.

She drained her glass and gave a final pat to her lips with her linen napkin, then refolded it and replaced it in its ring.

As soon as she stood, Sophie rose to her feet from her place by the door and waited until Gillian opened the door. She padded behind Gillian as she left the dining room. There were no footmen at Penuel Hall. She no longer noticed the dark stone walls surrounding her. After the first couple of months, she'd decided it was useless to expend her energies on things she was powerless to change.

She entered a small room where a fire had been lit for her. It was the only room with any semblance of coziness to it and she'd taken it as her sitting room. Somewhere at some point in the history of the Jacobean hall, some lady of the house must have taken pains to decorate it and make it habitable.

Gillian sat down to her needlework frame set up by the stone grate. A coal fire glowed. It warmed her feet through the screen.

Sophie found a place to curl up beside her. In a few moments one of her cats got up from his place on a Louis XV armchair and arched his body in a stretch. After a few wide yawns, he jumped from the chair and walked over to Gillian. She scratched his neck.

"Had a good nap, my boy?" At the sound of her voice the other cat opened his eyes from his place across the room and then reclosed them.

After working on her tapestry for a half an hour, Gillian rose and wandered to the armchair. She turned up the lamp and took the book she had started a few nights ago. She read for an hour then rang for a cup of tea. When it arrived, she sat at the card table in one corner of the room. She shuffled the pack of cards and laid out a game of patience. She would play until precisely nine o'clock and then she would retire for the evening.

She was debating the merits of placing her ten of hearts onto the jack of spades or the jack of clubs when she heard a carriage in the drive.

Immediately, she turned toward the windows, experiencing a momentary alarm. When she'd first come to the wilds of Yorkshire she'd gone to bed each night with a chair pushed against her door and a stout walking stick by her bed, terrified lest there be a new Luddite uprising in the region. It had only been a few years since textile workers had arisen all over the north, rioting, smashing factory looms with sledgehammers and causing fear of a French-like revolution in the country. But as the months went by and nothing untoward had occurred, Gillian had gradually been able to relax her guard at night.

But she never had evening visitors. Those few neighbors of the gentry who had called at first had been discouraged by her manner, and thus, in a short time, her daytime visitors had ceased as well.

She waited, not even daring to get up and peer through the heavy curtains that had been closed to keep out the cold.

The old servant's footsteps echoed in the hall and then the front door opened and a man's voice spoke.

Gillian dropped her cards and half rose, her hand to her throat. What must she do? More footsteps and finally the manservant's voice. Although it sounded excited, it didn't sound unduly alarmed, so the visitors must be familiar to him.

Should she open the door a crack or should she wait?

Deciding on the latter course, Gillian sat at the armchair, too restless to take up her book or resume her game.

She heard footsteps going up the main staircase in the great entry hall. What on earth?

A few minutes later the stoop-shouldered servant entered with a bow. "M'lady, I beg to inform you, t'maister nobbut brought in."

She stared at him blankly. "The master?" Had Lord Caulfield come all the way up here to see her? "Brought here? What are you saying?"

He cleared his throat. "Yes, m'lady. Lord Skylar. He be sommut ill. I've had him brought to the maister's room, tho' it ain't been made up. I've sent the missus to see to it, if that be all right with you, m'lady."

She had risen at his first words. "Lord Skylar here?" What was this crazy old man saying? "Ill? What are you saying? Speak clearly."

"Ech! m'lady," he replied impatiently. "Lord Skylar nobbut brought in a carriage by…by…" The old man's eyes grew round as he continued. "A blackamoor—a man as broad as a tree, and he done carried his lordship all the way up the stairs."

At the description of Lord Skylar's West Indian valet, reality began to sink in. Lord Skylar had come to Penuel Hall, and he appeared to be too ill to walk himself. Why had he come here, of all places?

Trying to collect herself, she took a step back and collapsed into her chair.

"M'lady, will you nut come see his lordship for yerself?"

"No," she said, hearing the cold, hard tone of her voice. "Lord Skylar's condition is no concern of mine. See to his needs."

The man stared at her a few seconds. Gillian deliberately took up her book once more and opened it to her place, removing the ribbon marker and setting it on the table beside her. Without looking at the manservant, she said, "You may go. I'll ring if I should need anything."

"Y…yes, m…m'lady," he stuttered, and backed out of the room.

She didn't look up until she heard the heavy oak door shut behind him.

Then she let the book drop into her lap and stared before her.

Lord Skylar under the same roof as she! What did he mean by coming here?

What was she to do?

She didn't think she'd ever have to see him again.

It had taken her a couple of weeks merely to feel clean again. There had been that horrendous journey north. The only thing that had made it bearable was the presence of her three beloved animals.

And now, after six months, her husband—the word caused a frisson of revulsion through her—decided to pay her a visit when he was too ill to walk. What did he want? For her to nurse him?

Well, he could die upstairs in his damp, unaired room, for all the aid she would give him.

She took up her book and once more began to read, the words dancing around on the page until she forced herself to focus on each one individually.

The next day her maid, Katie, began telling her as she dressed Gillian's hair, "Oh, my lady, you should see his lordship. The poor man, he's at death's door—oh, I beg your pardon. I mean, he is so poorly. And all he has to care for him is that giant black man and his heathenish ways." She pulled at Gillian's hair, causing her to flinch. "So sorry, my lady," she muttered, her mouth full of hairpins.

"What do you mean, his 'heathenish ways'?"

After she'd removed the hairpins one by one from her mouth and stuck them into Gillian's hair, she replied, "Oh, I hear him muttering gibberish over Lord Skylar's poor sleeping form when he thinks no one's around. And he's got something around the poor man's neck. Looks like witchcraft to me. It's no wonder the man's sick."

As Gillian was exiting her room later that morning, she started at the sight of Skylar's valet walking down the corridor.

She drew back against her door, but stopped when he saw her. His height and breadth overwhelmed her until she remembered who she was. She was mistress of this house. Her heart thumped wildly in her chest, as she realized no one else was about, but she was determined to stand her ground and not let him see how intimidating he was.

"Good morning, my lady."

The man's voice was low and gentle. She forced herself to

look up into his face. She was startled to find green eyes staring back at her from dark brown skin. They were an unusual green, like nothing she'd ever seen before—a mixture of brown and yellow, resulting in a light, golden shade.

"G…good morning," she replied.

"I beg your pardon I wasn't able to inform you of de master's arrival. I didn't know where else to take him."

Gillian stared at the man. "What are you talking about?"

"De master, my lady. This latest bout of fever struck so strong. I done everything in my power. I thought if I brought him here to you—"

"*You* took it upon yourself to bring him here?" She looked at the man aghast. "Lord Skylar didn't *ask* to be brought to Penuel Hall?"

"No, my lady. He hardly be conscious. De trip sapped de last o' his strength. I don't believe he any idea where he be."

"Oh, that's precious. I'm sure he'll be most gratified when he awakens."

If he noticed her sarcasm, he gave no indication. "If I might, may I beg some help with de nursing? Perhaps one of de maids?"

"Oh, take what you need. We have a whole troop of servants at our disposal." She numbered them on her fingers. "There's old Harold and his wife Edna, the retainers Lord Caulfield has seen fit to leave in charge of this drafty hall. There's a young girl who comes in from the village and seems incapable of understanding the simplest order. And then there's Katie, my own personal maid, chosen for me by Lord Skylar before he fell ill. Whom would you prefer?"

She thought she read sympathy in his eyes. But that was nonsense. What would a black servant from the Indies know about her situation?

"If you don't mind lending Miss Katie's services for a bit, I'd be most appreciative."

She smiled sweetly. "So, you'll take the best of the bunch and leave me with no servant."

"Only for a few hours a day, my lady."

She shrugged, suddenly not caring what the man did. "As you wish." She walked past him, but his soft words stopped her before she had gotten more than a few feet from him.

"Would you like to step in and see your husband?"

She pivoted back slowly. "No, thank you, I would most certainly not. You had no business bringing him here." Something else occurred to her. "Did Lord Caulfield know you were bringing him?"

"No, my lady. He wasn't around when I decided to bring him."

"How long has Lord Skylar been ill?"

"It been many weeks."

Her eyes narrowed. "Is this the same fever that struck him in the Indies?"

He nodded. "Yes, my lady. The fever hit him the first time before we left de island, but it come back since we been in London, but not as strongly as dis time."

"You mean he was ill when he was courting me?"

"At times, but only for a few days at a time."

She turned away again without saying anything more. Why hadn't she been told? She remembered the time she hadn't seen Lord Skylar for days and then he excused himself with the gift of the jewels and told her he'd been "indisposed."

Slowly, other details began to fall into place—how little he ate and drank. Why hadn't she seen this before? Had her mother known?

As she descended the wide stairway to the ground floor, the questions revolved in her mind. If she had been deceiving her future husband, had he, too, been deceiving her?

And now he was here. What would he do to her when he awakened? The terror that had finally subsided after so many months of the solitude of the Yorkshire wilds threatened her again. She looked down at her ring as she thought of the other jewels safely tucked away in her jewelry box. So many times she'd been on the point of pawning them to gather enough money to escape from her exile, but no matter how close she'd come, she hadn't yet taken that step.

Perhaps now the time had come.

But where would she go? That was what had stopped her.

A disgraced wife fleeing her husband had few choices.

Her mother wouldn't have her back. Not that Gillian had any desire to go back home. Her mother had written her a brief missive when she'd discovered Gillian's whereabouts.

I don't know what you've done to displease your husband. All he communicated with me was that he could by rights send you back to me.

If this rupture with your husband has anything to do with that Captain Hawkes, I warned you to stay away from him. He disgraced you before and now it seems he has ruined your marriage.

I told you one day you'd go too far. Your father over-indulged you.

Your only hope is to get with child by Lord Skylar, but I suppose there is no possibility of that now.

Your mother, etc.

Gillian had crumpled up the letter as soon as she'd read it.

She would be dead before she'd let Lord Skylar ever touch her again.

The next day, after Katie reported a few more tidbits of information to Gillian on Lord Skylar's condition, Gillian's curiosity got the better of her. The irony was too great to miss. Her jailer, who'd exiled her to the remotest corner of his properties, had now become the jailed, confined to his bed, on the point of death if Katie and that valet were to be believed.

When she was alone, she made her way down the corridor to the master bedroom. At the door she hesitated, but fearing someone would soon come by, she finally opened it a crack. With a quick glance about the room and down the hall behind her, she stepped in, closing the door softly behind her.

The moment she entered the shadowy, cavernous room, she wrinkled her nose at the musty smell. A large oak bed dominated the room, its hangings a gloomy dark velvet. Old tapestries covered the stone walls. She heard Lord Skylar's labored breathing, and was instantly reminded of the weeks before her father's death. The same smell and sounds of death.

Every instinct urged her to flee the decay. But curiosity and something else drew her forward. At the edge of his bed, she stopped short. She hadn't been prepared for how he frail he looked. If he'd been thin before, he was cadaverous now. His ebony locks, long and lank, hung from his head.

"Mmm…no…please…" His mumbled words came out with effort. Gillian leaned over the bed and touched his forehead. It was warm. He was indeed feverish.

Her gaze dropped lower and she spied a cord around his throat at the open neck of his nightshirt. Like a child reaching for something forbidden, she drew it out until she could see what was on it. Two stones, one black onyx perhaps, the other like coral, hung on the thong.

At that moment she sensed a presence near her. She jumped to find the giant valet beside her. "How did you get here?" she asked him sharply.

"I come in through there," he said, motioning to a side door.

"Oh." She turned back to Skylar, pretending indifference at the man's presence. "What is this thing?" she asked.

"It be a safeguard," he answered simply.

"I don't like it," she told him. "It scares me." She began to pull it forward, looking for a knot or clasp. Before she knew it, the manservant had stopped her, covering her hand with his large brown one.

She gave a shriek then quickly covered her mouth with her free hand. "Unhand me," she told him behind her hand.

"Excuse me, my lady, I didn't mean no harm. But it be better not to remove de necklace. The master be cursed."

She stared into those golden green eyes and felt a chill down her spine. "What kind of foolishness are you saying?"

"He be cursed. This amulet help ward off any evil against his lordship."

"What kind of evil?" she asked, remembering the maid's warnings.

"Very powerful evil." His green eyes, fringed by curling black lashes, looked into hers earnestly. "On de island there be many kinds of spirits. They can be sent to harm people."

"Is that what has happened to Lord Skylar?" she whispered, fascinated and terrified at the same time.

He nodded gravely. "I have tried to fight dis evil, but so far, I have failed. The evil must be very strong indeed. I don't know where we can find a spirit more powerful."

She let the thong go and immediately the valet released her hand. She had forgotten he still held her hand. Its warmth had been oddly comforting after her initial shock. Now, the cold penetrated her and she hugged her arms to her body.

"Well, I must go. I…only wanted to see how your master was doing." She paused. "He doesn't look well at all."

"No, my lady." The large man sighed and busied himself rearranging the covers. Then he poured a drink of water from a pitcher by his bed. He raised Skylar's head with his large hand and put the glass to his chapped lips.

The man's gentle behavior astonished Gillian. He wiped the water that had dripped down Skylar's chin and replaced the necklace beneath his nightshirt.

Slowly, Gillian backed away from the bed. She let herself out of the room, torn between a reluctant pity for the ghost of a man lying there and memories of his terrifying behavior on their wedding night.

The second time she went into his room, she was searching for her pets. She had looked for them through the entire manor house and called and called outside. She was beginning to get worried, when Katie told her, "The animals are in his lordship's room."

She quickly went to the master bedroom and paused a second before opening the door.

This time the valet was sitting at a chair by the bed. There was her dog, lying on the floor beside the large, four-poster bed. Her two cats were curled up at the foot of the bed. Annoyed at the traitorous behavior of her pets, she marched to the bed and gave the valet a brief nod.

"How is he?"

"The same," the valet answered.

"What is your name?" she asked the black man.

"Nigel, my lady."

She nodded. "Has Katie been able to relieve you?"

"Yes, she has been very helpful."

She reached down to grasp the dog's soft, red leather collar. She remembered the day she'd received it and how touched she'd been at Lord Skylar's thoughtfulness. Images of the day they'd rescued Sophie flashed through her mind.

Her gaze strayed to her husband. How could the two be one and the same man? Without conscious decision she reached out to touch Sky's forehead. At that moment, he opened his eyes. His deep brown eyes focused on her.

She stared back at him, wondering if he would recognize her.

She wasn't kept in doubt long.

"What is she doing here?" his voice rasped out. Before Nigel could rise and answer him, he said, "Get her out! Get her out of here!"

Gillian fell back as if he'd slapped her. Nigel immediately

stepped in front of her and blocked Tertius's view. His soft tone murmured, "Shh! She be your wife. She do you no harm."

"I don't want her here." Lord Skylar's agitation grew. "Where have you brought me?"

Nigel murmured as if to a child, "I done brought you home like I said."

As Gillian turned to leave the room, she could hear their two voices, Sky's demanding answers, and Nigel's reassuring him without giving any specific replies. All pity her husband's condition had aroused in her evaporated at his condemning attitude.

Well, he could rot in that bed before she came in again!

Chapter Ten

❧

The next morning, Gillian put on her warm cloak and went outside for a walk. The land was covered in snow and the air was cold, but she couldn't stand being in that house a minute longer.

She'd passed a sleepless night.

She left the stone mansion without a backward glance and walked down the gravel drive, past the frozen duck pond and the bare willow trees surrounding it. She gave a brief nod to old Harold at the stables before exiting through the tall iron gates.

Not until she was several feet outside the parkland did she breathe freely.

She had spent the first month of her exile in tears and despair, but through sheer will, she had managed to carve out a routine for herself in this forsaken land just to maintain her sanity. It was too much that now she was forced to live under the same roof as her tormentor and endure his absolute scorn and hatred.

She must escape. There was no other way.

An idea, which had been forming in her mind through the long hours of the night, had crystallized by dawn, and now her mind was resolute.

She walked a mile to the tiny village. Penuel Hall sat high on a hill. Below it, the village was wedged against the hillside above a long, deep valley. From its narrow cobbled street, Gillian could see the outlying buildings of the market town far down in the valley and the silvery thread of the river that bisected it.

She hated the sight of that town. A large stone mill sat by the river, its chimneys continuously spewing steam. To Gillian it depicted all the ugliness and isolation of the West Riding for a London-bred girl. On the first morning she'd ridden through it before arriving at the Hall, she'd seen only soot-stained stone buildings and sullen-looking children staring at her coach.

Despite her aversion to the town, she would have to make her way there and find a pawnshop. If no one there would take her jewels, she would have to find her way to the next town. Leeds was not more than half a day's journey away.

But she had no way of getting there. She hadn't a penny to her name. Her wealthy husband had left her a pauper in her exile.

She walked the stony track through the village. It, too, showed only signs of grim poverty. Tall trees, their stark black branches outlined against the gray sky formed a canopy over her head. All around her, snow-covered fields sloped downward behind the small, stone dwellings lining the street. Beyond, above the village, lay the still more desolate moors.

The village seemed an unfriendly place to her. She could barely understand the villagers' dialect with their "mun this" and "mun that." She rarely entered its few shops, preferring to let the housekeeper make all the purchases.

A large, stone church and graveyard beside it dominated the village center.

Evil-looking rooks sat in the black trees arching their spindly branches high over the graveyard, as if they were keeping the dead confined to their stone graves. Gillian hurried past the cemetery and followed a narrow track leading out of the village to the moors beyond.

The short scrubby heather, its leaves brown, peeked through the snow. Gillian continued walking until she tired and knew she had to return to the hall. She dragged her booted feet. Since Lord Skylar's arrival, the Hall no longer offered refuge from the staring villagers.

She resolved that as soon as she entered it, she would head for her writing table. She would enclose her letter in one to her closest friend, Charlotte, and ask her to send it on to the Guards' barracks. She had decided last night to send a plea to Gerrit. Perhaps if he knew her true situation, he would rescue her.

She wondered what he had thought when she had left London so hurriedly. The gossips must have had a field day. If she ever did return to London, her name would be so sullied by then that one more scandal would no longer matter.

She imagined the stories that would float around. *Lady Skylar runs off with an officer of the Guards.*

She was willing to run away with Gerrit if he still wanted her. Anything was better than being shackled to a man who despised her and kept her a virtual prisoner.

She remembered Skylar's deathly pallor. What if he shouldn't survive?

No matter how much she'd vilified him since he'd banished her, she'd never actually wished for his death. For her own, yes.

But now, it seemed fate was offering her a way out. Was there hope that she might be free again? Was there a chance for her and Gerrit this time?

Only one doubt niggled at her. What if Gerrit should leave her as before? Although his reasons sounded noble when he'd told her, a small voice inside her questioned his motives. How could a gentleman take a young lady's virtue and not stand by her and marry her, no matter what the opposition?

No, he had only been thinking of her—not himself, she argued against that voice.

If she were to be widowed, this time she would be of age, with her own fortune. She could marry anyone she pleased and no one could oppose her choice.

She shivered at the mere thought of it.

When she entered the hall, she had no sooner removed her outer garments than Katie came down the stairs.

"Oh, my lady, how glad I am that you've returned. We don't know what to do!"

"What is it?" she asked.

"It's the master. He's taken a turn for the worse. We must summon a doctor. Nigel says the master won't want one, but I say it's gone beyond what he's capable of knowin' or not knowin'."

Gillian stared at her maid, her heart thumping loudly. Could the maid read the guilt written on her face? She wanted to shout that she hadn't wished for Lord Skylar's death.

She turned abruptly from the maid and said more roughly than she meant to, "You two may decide whatever you wish. His lordship made his wishes very clear to me yesterday."

"Oh, please, my lady. You mustn't mind what a sick man says. He isn't in his right mind. Nigel won't heed my warnings. He says a physician won't be any help now, but I think we must do something."

Gillian stopped, her hand on the newel post, conscious above all of her duty. Her father would not have wanted her to do otherwise. She would do everything a wife would for an ailing husband. And if that weren't enough, at least his death wouldn't be on her conscience. She already had enough on it as it was, she thought wearily.

"Very well, Katie, send Harold to fetch the doctor from town. It might take a while for him to get here."

"Thank you, my lady. I shall have him go straightway." The maid didn't move and Gillian turned to her. "Well?"

"It's just…I was thinking."

"Yes?" Gillian prodded her.

"With his lordship doing so poorly, I had a thought of someone else we might send for."

"Who?"

"Lord Skylar's sister, Lady Althea."

"His sister?" Gillian stared at her. "I had no idea Lord Skylar had a sister."

The maid bobbed her head. "Yes, my lady. It's not common knowledge, but being in the household so long, I know more'n most. Lady Althea was Lord Caulfield's ward for many years. She grew up in their household since she was a babe.

"But as soon as Lady Caulfield passed away a few years ago, Lord Caulfield let it be known Lady Althea was his daughter. So, it's Lord Skylar's half sister."

"An illegitimate offspring?" she asked in disdain.

She blushed. "Yes, my lady, but ever so respectable a lady. And she's a nurse. She would be perfectly suited to nurse her brother. She has spent the last few years working in a Methodist mission in London, helping the poor, nursing and such."

Gillian's distaste grew. "A Methodist?" All she knew of them was they were heretics to the Church of England.

"She's a very pious lady. And begging your pardon, my lady, but with the heathenish ways of Nigel, I wouldn't think it amiss to have a good Christian lady at Lord Skylar's side."

"But Methodist?" she voiced her doubts. "What about the curate in the village?"

Her mouth turned downward. "I don't think he would rightly know what to do."

Gillian pictured the sickly looking young man with his brood of young children. "No, I don't suppose so. Very well, but how would I get in touch with this...Lady Althea, you say?"

"I have the address to the mission. I've been there before."

It would be good to have an experienced nurse in the house. "Give me the address, and I shall write to her."

As she climbed the stairs to her room, she realized she had two letters to write instead of the one she'd intended.

* * *

Despite her resolve to go nowhere near the sickroom, Gillian was drawn there once more, late that night. Through the walls of her room, she could hear Sky's shouts. He sounded terrified and she wondered if Nigel was harming him in some way.

Gillian put on her wrapper, took her candle and made her way to his room.

Nigel was trying to hold Lord Skylar down in his bed.

"He's delirious," he told her over his shoulder when he noticed her standing beside him.

The doctor had been and gone and offered little hope. When Nigel had refused to let him bleed the patient, he had left in a huff, saying he washed his hands of the patient's fate.

As if reading her thoughts, Nigel told her, "He won't know you. Perhaps if you helped soothe him."

Before she could decide whether to go or stay, Tertius burst out, "Get it away from me!" His hands tore at his chest and neck and the rest of his words were garbled. "…can't breathe…burning…"

Suddenly his hand groped at the side of the bed and, finding hers, grabbed it as if to a lifeline. Surprised at the strength of his grasp, she found herself powerless to remove her hand.

His eyes opened and he implored, "Water…I'm burning…anything for some water…"

Helpless to move from his grasp, she had to rely on Nigel, who brought the glass to his lips.

He gulped the water, his eyes never leaving hers. When he spluttered and coughed, Nigel removed the glass and brought a handkerchief to his mouth. During all this, Skylar didn't let go of her hand, and she didn't know what to do. Her position grew uncomfortable and she was finally forced to sit at the edge of the bed.

"Save me…"

Resentment warred with pity as she heard the plea. Clearly he didn't recognize her.

"Will you sit with him a while?" Nigel asked softly. "It's the first peace he's found tonight."

She looked at the black man mutely and hadn't the heart to refuse. "For a little while," she said at last.

He nodded, satisfied, and left her. She almost called him back in panic. What if Skylar woke again and recognized her? What if he hurt her?

She eased her position on the bed. Although Skylar had fallen asleep again, it was a tense sleep. He continued to mutter and she wondered what kind of dark place he was in. His hand remained curled around hers. She glanced down at it. His dark skin had faded to a pale, sallow color; only his cheeks showed a ruddy hue due to his fever.

His fingers were long and fine. She had never really looked closely at them until that moment, and she realized how beautifully shaped they were.

After a long time, when no one came to relieve her, she could no longer keep her eyes open. She eased herself down on the bed and curled up beside Skylar, seeking the warmth of his body.

It was getting near dawn when she awoke. She eased the kinks out of her neck and slowly sat up in the bed. Looking around, she saw Nigel fast asleep on a cot nearby. He had thrown a cover over her, she noticed, but otherwise not disturbed her sleep.

Realizing how closely she had lain near her husband, she hurried from the room, horrified at the thought of his body next to hers.

A week and a half later, Skylar's sister, Althea, arrived.

"I came as soon as I got your letter," she explained, greeting Gillian.

Gillian eyed her coolly, suspicious of the woman's piety. She looked nothing like Sky. Althea was much smaller in stature and blond and pale. She dressed in unfashionably dark and plain clothes and Gillian was put on the defensive immediately. Would she look on Gillian as frivolous?

The little she knew of Methodists was not favorable. She had heard of their frenzied worship and rantings of hellfire and brimstone.

"How is Tertius?" Althea asked, removing her plain bonnet.

"The same. The fever hasn't abated. We have little hope he will last much longer."

"May I see him?" she asked.

"Of course. Katie will show you to his room."

"I'm sorry, I haven't properly introduced myself or welcomed you to the family."

"I didn't even know Lord Skylar had a sister until a fortnight ago."

Althea blushed beneath the sprinkling of pale brown freckles across her cheeks. "I don't see the family very often now that I've moved to the mission."

Gillian turned from her. "Katie, take Lady Althea to Lord Skylar."

"I go by plain 'Miss Breton,'" Althea said gently.

Gillian stared at her. "I see. Very well. Show Miss Breton up," she said to Katie.

Curious to see what his sister would make of his condition, Gillian couldn't help following them up to Skylar's room.

Nigel and Althea had their backs to her as they stood beside the bed.

"How long has he been this way?"

Nigel described the condition and history of the illness. Neither noticed Gillian's presence.

"And he isn't being seen by a physician?"

"No, miss. He has seen many physicians and not one has been able to help him. He has lost much blood and I fear with de weight he's lost over de months, any more bleeding will kill him."

"You say he has had trouble keeping down food as well?"

"Yes, miss. No physician can make Lord Skylar well," the black man pronounced. "This illness not have its roots in nature. The truth is he be cursed."

"What do you mean?"

"It be powerful black magic that afflicts my master. He left a woman on de island when he come here to wed my lady, but that woman not willing to let him go."

"You're sure of this?" Gillian was surprised at Althea's attentive attitude toward the valet. She certainly seemed to be taking the black man's ridiculous theories seriously.

"Yes. I went to see a woman in London—a woman who can 'see' things. She saw dis woman and say Lord Skylar be sick with a powerful curse. She gave me remedies, but none was strong enough." He leaned over the bed and drew out the leather thong around his neck. "This is to ward off de evil. I think it's the only thing keeping my lord alive."

Althea leaned over next to him and examined the neck charms. Then she straightened and touched the valet on the arm. If she noticed Gillian's presence she gave no sign. "Do you know, there is something more powerful than this magic?"

Nigel's eyes looked at her with hope. "You know of a more powerful magic?"

Althea nodded, and Gillian was struck by the strength in her demeanor. "Oh, yes, Nigel, much more powerful. But it's not magic. It's spirit."

Nigel's eyes brightened in understanding. "Yes, it's spirit. Which spirit is this?"

"The Holy Spirit."

Nigel's eyelids closed in disappointment. "The Christian spirit not powerful against dis kind of evil."

Althea took the man's hand in hers with no apparent thought to the color of his skin. "Oh, yes, it is. You shall see."

She turned to acknowledge Gillian then. "Hello, Lady Skylar." She turned back to Nigel. "May I ask you to summon Katie for me? We shall begin by praying for Tertius. The 'prayer of the righteous availeth much,'" she told him with a smile.

A few nights later, Tertius woke and saw his half sister sitting by his bed.

"Althy," he said, his voice hoarse.

She looked at him with a smile.

"Papa's little by-blow," he added, wanting to wipe the smile off her face.

He didn't succeed. The smile faded, but somehow it lingered in her gray eyes.

"I thought I had dreamed you here the other night," he said.

"No, I'm real enough."

"Why did you come?"

"I heard you were very ill."

"Who summoned you?"

"Katie, your wife's maid. She knew where to find me."

He frowned at the mention of his wife. "Where is…Gillian?"

"She may have retired for the night. I'm not certain."

"I don't want her near me."

His sister didn't reply. Instead she helped him take a sip of water. Hating to be at her mercy but feeling his throat parched, he was forced to submit to her ministrations.

"Why should you want to take care of me?" he asked finally, too weary to pursue the topic of Gillian.

"Because I love you."

The answer annoyed him.

"I have never loved you," he told her bluntly.

"That's all right. I have enough love for both of us."

"You're mad."

"But it's a wonderful sort of madness." She reached forward and covered his hand with her warm one. "The Lord sent me to you. He wants to help you."

He gave a weary snort. "Who is the Lord?" An agitation seized him. "Why was I brought here? I don't want to see Gillian. I don't want her to see me like this."

"Shh. It's all right. She won't see you if you don't wish it."

He closed his eyes, but that way lay terror. So many terrible creatures inhabited his dreams. "I'm not going to make it, am I?" he asked finally.

"Of course you are." His sister's encouraging voice came to him from farther and farther away.

"Don't give me empty assurances."

"I won't. I am praying for you."

When he said nothing, she said, "Jesus loves you. He gave His life for you. Trust Him."

"How do I trust someone I scarcely know?" he mumbled.

"Just call on Him."

They were quiet a few minutes. It took too much effort to talk.

"I've always despised you," Tertius finally said. "Yet here you are at my sickbed. I hope you don't expect my undying gratitude." His laughter came out a wheeze.

"I always understood why you disliked me."

"You are discerning, at least," he said before the heaviness in his eyelids was too much and he slipped back into the netherworld that held him in its grasp.

Althea gathered them together and led them in prayer for Tertius every day. Gillian stood as an unwilling spectator more than participant. There was no change in Tertius's condition. They took turns sitting by his side. Gillian dreaded her turn, hating to see the fear, at times downright terror, in him.

He'd cry out, many times sitting up, his eyes abruptly opening but not seeing her. Whatever he saw tormented him.

She turned to Althea when her sister-in-law entered the

room and demanded of her, "Can't you do something? Doesn't God hear your prayers?"

"I know He does. No evil can prevail against Him."

Althea began to pray aloud and quote Scripture.

"Greater is He that is in me than he that is in the world." Her voice rang out through the somber room, lightening it for an instant before the shadows fell again.

Gillian noticed that soon after her arrival, Althea spent more and more time on her knees at her brother's bedside and began to fast.

But Gillian saw no change in Lord Skylar, and she wondered when the end would come. She didn't see how Tertius's weakened body could hold out much more.

Katie brought a pot of tea and some biscuits up to Nigel one evening, knowing he would be at Lord Skylar's bedside most of the night.

"I brought you a light snack," she told him as he rose to take it from her.

"Thank you," he said with a soft smile.

She busied herself pouring him a cup, which he set down at a small table by the bed.

"What are you doing?" she asked.

"Sewing on a button," he said, showing her. "Dis was— be one of Lord Skylar's favorite riding jackets. I noticed de button was loose."

She stood watching him a moment, hesitating. All her work was done for the day. Lady Skylar wouldn't need her until she went to bed.

Without a word she drew a chair up to the bed and sat, her hands lying quietly on her apron.

Nigel made no comment about her presence. Instead he said, "You should ha' seen Lord Skylar on de island. Sometimes he'd ride bareback like the wind. Other times he'd be dressed de finest gentleman."

"I never met him. I've been with Lord Caulfield's household since I was a wee girl, but Lord Skylar had already left for the Indies when I came."

"How old you be, Miss Katie?"

"I turned eighteen in the autumn."

After a bit, he said, "You know, you be de only person to eye me different when I first come to Lord Caulfield's household. You acted like I existed and weren't some stick of furniture."

She smiled, remembering the servants' comments when Lord Skylar had first brought him. "You were so large and...and different—"

"Colored?" he put in.

"Yes," she admitted. "I'd never seen one up close, if you know what I mean."

"It be hard to understand. At home we be all shades of brown. Those of your pale skin be far fewer."

"Tell me about your island."

She listened, fascinated with the place he described.

"You must miss it," she said, when he paused to knot a thread and break it off. She noticed the teacup beside him. "Your tea will grow cold."

"It doesn't matter," he said, laying the jacket in his lap and taking a long sip, which emptied half the cup.

He set the cup back down and took up the jacket once again. He shook it out. As he folded it in half, he frowned, eyeing it.

"What's the matter, discovered a tear in the cloth?" she teased.

He didn't say anything, but examined an inside portion of the hem where the garment was thickest along the jacket's facing.

Before she could ask him what he was doing, he took up a pair of small, sharp scissors and snipped at the threads of the hem.

Curious, Katie stood and leaned closer to him. When he'd gotten a good few inches loosened, he folded back the cloth. Katie drew in her breath at the sight of the small, cloth pouch flattened and tucked inside the hem.

She glanced up at Nigel's face and stopped short at the expression on his face. He looked terribly frightened.

"What is it?" she whispered.

He said nothing, but folded the cloth back to its original position and stood, looking around as if unsure what to do with it.

"What's the matter?" she asked more sharply.

"I found *it*," he whispered hoarsely.

"Found what?" Her own heart was pounding in inexplicable fear.

"De source of de curse." He finally focused on her. "It's what's causing his lordship's sickness."

She gave him a scornful look. "Now, don't give me that hocus-pocus, heathenish talk. We're in a Christian nation."

"That may be, but dis power be real." He spoke so seriously it gave her a shiver. But she got hold of herself and reached for the jacket. "Let me see that thing." Before he could stop her, she had unfolded the jacket and retrieved the pouch.

"It's just an ordinary cloth pouch," she said in disdain. As she spoke she loosened the drawstring and emptied the contents onto her hand.

"Don't!" He reached for her but it was too late. They both stared in fascination at the odd assortment in the palm of her hand.

A bit of curled-up dried skin, like that of a snake; a powdery dirt the color of clay; two colors of human hair entwined; a wizened spider; some torn bits of cloth stained with dried blood; and ashes.

"That be from a shirt of Lord Skylar's," Nigel said in awe. "De hair…it be his…and hers."

Katie shook herself from her stupor. "This is nonsense. Some witch's concoction! I know what to do with this." With those bold words, she poured the contents back into the sack and marched to the fire.

"What you be doing?" he asked worriedly, following her closely.

"I'm going to put it where it belongs, into the fire."

He grabbed her hand in a viselike grip. "You mustn't destroy it like dat. It could release de evil and there be no telling where it land."

She was stopped short by his wide-eyed look, the whites of his eyes in striking contrast to his dark skin.

"That's nonsense."

"That's what you think, but Lord Skylar's condition speaks differently."

They both looked toward the wan figure lying on the bed. Again she felt a shiver go through her.

"Very well, I won't burn it. But let me show it to Lady Althea. She'll know what to do."

He considered and finally gave a nod of his head. "Very well. But she must understand it be evil. Powerful evil."

When Althea came upstairs, Gillian followed behind, hardly understanding what her maid and Nigel had discovered and were in disagreement over.

"You say this is the evidence of the curse placed on Lord Skylar?" Althea asked, after listening to Nigel and examining the contents of the pouch as he spoke.

"Yes. The woman take various things—things that belong to Lord Skylar and other things—and declare a curse over his life, then she must put the things where they'll be near him. As long as the evil is not destroyed, his life be cursed."

"I see," she said softly. She, too, replaced the contents into the bag, but made no move toward the fire as Katie had done.

Instead she smiled at them, and Gillian felt a sense of shock that Althea alone of the four of them seemed to feel no fear at the harmless-looking object in her hand.

"The Lord has answered our prayers. He has revealed the source of the evil and now it's up to us to consign it back where it belongs."

"You must be careful, my lady," Nigel said with urgency. "You mustn't release de evil contained there."

"Do not fear, Nigel, for 'greater is the One in me' than the one who put this together."

"You don't understand, Miss Breton—"

"The Lord has given us 'power to tread on serpents and scorpions and over *all* the power of the enemy.' He has promised, moreover, that nothing shall by any means hurt us. Do you understand that, Nigel? *Nothing. Absolutely nothing.*"

Before Nigel could argue further, she closed her eyes and held out the pouch before her.

She began first of all to give thanks to God for revealing the object to them.

"Heavenly Father, I take the authority You've given me through Your son, Jesus, and I bind the power of darkness at work through this bundle. I send that power back to the pit where it belongs just as I confine this object to the flames to be consumed."

As Nigel gave a start and made to reach out, her words stopped him.

"I declare You sovereign, Lord Jesus, over my brother Tertius, over his body and soul. I declare, in Your name, every attack and power of the evil one turned back, destroyed, and rendered completely useless against Tertius or anyone in his family or in this household. I break every curse spoken over his life. And I thank You for Your precious blood, Lord Jesus, which cleanses and heals him and sets him free."

With those words, she opened her eyes, took the pouch and threw it into the fire, where it sizzled against the red coals before it burst into flames.

There was no visible change in Tertius.

Gillian realized she had somehow expected him to suddenly awaken and reappear his normal self. Of course, no such thing would happen! She glanced at Althea contemptuously.

But her sister-in-law did not seem disappointed. She told them, "I shall stay with my brother tonight. We must believe the curse has been broken."

Tertius was back on the ledge, fighting to keep from falling. This time he was naked and manacled and it was so hot he felt the surface of his skin would blister. Sulfurous fumes rose from below, suffocating him.

Every time he moved, the heavy chains attached to the manacles weighed down his limbs. A metal band choked him around the neck. He clawed at it, seeking some give in it.

Agonized cries from down below told him, however bad his situation, there was worse if he fell off the ledge.

As he pressed his body away from the edge, there was movement from the void below. He watched in horror as gargoylelike creatures rose and came at him. He batted them away, while struggling desperately to maintain his hold on the ledge.

The little beasts tormented him, pecking at him, pinching him, shrieking at him. He caught sight of his sweat-soaked skin. It was covered with blood-sucking leeches, writhing and bloated on his body.

He could no longer fend off the mind-numbing panic.

He screamed and screamed and screamed.

As if from a distance, he could hear his sister urging him, "Jesus! Tertius, you must call on the name of Jesus!"

He tried, tried so desperately, but the demons wouldn't let him. They clawed at his mouth, spitting venomous slime on him. With his last reserves of strength, he pushed his arms away from himself to fend them off, but in doing so, he lunged over the edge of the ledge.

"Nooo!" His silent scream echoed in his mind as he fell into the choking fumes. The screams of those down below grew louder, and he knew they were the agonizing cries of the damned.

"Jesus!" The word sprang from his burning throat.

Immediately, a shaft of light burst through above him and he instinctively reached upward. The shrieks around him intensified even as the hold of the demons clinging to him seemed to slacken. It gave him the chance to reach his arm above him.

He felt pulled out of the darkness and toward the light. He sped through the space, traveling upward in what seemed seconds.

He came to a place of pure light. He was surrounded by it; it seemed to shine through him, making him feel as fragile as glass. He fell to his knees, the shackles gone.

He experienced an overwhelming sense of his filth, crouched there naked before the brilliant light.

He felt a touch upon his face, lifting it. And then like a spectator he saw the panorama of his life, from the memorable events to the trivial. Shame engulfed him, and he wished there were somewhere he could hide. But everything was transparent.

Selfish motives permeated almost every act. Here and there stood a few acts of kindness which he'd long forgotten—defending a schoolboy against his tormentors, feeding a stray cat until the servants had it drowned, throwing a few coins to a beggar, rescuing Nigel from the cane fields; but all these acts were the exception. The overwhelming majority of his actions were a dissipation of the talents and opportunities he'd been given since birth.

He realized the great privilege and wealth he'd been born to. The injustices committed by his family upon the hundreds of workers in its employ flashed before him. His heart felt consumed by shame at the name and crest he had been so proud of.

He saw every wench he'd bedded and experienced their degradation and felt the violation against his own body. The young actress, Laurette, treated so callously by him, had been filled with fears and uncertainties of her own precarious future. Remorse engulfed him, forming a weight so heavy he thought he'd never be able to rise again.

He relived his wedding night and experienced his bride's terror and humiliation on a night that should have been the most special of her young life. Sorrow constricted his heart, and he felt an overwhelming desire to go back and change things.

All he could do was bow down on his face and weep and weep. The demonic torment was what he deserved.

But again he felt his face lifted. What he saw now was his old life being burned away completely, as not worth saving. Like a piece of paper aflame, it curled inward, turning black, until it was fully consumed and crumbled to nothing.

He found himself plunged into a pool of clean, cool water, fully submerged. The splash of droplets burst upward as his body emerged forth again, a new life being born.

He stood before his Lord and understood without words that the new body being given him was a holy temple. A clean garment clothed him and covered his nakedness. *I have purchased these robes of righteousness by My very blood* was intoned into his spirit. Then the Lord breathed on him. *Receive My Spirit.*

He felt filled to overflowing, complete and lacking nothing, more alive than he'd ever felt. The Lord's light and love overwhelmed his being. His whole body felt elevated, rising from the void and into a plane far above anything he had ever known.

Then he was viewing what his new life was to be. Purpose and meaning were given it. He gazed in awe at the tasks ahead.

Then the Lord gave him an image of his wife. *Wife.* The word, which had filled him with rage and disillusion, gained a new, special meaning. *As I have loved you, you are to love her. As I gave Myself for you, give yourself to her.*

And his immediate response was, *Yes, Lord.* He would do anything for his Lord, who had saved him and who had loved him and who had taken away his reproach.

Chapter Eleven

❧

Gillian broke off the thread she'd knotted and arched her neck back, kneading the aching muscles with her fingertips. She was tired of watching vigil over a man who seemed closer to death than to life.

She was tired of being around people who, instead of relying on the traditional remedies of a physician, spent all their time either mumbling incantations or speaking out Scripture.

She looked wearily at Tertius's sleeping form on the bed beside her. Clearly, his sister's little prayer ceremony the evening before had done no good.

Just at that moment, her husband opened his eyes.

"Tertius!" The name slipped out unthinkingly. She'd grown accustomed to hearing Althea saying it.

"Gillian." Her name came out sounding cracked, but his eyes were fully conscious and filled with humor.

"We thought you were going to die," she said stupidly, too shocked by the lucidity in his eyes to know what to say.

"I *did* die," he said in his low, rough voice.

She went on unheeding. "So many strange things happened—but you wouldn't know…" She got up to feel his forehead. It seemed normal.

She couldn't believe that Althea's prayers…her commands of the night before…that little, harmless-looking pouch with its bizarre contents—no, it couldn't all be true! "Let me get Althea."

"Althea? She's here?" He smiled. "Yes…I seem to recall speaking to her…and she to me."

"She came about a fortnight ago, when we thought you were going…to die." As he digested this information, she added, "I didn't even know you had a sister."

His gaze met hers once more. "Yes. There's so much I need to tell you."

She tore her eyes away from his and began to fold up her sewing, feeling a sudden desire to flee the room.

"Might I…trouble…you for…a sip of water?" He spoke like someone unaccustomed to using his voice.

"Yes, yes, of course." She stood nervously, set down her sewing and picked up a glass and pitcher, surprised to find her hands shaking.

Carefully she lifted his head and brought the glass to his dry lips. His hair had grown and his beard, too, in the past few days, when Nigel had been afraid to shave him for fear of hurting him. The dark beard was scratchy against her fingers.

He lifted a hand to help guide her hand to his mouth. The touch, though featherlight, sent tingles through her. Maybe because it was the first time he had touched her consciously since…since their wedding night.

His hand fell back onto the coverlet. "I'm so da—" The word died on his lips. "So weak," he finished.

"It's not surprising," she said. "You've been sick for quite some time," she explained, taking a handkerchief out of her pocket and wiping his mouth as she laid his head back on the pillow, aware of his dark eyes fixed on her the entire time.

"How long have I been out this time?" he asked, his voice smoother.

"Weeks, it seems," she replied, uncertain herself. "The days seemed to flow into each other. I don't know how long you were ill in London before Nigel brought you here."

"Nigel brought me here?" He frowned, as if trying to remember. "I'm in Yorkshire? I've had so many dreams…it seems a lifetime has gone by."

"Well, you are at Penuel Hall," she answered shortly, her reasons for being where she was beginning to reassert themselves. Before she said something she shouldn't to a man in his weakened condition, she explained, "Nigel brought you here of his own accord. Your father didn't even know. I wrote to him afterward. He has replied, sending you his best wishes for a speedy recovery."

"Has he?" he asked in an absent way although his eyes seemed to be observing her keenly.

Again she felt herself blushing, with no good reason, and it annoyed her. "Well, I shall summon Althea or Nigel, who are your primary nurses. I'm sure they'll see you need something like beef tea—"

His hand reached out and loosely encircled her wrist. She

flinched, then willed her arm to remain unmoving, reminding herself this was an ill man, too weak to do her any harm.

"Gillian…thank you. I think there are things…things we need to talk about…" His hand let her wrist go and she realized how frail he truly was.

How much did he remember of everything he had done to her?

"Well, it can't be right this moment. You're weaker than a newborn lamb," she said briskly, and stepped away from him. "I'll get Nigel and Althea. I'm sure they'll be overjoyed with your recovery."

"Gillian—"

She turned back to him. "Yes?"

"God healed me."

She smiled thinly. "Your fever seems to be gone, but as to being healed…" She splayed her hands in question.

"This body might not know it yet, but it is healed. It has been reborn."

She left the room, disregarding his extraordinary statements, more intent on her own confused emotions.

Tertius had survived, against all reason. Where did that leave her?

Since his condition had deteriorated so much, she had begun to believe she might be a widow, and now she was suddenly presented with a living husband once again.

She pushed her disheveled curls away from her face, wishing she could push her thoughts away as easily. Guilt swirled through her brain, heedless to her logic. She'd never wished for Tertius's death, her reason argued back. She'd never wished to deceive him. She'd never wished to be married to him.

But she was powerless to stop the insidious voice insinuating that she was guilty.

She wasn't guilty! she wanted to scream. All she wanted was that somehow none of this had ever happened. How could she ever undo what she'd done?

Tertius heard the door close behind her and moved his focus upward toward the bed's canopy.

"You brought me back, Lord," he said aloud, feeling God's presence. "I thank You. Oh, God," he breathed, remembering everything. "I thank You…I worship You," he repeated softly, feeling the tears already welling up in his eyes at the memory of what he had experienced.

He looked around the strange bedroom, trying to orient himself. He had sensed less than happiness in Gillian, and he realized she must be in some sort of shock at seeing him alive. Well, he was, too.

He felt a pang of sadness, remembering what he had done to her, but knowing if God had seen fit to bring him back, there was hope for his relationship with his wife.

Hope and joy and an overflow of love were the primary sensations running through him at that moment.

When a couple of days went by and he saw nothing of Gillian, although he asked for her every day, he began to sense the rift between them went deeper than he'd imagined. He'd been too consumed with his own hurt and disappointment for so long that he'd never thought what she must have been going through.

Most days he sat with Althea, with Nigel hovering nearby. He shared his experience with her, and she understood perfectly. She told him the story of her own encounter with her redeemer.

"I was listening to a preacher and felt the convicting power of God and fell to my knees at the altar. I laid all the loneliness and pain and shame I'd grown up with there and felt a love and acceptance such as I'd never known in my life."

He reached out a hand to her. "Poor Althea. We treated you contemptibly, Edmund and I. We never considered how you must have felt—a child, having come to a strange home in a strange country. I hated Father for bringing you to our house, and it was easier to blame you, a helpless child."

She squeezed his hand. "It's all in the past. The Lord filled me with His love and has kept me filled since that day at the altar."

"I am sorry for the suffering I caused you," Tertius told her. "Can you ever forgive me?"

"Oh, Tertius, I can only rejoice that the Lord has answered my prayers." She smiled. "I've prayed and prayed for you for a long time."

"Thank you, dear sister." He shook his head, still feeling overwhelmed with his new self. "You know, I feel a completely different person. The moment I awoke, I was about to utter a silly profanity and the word died on my lips." His expression sobered. "Althea, can you ask Gillian to come and see me?"

She looked downward, and he was aware that she must have sensed the estrangement between him and his wife. "Of course, I shall get her immediately."

Nigel found Althea leaving his master's room, and he approached her.

"Miss Breton?" he asked when she had stopped attentively before him.

"Yes, what is it, Nigel?"

"I wish to know your God."

"Oh, Nigel, of course. I shall be glad to introduce you," she said with a smile.

"He be more powerful than all de evil I have seen on de island."

"Yes, He is." She considered then said, "I have an idea. Lord Skylar is eager to know about His God and I have been reading to him from the Scriptures. Why don't you join us and you can discover Him together?"

He nodded eagerly. "I should like that above all." He hesitated. "May I ask permission for Miss Katie to join us as well? She believes in dis God but says she has never seen de evidence of His power so clearly."

"Of course she may join us. How wonderful. We shall have a Bible study together. Let us gather together this evening."

Gillian looked up from her game of patience. Although the snow had nearly all melted, it was a cold, rainy day, and she was confined to the house this afternoon.

Althea entered the sitting room. "I don't mean to disturb you, but I wondered if you wouldn't mind sitting with Tertius a while, perhaps read to him for a bit? It is tedious to be lying in bed, yet he's still too weak to get up."

"I'm sorry, but I'm occupied at present," she replied, flipping over a card from her pile.

"You could finish your game in a little while, couldn't you?"

Gillian felt the resentment well up in her bosom. She

looked Althea straight in the eye and said in a hard tone, "No, I'm afraid I couldn't."

"I beg your pardon," Althea replied immediately, clearly taken aback by Gillian's tone. "I didn't mean to disturb you."

"That's quite all right. You didn't disturb me at all," she answered serenely, and turned her attention back to the cards laid out on the table.

Althea returned to Skylar's room.

"Well?" he asked as soon as she'd entered the room.

"I'm sorry, but she's…occupied," she answered lamely, sitting back down and smoothing her skirts.

"I see." He looked beyond her with a sad smile. "I shouldn't have sent you."

"Don't worry about that, but Tertius, what is the matter between the two of you? I realize you are recently married and you've been sick most of that time, but I don't understand."

"There was a misunderstanding between us. Quite a major one, as a matter of fact. I haven't treated her very well, I'm afraid. I have much to make up for." He gave a rueful smile. "But it seems she isn't going to make it easy for me. And I'm too weak yet to do much but lie here and wish I could do better."

"Don't be impatient. Your body needs to grow strong. And think, this time isn't wasted. You are learning about your Savior. Each day you're gaining insights that it took many of us years to learn."

He nodded. "I thank God every minute for the privilege of knowing Him. For so many years, I misjudged you. I dismissed you as a pious evangelical—a heretic even—when all along, you were the only one of us who knew the truth."

He sobered. "What about Edmund? Did you ever get to talk with him?"

"A little. He didn't seem to feel he had anything to be saved from."

"Poor Edmund. He had everything and for so long I envied him—or at any rate, I measured all my accomplishments against his."

"I never realized that. I always saw the two of you in much the same light—two aristocratic young men with no blotch on their name—two full brothers with no need to recognize an illegitimate half sister."

He reached out his hand and she met it with her own hand and they smiled in understanding at each other.

"It's good to have a full-fledged sister."

"It's good to have a brother," she replied.

Gillian groaned in annoyance. These days she could never count on having her pets beside her. She knew where she'd find them!

Always curled up on or around or under Skylar's bed!

Well, she'd had enough. She wouldn't be cowed from going and fetching at least one of them.

But when she stood outside his door and heard the voices and the laughter, she paused, as if suddenly faced with a ten-foot-high wall instead of an opened door with light spilling from it.

She viewed the scene around Tertius's wide bed. There sat Althea with her Bible in her lap, her face smiling and animated as it never was when she was with Gillian. As usual she was expounding on some portion of Scripture. Gillian gaped at Tertius. His face was more expressive than she'd ever seen it. He was laughing. He, too, had a Bible on his lap where he lay propped up in the bed.

She surveyed the rest of the immediate area surrounding the bed. There on the other side sat the black valet, a Bible on his lap! He, too, was smiling and asking a question of his own. Beside him, on another chair, with her Bible, sat her own personal maid, Katie, her eyes fixed on Althea as if she were relating the most fascinating story.

Since when did one sit with one's servants as if they were one's equals? And since when did reading the Scriptures become a festive occasion? They seemed to be having more fun than at a party.

Gillian almost drew back from the cozy tableau, but then annoyance grew in her. This was her home! She had been relegated here as a virtual prisoner and now she was being made to feel she was the intruder.

She would see about that!

Taking a deep breath, and ignoring her beating heart, she stepped into the light. Immediately all four pairs of eyes turned in her direction.

"Good evening," she said through stiff lips.

An immediate chorus of "good evening" greeted her. As she stood there, hesitating about crossing that large expanse between the door and bed, Tertius said, "It's good to see you, Gillian."

She cleared her throat, her fingers playing with the ribbon hanging from her dress. "I just…just came to look for my pets."

Tertius waved to the two sleeping cats at the foot of his bed. "Here they are, as comfortable as you please. Won't you come in and join us?"

She looked away from him. "No, thank you. I'll just take one of the cats, if you don't mind." Why was she so unsure of her actions? She marched across the room and scooped up one of the furry balls curled up by Tertius's legs.

"We'd love to have you join us." Althea's soft invitation came to her.

She used the cat to hide her face in as she answered. "No, thank you just the same."

She left, their silences, like their expressions, weighing on her and angering her. By the time she entered her own room, her cat scrambling to be let down, she felt as if she were flee-ing. Fleeing her own domain!

What did he want? Why had he come here? Since he'd regained consciousness, she felt his presence wherever she went in the house. Why hadn't he remained in London? Why couldn't she go back to London?

She *must* go back! Somehow she must find the means. Once more she went to her jewelry box and removed the necklace and earrings. She would find a way to sell them. Perhaps tomorrow.

In the light of her lamp she glanced down at the rings on her finger. A pinpoint of red light reflected off the diamond from where the lamplight hit it. She shifted her finger a fraction and the pinpoint turned bright blue; another frac-tion and it transformed to brilliant green, then back to red. Gillian continued shifting her hand back and forth, watch-ing the colors in fascination.

Suddenly she stopped and yanked the rings off her fin-ger. Why was she still wearing them? She was nothing to that man lying in the next room and he was nothing to her.

Husband! The word was an affront.

As she began to lay the rings beside the necklace in her jewel case, she noticed the inscription inside the wedding band. She had never realized it contained an inscription.

Slowly she picked it up and held it up to the light, deciphering the minute script.

To Jilly Girl, My Wife.

The words brought a sudden lump to her throat. Was that how he had thought of her before…

The endearment conjured up a loving partner, a man to honor and cherish her. How she had longed for such a man to love and be loved by.

Through her own perfidy and lies, had she been the one to forever destroy her chances at having such a husband?

She wiped angrily at a tear that ran down her cheek.

Her father had always called her Jilly dear.

Without giving it conscious thought, Gillian replaced the wedding band on her finger, telling herself it wouldn't fetch much anyway, an inscribed band of gold. She gathered up the other jewels and put them in her reticule.

The next afternoon, Althea knocked on the side of the sitting-room door and asked, "May I come in?"

"Of course," Gillian replied, where she sat sewing. Once again her plans for going into town were thwarted by rainy weather.

Althea took a seat beside her. "Tertius is coming along very nicely. He even was able to stand this morning. Soon we won't be able to keep him in bed."

Gillian concentrated on her stitches. "How nice."

"I wanted to ask a special favor of you."

Gillian met her gaze then. "Yes?"

"Could you take a turn at reading to him? He is getting

tired of lying abed, and I'm afraid my voice will give out." She gave a hesitant smile.

Gillian looked away, wondering how to turn down her sister-in-law's request. Why did she fear being in Tertius's presence? Would he be able to read the treachery in her eyes?

"I'm afraid I'm not much for Bible reading," she finally replied.

"You don't have to read the Bible." She glanced around at the tables in the room and, seeing the books, suggested, "You could read to him whatever you are reading."

"Are you sure he'd be interested? It seems to me all he cares about now is hearing Scriptures," she asked in an acid tone.

"That's what he cares about most, but I'm sure having your company would be far more important than the subject matter you were reading."

Gillian sighed, suddenly tired of dissembling. "My husband almost died, and if he had, I would have had my freedom. As it is, I am still his prisoner. So don't expect me to share your joy at his recovery or join your cozy Bible parties upstairs. As far as I'm concerned, his life is at the expense of my freedom."

She jabbed her needle into the muslin to punctuate her point. There! Let the good Althea think the worst of her. It was no more than she deserved, she thought, remembering the letter she had written to Gerrit.

She saw the shock and distress in her sister-in-law's eyes and felt a perverse satisfaction. It would come as no surprise, then, when Althea found out Gillian had run away from her husband.

"He's your husband. The two of you were joined in holy matrimony," Althea began quietly.

Gillian stood, unable to bear the confines of the chair. "My husband, as you call him, is a brute! I was forced to marry him, but I never dreamed he'd be such a monster. I hate him! I hate him!" The more she voiced the feelings that had been pent up inside her for so long, the more justified she felt.

"I'm sorry, my dear. I'm sure Tertius didn't mean to hurt you—"

Gillian covered her ears. "I don't want to hear any more. Leave me alone! All of you! I shall soon leave here and you can have your private little gatherings, spouting Scripture!"

Unable to bear Althea's sympathetic expression, Gillian rushed from the room.

A few days later Gillian finally received a reply from her friend Charlotte. Gillian's heartbeat quickened. Could it contain a reply from Gerrit?

She took it up to her room and locked the door behind her. Breaking open the seal, she breathed a sigh of relief when from the letter fell another which had been tucked inside the first. Her salvation had come!

She immediately recognized Gerrit's handwriting on the inside letter. He had answered her letter—her plea—for help!

She unfolded it and scanned its contents.

My dearest Gillian,
You'll never know the joy your note gave me. When I saw you last, I thought you would never consent to see me again. My heart was broken for a second time, thinking you lost to me forever. Then I received your letter, describing your cruel treatment and I was ready

to go and snatch you from your prison. But your next words stopped me. Now I await the day you will be free again. My heart has been true to you all these years. Fighting on the battlefield, torturing myself with thoughts of you with other loves. I await the day we will be together again.

Yours forever,

Gerrit

Gillian hugged the letter to her breast. He still loved her! He would wait for her! She did have a place to go! She needn't be left to feel an outsider by these people around her.

She sat at her desk and reread his letter. He still thought Tertius lay at death's door. Of course now she would have to tell him of Tertius's miraculous recovery. But if Gerrit loved her, it shouldn't make any difference. They could flee England together. Now that Napoleon had been defeated, they could live in France or Italy. Isn't that what so many others had done in the past for the sake of true love? Even Princess Caroline, the Regent's poor wife, was living the life of a virtual exile since he wouldn't grant her a divorce. And hadn't the poet Shelley eloped this summer with Mary Godwin, even though he already had a wife and child?

She and Gerrit could have a good life on the Continent. Anywhere but here. Her fevered thoughts grasped at this opportunity to escape.

By mid-March spring had come to the West Riding. The grass turned vibrant green, and the sheep were let out to the pastures on the sloping fields.

Tertius was determined to regain his strength as quickly

as possible. He felt an urgency on him to do the work the Lord had for him. For the first time in his life, he felt he had a purpose to fulfill, a purpose with eternal value. But he knew he could do nothing without first making things right with his young wife.

Althea and Nigel continued to nurse him, but he no longer wanted to be treated like an invalid. The times he enjoyed most were gathering together, the four of them, he and his sister with the two servants and discussing what they had read in the Bible. Second to this was reminiscing with Althea about their childhood.

He was unprepared, then, for the day Althea told him as the two sat in the drawing room, "I must return to London."

He turned from surveying the parkland from the window. He'd been watching Gillian walk along a tree-lined lane toward the moors.

"What? When?" he asked in alarm.

She smiled. "I left many things pending when I came here so hurriedly."

"What kinds of things?"

"At the mission. I have many responsibilities there."

He came to sit beside her. "Forgive me. I haven't asked you much about your present life. I'm sorry you had to come here in such haste."

"Don't be. I came here gladly. I know the Lord led me to you. He has blessed me with seeing the fruit of my prayers," she said with a smile, then sobered. "You know, I don't wish to leave so soon. You haven't fully regained your strength, and I don't want you to overtax yourself. Give your body time to heal properly. You also have only just begun your discipleship. I hate to leave you only a babe, but I sense the Lord would have me go at this time."

"But what am I to do without my teacher?" he asked, merely half in jest.

"Depend on the Lord even more. He shall teach you Himself." She opened the Bible that was never far from her side and flipped through it. "Listen. 'The anointing which ye have received of Him abideth in you, and ye need not that any man teach you: but as the same anointing teacheth you of all things, and is truth, and is no lie, and even as it hath taught you, ye shall abide in Him.'"

He took the book from her and read for himself. "I never would have understood these words before. They were meaningless to me. It's about revelation, isn't it?"

"Yes. The Lord has opened up the Scriptures to you. He has much, much more." She smoothed down her skirts, as if still wishing to say something more.

"What is it, Althea?"

"There is another reason I feel I need to leave now."

He waited.

"You have a lovely young wife who has been deeply hurt. I believe the two of you can begin mending things the sooner you are alone together." She sighed. "But I shall miss you, Tertius. I feel I've only just begun to have a brother."

"I shall miss you, too. Terribly," he said with a grin. "But we'll see each other again soon in London. I promise."

"I look forward to that. I shall be praying for you and Gillian."

"Thank you. I shall be praying for you and your work, too, dear sister."

Chapter Twelve

The evening after Althea left for London, Nigel came into Gillian's sitting room.

"Yes?"

"The master requests you come and read to him for a little while."

"Tell him—" She had been at the point of telling him that she was not going to take his precious sister's place, but she stopped herself. She had hardly seen Sky since he'd recovered, and she was curious to see if he indeed was "cured."

Part of her wanted to crow over him now that his closest ally was gone. Perhaps he needed to see who was in charge.

She entered his room and had her first surprise. Although he was abed, his aspect was already so much different from when the fever had left him. His face was cleanly shaven, his hair neatly combed, but it went deeper than that. As he smiled at her in welcome, she realized she had never seen quite such a genuine smile on his face.

His face looked young and open—there was no hint of the irony or mockery it had habitually contained.

"Thank you for taking pity on me and agreeing to read to me for a bit."

She sat down, the book she had brought in her lap. "Well, don't expect a long reading of the Scriptures," she snapped. "I'm in the middle of *Waverley* and if you wish to hear something else, you shall have to read it for yourself."

He chuckled. "Read anything you wish. I'd rather listen to your voice."

She glanced at him at that, but at the warm look in his eyes, she quickly opened the book to her bookmark and began to read.

"Chapter Eight…"

She didn't stop until she had finished the chapter. Despite her reluctance to read to him, she had gotten caught up in the story and forgotten Tertius's presence. He hadn't spoken or made any sound to distract her.

She placed the book upon the night table and poured herself a drink of water, realizing how dry her throat had become.

"Why don't I ring for some tea?" he asked, his hand already on the bellpull.

"If you wish," she said, eyeing him warily as she placed the glass back on the table.

"You have a nice reading voice."

"I'm sure it's not as inspired as Althea's," she couldn't help commenting.

"I read *Waverley* when it first came out last year."

"So did I," she retorted, "but since I didn't have time to pack my books, and your library here seems not to have had any new additions for at least a century, I've had to content myself with rereading those few books I did bring."

An awkward silence fell as they both thought of the reasons she had been brought there.

"I don't remember the last time I was here at Penuel Hall," he remarked. "I daresay my father rarely visits."

When she said nothing, he cleared his throat. "Did I hurt you very much…that night?"

She stared at him, hardly believing what she heard. How dared he bring up that night? All the pain, the humiliation, the absolute terror he'd put her through came rushing back as if it were happening all over again.

Without a word, she stood, the book falling with a thump to the floor, unheeded by her. She ran from the room, ignoring his "Gillian—"

The next evening as she looked in vain for her book, Nigel again appeared at her door. "If you would be so good and come read to the master again, he would be most grateful."

That's where she'd left the book! Swallowing her exasperation, she finally decided to fetch her book.

She'd retrieve it and leave straightaway, showing him by her action that he no longer had the power to frighten her.

But when she entered the room, and glanced toward the table for the book, refusing to look toward the bed, she heard Tertius's voice. "Good evening, Gillian."

She looked at him reluctantly. There in his hands was her book. She'd have to approach his bed to retrieve it.

"Thank you for coming."

"I left my book here last night," she stammered, her hands clasped in front of her. She felt a vast space separating the two of them, and the only way to retrieve her book was to cross it. Shaking aside the ridiculous thought, she walked boldly to his bedside and reached out her hand for the book.

Before he gave it to her, he said, "Forgive me, Gillian, for hurting you that…night—and for bringing up a painful subject. All I can say is that I wasn't myself that night. I was so angry to think I had been made a fool of…I wasn't capable of thinking of anyone but myself at the time."

She said nothing, fighting with herself not to yield to his gentle tone. Did he think a simple apology would wipe away that night of horror and shame? Would it wipe away the months of solitude and utter separation from every familiar face?

She must have taken a move backward, which she wasn't even aware of, for he said suddenly, "Please don't leave. Will you read to me some more, if it's not too tedious for you?"

He handed her the book, leaving the choice up to her. She took it from him and found herself sitting back down on the chair instead of leaving the room as she'd intended.

Well, no matter, she told herself, she was only there to read the story. She had wanted to continue it that evening and whether in this room, or another, made little difference.

When she'd finished her chapter, he said, "Would you like to continue?"

"No, I must go back down." But she didn't rise from her chair immediately.

"I'd like to ask you something," he began, "but find myself oddly hesitant at the thought for fear you'll get up and leave before hearing me out."

"What do you want?" Suddenly she was nervous. Did he somehow know of her correspondence with Gerrit? If he did, what would he do this time? Kill her?

He glanced down at his hands lying on the coverlet. "I'd like to ask you…if—" he faltered then recommenced "—if you think it might be possible, during my recuperation, to pretend that we'd never met until this moment and imagine how it might go this time around?"

The question was so different from what she'd been thinking that she slumped in relief. Then she realized what he was asking. "That we'd never met?" She made a sound of disbelief.

He glanced at her ruefully. "I was afraid you'd react that way."

"Well, you must agree it would take a stretch of the imagination."

"Perhaps. But what if it were so?" he said. "What if you and I had met at a dance or assembly? Let's say it wasn't even in London, but here in the West Riding."

Despite the absurdity of the game, she said, "It could have been at someone's country house."

He leaned back against his pillows, fingers to his lips, and mused aloud, "It was not even during the season, but at a local squire's ball. I had almost decided not to go, the squire was known to be tedious…"

She added, intrigued by the game, "And I almost didn't attend, but a friend begged me to accompany her."

"It was when you came in, a few minutes after the company was gathered, that I spotted you across the room. I interrupted my conversation with my host—"

A smile tugged at her mouth. "The tedious squire."

"The tedious squire." He smiled back. "I thought to myself as I saw you, 'what a pretty brunette. I haven't seen her before.'"

"I was visiting from London," she added, her imagination taking hold.

"I knew then that I wanted an introduction."

"I didn't notice you right away," she was quick to point out.

He waited, a dark eyebrow upraised.

She smoothed back a curl behind her ear. "There were so many people present that night," she explained. "My friend introduced me to her many acquaintances. It was hard to remember everyone's name."

"But I was persistent. I pressed through the crowd surrounding you and gained an introduction through our host."

"The tedious squire—" they both said at the same time and then laughed.

Before she could rein in her laughter, he went on, "I asked you for the allemande."

"I hesitated," she replied, immediately caught up again in the scenario. It was like reading a romantic novel. "You didn't seem like a gentleman I'd care to know," she added, mixing fact with fiction, as she remembered her own initial reaction to him.

"What was your impression?" he asked her, as if sensing that somewhere along the way they had passed from fantasy to reality.

"Cold and arrogant."

"At least you didn't say 'too old,'" he said wryly.

"I could have thought it but been too polite to say it," she countered.

"True." He laughed, his head thrown back against the pillow. She noticed the fine line of his jaw and tendons in his neck as her gaze traveled down to the open collar of his white nightshirt.

His laugh was a hearty laugh, like that of a man enjoying himself thoroughly. She'd never seen him laugh like that. His sense of humor had always struck her as tinged with mockery, either self-directed or directed at those around him and always restrained.

His laughter ended and he met her eyes. The humor still lit his face as he continued looking at her.

She rose, realizing how comfortable she was beginning to feel with him again. She wouldn't let herself be fooled by him a second time.

"I must go."

"Must you?" he asked softly.

"Yes," she said firmly, remembering to take the book with her this time.

She was destined to hear that laughter again in the days and weeks that followed.

As spring came to the West Riding, Gillian was amazed at the progress in Tertius. He refused to stay in bed, but was soon dressed and coming downstairs before his legs could hold him. Before long, he was walking outside. After his first venture outside, he asked her to accompany him on his walks.

"In case I fall on the moors and no one knows where to look for me," he quipped.

"Very well, but if anything happens to you, I can't be held

accountable. The moors are muddy now. I'm sure a physician would say you are mad to go out so soon."

"Since it wasn't a physician who was responsible for my recovery, I think I can dispense with whatever advice he would give."

"And whom do you credit with your recovery?" she asked.

"Jesus," he replied simply.

"He decided you were worthy of healing?" she challenged.

"He saw my unworthiness and gave me life in spite of it."

"Soon you'll be taking holy orders, the way you talk," she said with a light laugh, though she didn't see the humor of it at all.

On Sunday morning, Tertius appeared at the breakfast table dressed in a dark green cutaway coat, buckskin trousers and starched cravat. Gillian had to restrain herself from staring at him. He looked as if he'd walked in off a London street. She was surprised at how quickly he was regaining his strength.

"You appear fitted out for a stroll down Bond Street this morning," she told him dryly, buttering her piece of toast.

"I am going to church. Care to join me?"

She did stare at him then, the bread halfway to her mouth.

"I didn't know you attended services regularly," she said at last.

"I didn't. I had become quite deficient of late. But that is something I am about to remedy. So," he said, unfolding his napkin, "would you care to come along? I've already given orders for the carriage to be brought round."

She remembered herself then. "No, thank you. A Sunday

service in a third-rate parish with a third-rate curate does not appeal to me."

"A pity." He turned his attention to his plate. She watched him dig into his ham and eggs. He ate with relish, and she remembered how abstemious he used to be at the table.

"You seem to have regained your appetite."

He looked up and smiled, and she had to harden herself against that open smile—it almost made him look boyish.

"Yes, thank God. He has healed me so completely I am able to eat anything. It wasn't too many weeks ago everything used to disagree with me."

He returned to his food, and Gillian quickly finished her tea, no longer having an appetite for what remained on her plate. She excused herself and left him to his breakfast.

She watched him from her window when he departed toward the village. A part of her felt resentful at being left behind, which she knew, of course, was nonsense. She reminded herself he was still her jailer. His very invitation to church implied she could only come and go at his pleasure.

She would show him. Tomorrow she would take the carriage to the market town in the valley.

When they met at luncheon, he came into the dark-paneled dining room, rubbing his hands together. "Well, what has our dear cook prepared for us this day?"

"Our dear Mrs. Mudgeon has most likely prepared the usual fare of boiled mutton and potatoes. Her repertoire does not seem to extend to anything beyond that."

He laughed and spoke a few words to Harold, who served them.

"I suppose we really should see about increasing the staff if we are to continue here a few weeks more."

"We?"

He looked at her seriously. "I hope you will use your full prerogative as mistress of this hall to order what you see fit."

"That's rich, for someone who left me without a farthing," she commented, taking a bite of her boiled mutton.

"I'm sorry. I had no right. I shall rectify that immediately. Now, what about hiring a housekeeper?"

"You may do whatever you like. I have no interest in the day-to-day running of this estate."

"Very well." Again her words seemed to have no effect. He ate heartily for the next several minutes, and then sat back as the old servant cleared away the plates and brought the pudding.

"Have you been to the village church?" he asked her.

"The first Sunday," she replied.

"You haven't returned?"

"No." She took a careful bite of the pudding.

"Why not?"

"I found the dank church depressing, the curate a young, underfed-looking man with a shabby appearance, and the local congregation composed mostly of very poor laborers." She did not add that the main reason was the way everyone looked at her as if she came from some strange land.

"The curate *is* very young," he conceded. "The rector has two other livings, so he has put this young man in charge of this parish, the smallest of the three.

"He's a thoughtful young man," he added. "His bent is evangelical."

Gillian made a sign of disdain. "Low church. At least he's not a Methodist like your sister."

"No, he's not Methodist, but his thinking is very much like Althea's. I've invited him here to visit."

"You what?" She wrinkled her nose, determined to be disagreeable. "Doesn't he have a lot of young brats?"

He smiled faintly. "Yes, my father would be envious. He has four children. His wife seems a very nice lady, well educated and modest. She must be lonely in a little village like this. She is from Leeds."

"You certainly discovered a lot about them in one morning."

"I merely asked—and listened."

"Well, do as you please. I'll endeavor to be out that afternoon. By the by, I shall be going into town tomorrow, if I may have use of the coach."

"Of course. Shopping?"

"With no money?" she asked caustically.

"I'll give you money as soon as luncheon is over."

She looked away, reluctant all of a sudden to take money from him when she knew it would be used to help her escape from him. Why the sudden scruples, she wondered. Wasn't she going to pawn the jewels he'd given her?

She had a right to that money, she argued to herself. Hadn't he taken control of her whole fortune and left her virtually penniless? she countered, jabbing at her pudding.

"It looks to be a beautiful afternoon," he commented with a glance toward the window. "Would you care to come for a walk upon the moors this afternoon?"

"No, thank you," she answered, her mouth drawn tight into a prim little line.

They ate in silence again. When the last dishes were cleared away and right before Gillian stood from her chair, Tertius said, "I was thinking of doing a little entertaining."

She finished patting her mouth with her napkin and laid it down on the table. "You mean with the curate?"

"No, I was thinking more along the lines of a dinner party. We could invite the local families and maybe have a little dancing afterward."

"By all means. Let us invite all the gentry, along with the curate and his sniveling brats. It sounds delightful. A bunch of country squires and their disapproving wives who have no conversation."

"I thought you might enjoy some company after the long, solitary winter."

She rose. "I've grown to enjoy my own company. But by all means, plan your little party. It's your house, after all, and I am merely your chattel."

Tertius sighed after she'd closed the door behind her.

That afternoon, he went for his walk alone. As soon as he'd left the ancient hall and its oppressive atmosphere, he felt better.

It was the end of March, but the days were already balmy and the grass a deep-hued green. When he left the stone-fenced pastures behind him and began to climb a worn path toward the moors, his spirits lifted. The heather was still brown and lifeless on the moorland. Soon the path disappeared and he walked through the ankle-deep plants.

He wanted to rebuild his strength quickly. It sometimes seemed as if he'd wasted half his life and now he had much to make up for. He knew the Lord wanted him to exercise patience, but part of him wanted to soar now that he knew the truth.

The blue sky above him reflected the expansiveness of his soul. He hummed a few bars of a hymn Althea had begun to teach him. The heavens truly declared the glory of God—and he had been too blind before to see it.

How he wished Althea had stayed a while longer. He had gleaned so much from her knowledge of the Scriptures. He still read voraciously but felt he needed someone to teach him. Althea had promised to introduce him to those at the mission once he returned to London.

He stood on a rise, which led to some rocky peaks farther up. He didn't feel strong enough yet to attempt the climb. The stones were great broken, sharp-edged slabs, which reminded him of a giant pair of Ten Commandment tablets hurled down and smashed against the earth, to lie in a jagged mound. Between and around them grew the stubby brown heather.

From his vantage, Sky could see miles around him, acres of heather that would soon spring to life into thousands of blossoms. Far down below were the green squares where sheep grazed, tiny dots in the distance, with a solitary stone farmhouse far beyond.

The only sound was the twittering of birds and the constant sifting of the wind like flour being passed through a sieve.

Beyond what he could see, miles down in the valley, sat the mill town. He knew a part of his mission lay there, in the mill owned by his father…by his family.

He remembered the cry of the poor and downtrodden in his vision.

He took a deep breath. First he must regain his strength, he reminded himself. Reluctantly, he left the spot where he stood and began his trek homeward. He stooped down to examine the heather every once in a while, wondering how such dead-looking plants could spring to life in a matter of a few weeks. But there were already signs, a slight tint of green at the tips here and there, hinting at new growth, and the pale white showing at the edges of yet unopened buds.

He had come farther than he'd realized. He had a few moments of doubt, wondering which way to turn, when the land dipped down and he lost sight of the sheep fields. It seemed then he was in a vast ocean of rolling moors. He had lost sight of any worn paths as he waded through the moors.

His legs began to feel weak and he wondered if he had been foolish to walk so far. His legs felt as if they would buckle under him at any moment. It was with a sense of relief he came finally to a stone fence at the beginning of a dirt track. He lowered himself onto it.

He had only been there a few minutes, losing himself in prayer, when he heard a dog bark. It was Sophie, Gillian's dog. He felt a sudden surge of gladness.

Far in the distance the dog came bounding toward him. Farther back, he could see Gillian following. His joy at seeing her turned almost immediately to a grimace. Would that look of dislike on her face ever be erased from her pretty features?

He didn't even require a grand passion with her, just a simple regard and mutual respect. That's all he'd ever wanted from a wife. But that seemed an impossible dream now.

Oh, God, he prayed, *we've been joined in holy matrimony. Yet we're living like strangers and enemies. Can You heal this rift between us? Can You bring Gillian to a place where I'm not wholly distasteful to her?*

She spotted him when Sophie ran up to him, barking and seeking to be petted by him. Tertius obliged the dog, as he waited for the inevitable confrontation with her mistress.

Gillian finally reached him. "What are you doing all the way out here?" she asked sharply.

"Resting."

She frowned. "What's the matter?"

He smiled ruefully. "Perhaps I overdid it a little today on my walk," he admitted.

"Can you make it back?" she demanded, no hint of sympathy in her tone.

"I shall endeavor to…in a few minutes. I'm glad I saw you. It means I must be on the right way home."

"Yes, you're not too far from the first farm."

To his surprise she sat beside him on the fence.

"You don't have to wait here. You haven't finished your walk."

"It doesn't matter. I'm not going to leave you out here alone."

He said nothing, afraid to bring on an acerbic comment.

They sat quietly for several moments, watching Sophie run about and nose around the heather and bilberry plants. Finally he tried to stand, but found he still had to support himself on the stone.

She stood immediately beside him, concern in her pale green eyes. "How do you feel?"

"Pathetically weak," he said, trying to make light of it.

"Well, as I said, it isn't too far back, perhaps a mile,"

she said briskly. "Here, I'll help support you if you think you can walk a bit." As she spoke, she guided his arm around her shoulder and the two began to walk back slowly.

"I'm sorry about this," he ventured, imagining how disagreeable it must be to her to help him.

"Never mind about that."

They walked excruciatingly slowly through the rough heather plants. Tertius found himself concentrating on putting one leg in front of the other without falling flat on his face before her.

"You seem to know exactly where to go," he remarked in admiration.

"I ought to by now. It's been one of my few occupations these last few months."

One more thing to regret, he thought. How many times might she have been lost or stranded out here on these treacherous, lonely moors during the long winter months?

He noticed how good and right she felt nestled under his arm. So small compared to his frame, but so right, tucked in his embrace.

Suddenly they both stepped into a boggy patch, the cold water rising immediately around their ankles.

"Oh, bother!" she cried, as the two tried to find a dry spot. As they only succeeded in getting their feet wetter before stumbling to higher ground, she began to laugh. "I told you the moors would be wet and muddy this time of year," she scolded.

"So you did, which is why I wonder that you should be out here alone."

"I usually manage to avoid the wet spots," she said.

"If I were half the man I used to be, I'd carry you over this wet patch. Instead, here you are half carrying me," he muttered.

"Come, I think it's dryer here." She tugged at his waist with her arm and led him along another route.

When they finally made it back to the hall, she seemed to sense how light-headed he felt. Without a word, she led him to her sitting room, where the warmth of a fire permeated every corner. She assisted him onto the couch.

"I'll ring for some tea," she said with a sigh of relief as she helped him off with his greatcoat. Then she proceeded to help him off with his boots and stockings.

"Here," he said, trying to stop her, "you can call Nigel." He felt embarrassed suddenly at his bare feet.

"It's all done," she said, spreading a throw over him before carrying his boots and stockings to the hearth.

"You are wet as well. Why don't you go and change? I'll be all right now."

Rather than reply, she removed her own hat and pelisse and rang the bellpull. When Katie came to the door, Gillian instructed her to bring some tea. Katie looked in surprise and concern, over Gillian's shoulder, toward him. "Oh, yes, and please bring some dry socks and slippers for us both and some papers to stuff into our wet boots. That will be all, thank you."

When she closed the door behind her, she went to a chair by the fire. As if she had forgotten his presence entirely, she bent to remove her own half boots and stockings.

He could feel the heat rising in his face at the sight of her slim arched foot and the curve of her calf. She worked quickly and efficiently, first one foot then the other, but not quickly enough to prevent Tertius from being overwhelmed by a swift, fierce desire for his wife.

It was over in a few seconds. Two pairs of boots stood neatly by the fire, two pairs of stockings draped over the fender. What a sign of domesticity, and it came to him with a sudden, jolting clarity that a platonic sort of respect and affection from his wife wouldn't satisfy him. He wanted a passion to match the one he was feeling.

She turned to him and he quickly closed his eyes, feigning sleep. Sleep was the last thing his pounding heart was capable of at the moment. He heard her rise and pour something into a glass.

She approached him and crouched by him, gently placing her hand under his head and raising it. "Here, drink this," she directed softly.

He drank a sip of the liquid, his light-headedness disappearing.

"Thank you," he said, lying back against the cushion she had placed for him.

"Would you like me to read to you?" she asked when she had set the glass down.

"If you wouldn't mind."

She retrieved her book and brought a chair up close to him. As she began to read, almost without conscious thought, he took her free hand in his and held it loosely.

She didn't draw her hand away, but continued reading as if nothing had occurred. He felt the wedding band between his fingers and began to play with it idly. His eyes focused on it and he was grateful she was still wearing it. But what of the other? he wondered, thinking of the ruby and diamond ring he had given her. His gaze strayed to her bare foot peeking out from the hem of her gown and he forgot about the ring.

At length he drifted off to the sound of her soothing voice, at peace, his fingers still loosely entwined with hers, knowing the warmhearted girl he had fallen in love with hadn't disappeared. The girl who'd risked her life for a flea-ridden stray was still there beneath the hurt and bitter exterior.

When had he fallen in love with her? Was it when he'd seen her petting the dog, oblivious to its dirt and fleas? Or when she'd confessed shyly to wanting a home and children of her own? Or when the Lord had filled him with His love—such a love that overwhelmed and overflowed until it couldn't be contained but had to touch others?

I'll make it up to you, Jilly girl, he promised in an inaudible whisper before drifting off to sleep completely.

Chapter Thirteen

❧

Tertius surveyed Gillian across the great hall of the house. She was laughing at something an older gentleman was saying to her. Suddenly she caught his eye and her own twinkled back to him, as if telling him, *See, here's our tedious squire.*

He bowed his head to her and turned back to the group of gentlemen he was standing with.

"You're lucky you weren't here during the Luddite uprising," old Mr. Haversham said in a throaty growl. "We were afraid to go to bed at night, for fear they'd torch us. We had the militia patrolling every night."

"Those Luddites were a fiery rabble. Demanding we shut down the factories and return the hand loom to them!" Another well-fed squire snorted into his drink. "Against all progress. They were lunatics. Hanged a bunch of them and transported the rest. Good riddance, I say."

"You should be grateful you were out in the Indies. Though you had to face slave uprisings, no doubt."

"Yes, that was an ever-present danger. When you take away a man's freedom, he is bound to rebel," he added quietly, his mind going to his wife.

As the men looked at him askance before resuming the topic of the Luddites, Tertius thought about Gillian. He knew he must allow her back her freedom, but he didn't feel able to let her go quite yet. If only he could have a little more time to win her forgiveness.

"Excuse me, gentlemen," he told the company, "but I believe I promised this dance to my wife."

"A most gracious lady, the new Lady Skylar," the men all remarked. "We congratulate you."

"I thank you," he told them with a bow before making his way across the room.

"May I have the honor of this dance?" he asked, taking her hand in his.

"Very well, my lord," she answered. "I must leave you, Sir George," she said to the portly gentleman at her side.

"I wouldn't dream of keeping you from your charming husband, my dear lady."

Tertius escorted her to the set. "I'm sorry to interrupt your tête à tête with the amiable Sir George."

"If you hadn't rescued me from his tiresome conversation, I should have accosted the first gentleman to pass by and demanded a dance."

"I'm glad I saved you from that fate," he answered lightly, leading her in the steps as the music started up. It was a lively country dance so they had little chance to talk.

He enjoyed watching her and feeling her hands in his each

time they came together. Although she had not been involved in any of the preparations for the house party, she was behaving as the model hostess. He realized for the first time what an ideal wife she was for a man of society. She had spoken to each of her guests for at least a few minutes and had let none of them commandeer her company for very long. She put the matrons and their plain daughters at ease, so although she was clearly the most fashionable among them, they warmed to her.

When the dance ended, he bowed again and said, "Perhaps another?"

She gave a fluttery laugh. "What, two dances in a row? Of course not, or we run the risk of being like those unfashionable husbands and wives who monopolize each other's company at a social function."

As she walked away from him, already in conversation with someone else, he felt a pang. He shouldn't feel the hurt at her careless remark, clearly addressed more for the benefit of those around them than for him.

As he watched her get in line for the next set, he told himself that her behavior only reaffirmed something he'd known all along—he was too old for her. He'd spoiled her youth. He'd left her alone for so many months. He still had no clue about her disgrace and no longer thought it important. Perhaps because God had shown him the extent of his own sin, hers paled by comparison.

The best thing he could do for her would be to take her back to London as soon as possible where she could be among her own kind.

But he hated the thought of giving up the tenuous closeness they had achieved in this wild and lonely house on the edge of the moors. In London he'd likely rarely see her, if this gathering revealed anything of her social nature. How would he ever restore his marriage in London? he cried silently to the Lord. But he couldn't shake the feeling that he was being selfish in keeping her isolated here. He must give her back the freedom he'd taken away from her.

Gillian continued dancing every set after that, with whichever gentleman asked her, from old wheezing squire to pimply, stammering youth. As long as it wasn't with Tertius, and as long as it kept her from him.

The dance had been too unsettling. Each time he'd taken her hands or held her close, she'd felt shaken. It confused her. It had all begun the afternoon he'd taken her hand in his.

She wouldn't let him weaken her resolve at this late date. She was going to leave him. She swore it. It would be fitting retribution for all he'd put her through.

Although she kept far away from him, she couldn't help observing him. He was a charming host. She noticed he didn't dance anymore. She also noticed that although spirits were served, he partook of very little. It seemed more as if he enjoyed watching the others enjoy themselves.

Humph! He probably thought he was above all forms of earthly pleasures now. There would undoubtedly be no more card games as well. He'd become like that sister of his in her plain dresses and quiet manners. Althea would be halfway pretty if she took a little trouble over her appearance, but then she probably enjoyed the fate of a spinster doing her good deeds.

Gillian turned to the young gentleman approaching her

and graciously accepted his compliment. She'd had enough of these evangelicals for one evening.

Late that evening, when she and Tertius waved to the last departing guest, they reentered the great hall.

The new footman Tertius had hired locked and bolted the large double doors behind them.

"Will there be aught else, my lord?"

"No, thank you. Go on to bed."

"Very well. Good night, m'lord, m'lady," he said, bowing to each in turn.

"Good night." Tertius turned to her with a smile—too warm a smile. "Although he doesn't yet have a proper livery, I think he adds quite some elegance to the establishment, don't you?"

"Oh, yes, with his broad Yorkshire accent," she replied disdainfully. "I vow, I can hardly understand half your tenants when they speak."

"You've met them?"

She floundered around for a reply, flustered for some reason. "Isn't that what the lady of the manor is expected to do, visit the tenants?" she countered.

"Yes. It surprises me a little, is all," he said.

"That I should have seen to my duties? Don't be unduly alarmed. I didn't go out of my way. I've only met a few on my walks." She didn't want him thinking anything good of her at this late date.

"How did you find their living conditions?"

"Deplorable—what little I saw," she answered in an offhand way, already turning away and heading toward the staircase.

"Come, sit with me a few moments in the sitting room before you retire," Tertius bade her, as she reached the first steps. "I don't know about you, but I'm too keyed up at the moment to sleep."

She struggled for a moment, a part of her wanting to accept. "Very well." She didn't want to be alone with him, and yet suddenly neither did she want to go up to her bed.

She preceded him into the room but didn't sit down immediately, too aware of being with him in a house where everyone else had retired.

"Your party was a success," she told him, standing behind the couch, her hand resting on its back.

"Thanks to you. You were a wonderful hostess," he said, handing her a glass.

He touched his glass to hers and they each took a sip.

"Did I tell you how beautiful you look?"

"Only about three or four times," she replied, refusing to let him see that the words meant anything to her.

"Then let this be the fifth." He raised his glass to her. "You are a beautiful woman, Gillian."

"La, sir, but you are most unoriginal in your compliments," she said, turning away from his warm look, conscious of her evening gown. It was the first time she was wearing anything remotely fashionable since London.

She walked to the far end of the couch and sat down.

He came and sat beside her, leaving enough space between them to turn and face her.

"Tonight I saw the Gillian who has probably been gracing the London ballrooms for the past few seasons, charming all and sundry of the ton."

"Is that a criticism?"

"Not at all. It's a compliment."

"You can save your Spanish coin," she said stiffly, determined to hang on to her resentment. He wasn't going to make her relent of her plans with all this softness and tenderness. She wasn't going to forget what he'd done to her.

He watched her for a few moments in silence. "Tell me, Gillian," he asked finally, "what will it take to put a smile—a real smile, not those false smiles you wore for our honorable squires this evening—on your face?"

She felt an irrational anger swell inside her. "You dare ask me that, when you've taken away my freedom and held me a virtual prisoner in this tumbledown hall of yours for the past seven months, two weeks, and five days!"

Suddenly she felt the full extent of her frustration. Its force overwhelmed her. Every dark thought she'd thought about him over the months since her banishment rose to the fore.

She stood and turned on him. "I'll tell you what you can do! Let me go! I never wanted to be married to you. Mama forced me to. And you proved yourself an absolute brute."

She moved away from him. "I never want to talk about that—that awful night, but I want to make it absolutely clear, I shall never forget what you did to me! I shall *never* forgive you for that."

She held out a hand to stop him from whatever he would have replied. "As if that wasn't horrible enough, you sent me so far away…away from any friendly face, with no money, with not even my personal maid—" Her voice broke then as she remembered, but she backed away from him when he stood. "Don't come near me. I can't bear it when you touch me."

He drew back immediately, and she felt a curious satisfaction that she had managed to hurt that manly pride of his.

Her voice grew quiet. "When they brought you here, I thought you were going to die. It was the only thing that gave me hope—to be your widow. But that's not going to happen now, is it? Your great, merciful God has played a fine trick on me. I hate you. Do you understand? You've ruined my life—any chance at happiness."

"I'm sorry, Gillian," he began, but she didn't let him finish.

"All I want is my freedom. I'll go away somewhere," she entreated, "to the Continent, where you needn't ever see me again."

She saw his face work, his jaw tighten, and again she felt gratified that she had succeeded in robbing him of his newfound joy. He looked a bit like the old Tertius even, the enraged one of her wedding night. But he didn't come near her or touch her, although she noticed his clenched fists.

"Good night, Tertius," she said coldly, then turned and left him.

When the door had shut behind her and the final timbre of its closing had died, Tertius brought his fists up to his face.

Oh, God, I've tried everything I know. How can I get through to her? She wants nothing to do with me. Is it Your will to let her go as she asks, to give her a divorce? The ugly word brought a shudder through him. *Is that all that's left to us?* he cried in despair, pacing the confines of the room. *Just when You've given me love for her, all she feels for me is hate. Divorce will only bring her more disgrace than me. How can I do that to her? Yet, she will be satisfied with nothing less than total separation from me.*

Finally he knelt at the couch, at the place where she'd been sitting, seeking the Lord's guidance for his life and for his marriage.

He didn't see Gillian the next morning at breakfast and assumed she was sleeping late after the party. He went to work in his office, reviewing what little he could find on the running of the hall over the past ten years. It wasn't until dinner that he saw her.

"Hello, Gillian," he said with a nod. She stood by her chair, presumably waiting for him.

They were seated and the food was served. He bowed his head to pray—following the example his sister had shown him. When he raised his head to begin his meal, he noticed Gillian had started without him.

They ate in silence. He noticed she ate little. He, too, had little appetite. How long must they endure this uneasy stalemate?

When the final dish had at last been cleared away, he sat back in his chair and asked for God's grace to say what he had resolved in the course of the night.

"Gillian," he said, before she could rise.

She looked at him without speaking.

"I've been thinking of what you said to me last night." As soon as he mentioned the subject, she looked down at her lap.

"I can't rectify the past. I shan't refer to what is painful to you. All I can hope to do is change the future.

"I have always intended to return you to London. I was wrong to send you away—and in such a brutal manner.

"Although you've never told me what…happened to

you…prior to our wedding night, I won't ask you about it. I would like to hear about it, if you ever care to tell me. I give you my word I won't condemn you."

He cleared his throat, having received no reaction from her. She seemed determined to keep her head lowered, her hands in her lap.

"As I said, I promise to return you to London as soon as possible." At these words, she raised her eyes and he could read hope in them. At his next words, the hope died. "There we can discuss your 'freedom.'" Clearly, she didn't like the implications that he wouldn't give her her freedom right away.

Now he, too, bowed his head and studied the lacework on the tablecloth in front of him. "We were thrown together, you and I, by our parents and the customs of our family. Perhaps we were unsuitable. You were more to be pitied than I, I suppose. I could have stopped the marriage with a word to my father. I was long past the age of majority.

"I'm sorry you were forced into a marriage against your will. You probably had little choice, being subject to your mother, the duchess." He gave a grim smile. "I am not well acquainted with her, but I think it unlikely you could have opposed her wishes. I had hopes during our short courtship that you didn't find me thoroughly distasteful and that we could manage a marriage of mutual regard and benefit."

He gave a short, hollow laugh. "Unfortunately, I no longer find that kind of arrangement to be enough for me."

He smoothed the table linen with the flat of his hand, coming to the heart of the matter. "That said, we are married now and cannot undo that contract. I will do my utmost to give you what you want.

"However, I ask something of you in return." At those words, she looked up and he almost smiled at the alarm in her eyes.

"I need a short while longer to fully regain my strength, no more than a month, I should think. Perhaps a little less, perhaps a little more. All I ask from you is your forbearance for this short period of time. And that you help me."

"How?" Finally she spoke, although in a low tone, full of suspicion.

"Pretend we are getting acquainted for the first time— the way we played that evening. Let me show you the kind of husband I can be. I'm not the same man I was, Gillian."

Was he getting through to her at all? Fighting despair that his words were merely hitting an impenetrable wall, he continued doggedly on, knowing only that he must be obedient to what the Lord demanded of him.

"All I ask of you is to be patient for a short while longer. And that you behave like a wife." He rushed on before she could misinterpret, "Not in the bedroom, but in our daily life. Can you smile and be my helpmate for a few weeks? Can you do that for me, Gillian? You've given me more than half a year of your young life already. Can you give me a few more weeks? Then, I promise you, I'll take you back to London and discuss your future."

"You give me little choice," she said at last, when he'd given up hope that she would even answer him. She stood and stepped back from her chair. "Very well, my lord, I shall remain with you until you regain your strength. I shall endeavor not to act disagreeably," she ended in a whisper.

He stood. "Thank you, Gillian. I ask nothing more."

When she left, he sat back down, feeling as if he hadn't gained anything but a short amount of time—too short.

There followed days of walking the moors, of visiting the tenants, of going to the village church on Sunday and returning calls.

At times Tertius could almost fool himself they truly were a married couple, Gillian acted so pleasantly with him, especially when they were around other people. He began to be acquainted with her, the impetuosity and enthusiasm of her youth and of her own particular character, her likes and dislikes—how she firmed up her mouth but said nothing when something displeased her, or how her eyes lit up when something pleased her.

The more he got to know her, the more he longed for her regard.

But he couldn't fool himself that theirs was more than a temporary arrangement, when evening deepened and she bid him good-night and went her separate way.

No, they were still merely fellow inhabitants of the same manor, and he was still very much on probation.

Sometimes he railed at the arrangement. Why must he continue to prove himself to a mere chit of a girl, who had probably up to now been used to having her every heart's desire? But then he read the Scriptures and understood that he must bow in obedience to the Lord—and submit and trust in the Lord to change Gillian's heart.

Their short walks between the green fields bisected by stone walls and dotted with sheep grew to longer walks. Gillian led him along the paths she had discovered across the moors where only a lonely sheepherder's hut broke the desolation of the fields of sweeping grass.

Although the days grew longer and warmer, the wind was a constant presence, blowing the meadow grass in waves. With each passing day, he felt himself grow stronger. He always carried the small Bible Althea had left him and he'd lie on the grass and read while Gillian sat dozing or looking for the first wild flowers. Sometimes they sat by a brook and she threw twigs into the swirling water. So often, he wished he could read passages to her—passages that stood out to him and gripped him with wonder. How had he never understood what the Lord was speaking to him before?

But the words died on his lips, knowing she would only rebuff him if he suggested reading a verse to her.

He told her of his childhood and listened to stories of hers. He understood the special relationship she'd had with her father, as he figured most prominently in her narratives, and he came to see how much she still missed him.

"It's not far to go to the most distant stone hut," Gillian told him one day as they sat on some large boulders overlooking the brook. A narrow waterfall tumbled down into the brook from a gray cliff above them. They sat on a rock formation creating a bridge over the brook.

He glanced at her, wondering if she was as eager as he to see him fully fit. Was her helpfulness due to her desire to return to London? Hadn't she enjoyed these days as much as he?

"When I first discovered this place," she told him, "I considered throwing myself down into that ravine and crushing my skull against the rocks." She pointed to the boulders at the base of the waterfall. "I saw how easily it could be managed."

He watched her profile as she spoke the words matter-of-factly.

"I imagined how sorry you might be then for all you'd done to me."

"What finally stopped you?" he asked, amused at her childish desire for revenge while simultaneously terrified at how easily she could have caused herself irrevocable harm.

She shrugged. "I decided I wouldn't give you the satisfaction of taking my life while you got off scot-free. There must be a sweeter revenge."

He chuckled. "I'm glad you came to that realization. Did you come up with a method?"

"No—yes. I mean, your sickness seemed revenge enough," she added hastily, and he wondered at her confusion.

"And then I went and recovered. What a shame. You could have found yourself a wealthy dowager countess with a chance at happiness with another man." He threw a pebble into the rushing brook. "But the good Lord has shown me I'm not to die yet. I have a lot of work before me. It won't be easy, He's made it plain."

"What kind of work?" she asked curiously.

He nodded toward the way they had come. "Down in the valley, for starters. The mill," he explained to the question in her eyes. "There are too many people starving and mistreated while my father and I grow richer with each passing year, oblivious to their lot."

"Oh, dear me, don't tell me you are going to become as fanatical as your sister. Will you renounce your title and go live in poverty in the East End as she has done? Do you expect me to go about wearing only gray or brown and hand out tracts on street corners?"

He smiled at the picture she drew but didn't bother to argue against the preconceived image she had of evangelicals. They were detested by the aristocrats and gentry and looked at suspiciously by many of the common people. He, too, had had the same mental images.

"I know the Lord has spared my poor life for His purposes, not my own paltry ambitions. What had I done but squander what He'd given me?"

"I thought you had done quite well running a plantation out in the Indies."

"At what price? That of forced labor, men and women who have no freedom to choose their lives, because they were born with the misfortune of a darker shade of skin?"

She was staring at him as if he were a creature she had never seen before.

"You can't mean to go against all your family owns?" she whispered. "Like Wilberforce and the Clapham Sect and all those who are fighting slavery in Parliament?" He couldn't tell if it was horror or fascination in her eyes.

He looked back down the narrow ravine they had climbed and spoke above the sound of rushing water. "I know what the Lord requires. I know it will be difficult. He has made it plain I will come up against nothing but opposition. That's why I must be strong in both body and spirit. He's given me His spirit and this time here to rebuild my body."

"So you propose to give away all your wealth and leave us in the poorhouse?"

He smiled. "You needn't fear. The Lord doesn't begrudge His children any good thing. But He wants us to be good stewards of all He has given us. There's only one thing we can take with us to Heaven—our deeds toward our fellow man.

"I'm sorry in some ways that the Lord didn't take me with Him that night I almost died. He gave me a glimpse of Heaven and its glories. But He has also shown me great mercy by giving me a second chance on this earth—to do better this time around with the talents He's given me.

"I won't leave you in the poorhouse, Gillian. I'll see you always have whatever you desire that money can buy. I deeply regret I left you with nothing when I sent you up here. You'll never be in that position again. In fact, as soon as we return to London, I'll see that you have control of your own fortune, which is not inconsiderable."

He took a deep breath, knowing the next words were going to cost him. "You may even set up your own household independent of me, if you wish. I hadn't meant to discuss these things with you until we arrived in London, but..." He shrugged.

"I would prefer we make a marriage together," he added.

"And if we can't?" Her tone was unyielding, as if the past few weeks had meant nothing to her and she had only been waiting for this day.

He reached out his hand but stopped himself before laying it on her arm. "If we can't, then I would do the best I can for you.

"I wish I could give you your freedom, but short of dying, I don't believe divorce is in your best interest. If you remain my wife in name only with your own household, as I said, every door in society will be open to you. Divorce would only lead to ostracism for you. You know society treats the woman more harshly than the man."

She was silent, looking down at the rushing waters of the brook. He watched her profile, her chin in her hand, wishing for the hundredth time he knew what would reach her.

She finally turned to him. "And if I would desire children someday?"

The question caught him off guard and made him realize he had never pictured Gillian bearing any children but his own. "I assume you don't mean mine?"

"You assume correctly." Again that hard little voice.

He looked down at his knuckles. "I realize you are young and beautiful and if you choose to live a life apart from me, it is likely you'll soon meet someone whom you do desire as the father of your children."

"And what then?" Her tone was taunting.

His knuckles tightened, showing white. "I cannot answer that now." All the patience he thought he'd gained disappeared in those few moments, and he realized how little he was truly resigned to losing her.

She stood as if all the rest he'd promised her were nothing but chaff to be dusted off her skirt before resuming her walk.

He got up more slowly beside her, feeling as if time were running out and he'd gotten nowhere.

As if by mutual consent, they turned homeward then. When they left the moors and entered the emerald green fields, the day mocked Tertius. The air was filled with the trill of birdsong; clumps of daffodils appeared at the edges of farmhouse yards; everywhere were the signs of recommencing life.

They came upon a stone-enclosed field, and Gillian suddenly turned to it with an exclamation of delight. Tertius followed more slowly, wondering what the attraction was.

Suddenly he saw, and his heart twisted in bitter agony. The enclosed field contained a few dozen ewes with their lambs. Most were seated in groups of three: the mother with her two babes by her side.

Gillian leaned against the gray, lichen-covered stone fence, her face filled with awe at the sight; and he realized with a deep, gut-wrenching understanding that she was born to be a mother. It was only a matter of time before she would no longer be satisfied rescuing pets, but would crave her own offspring.

Would he have to relinquish all honor and self-respect of a man, a husband, and see her bearing another man's children while still married to him?

It happened all the time in their class. Tertius knew that. How many bastards were raised by their "stepfathers" and were afterward given titles of their own and perfectly accepted into society, when everyone knew their illegitimate origins?

Hadn't it happened in his own family? Hadn't his father brought his half sister to live with them under the guise of "ward"?

And now his young wife expected him to acquiesce to the same arrangement.

"Oh, aren't they adorable?" Gillian gushed, reaching out a hand toward a little lamb nearest the stone. "Come here, little fellow, and let me pet you." She turned to Sky with a wide smile. It was the first smile of pure enjoyment she had given him since they'd been married.

"Yes, they are adorable," he agreed quietly. The lambs were white with black legs, their fur, still pure and unsullied, whiter than their mother's.

Tertius had a mental picture of his Lord, a lamb led to the slaughter for Tertius's sins.

He had been washed of his sins and set free of his past. What right had he to expect anything more? He turned his eyes heavenward and praised God, and his spirit felt lighter.

"My grace is sufficient for thee…" he repeated the promise to himself as Gillian rose, and they turned to continue their walk homeward.

Chapter Fourteen

Gillian paced her room. She felt an anger and frustration building up within her. When was Lord Skylar going to take her back to London?

She didn't like what she was made to feel here. The more time she spent in Lord Skylar's company—she refused to call him by his given name—the more torn she felt.

Torn was the last thing she wanted to feel. She wanted to pay him back for what he'd done to her and then be free of him, rid of him for good. She wanted to run into Gerrit's embrace and rejoin the man she had given herself to once before.

Why did this have to happen? Why did Lord Skylar have to recuperate and then be so kind, so considerate, so thoughtful? Every time she deliberately baited him or spurned his subtle attentions, or exercised any of the myriad petty cruelties each day, just to get him to say an unkind word or lose his temper, he only ignored her bad behavior and smiled at her sympathetically as if he understood exactly what she was doing.

She fisted her hands, wanting to smash something. How much she wanted to prove he was the same man who had treated her so vilely her wedding night.

She would have no compunctions leaving such a man for another.

But this man, this new Tertius—the name slipped out unbidden, and she almost bit her tongue in futile fury—had remained the same, day in and day out, since his recuperation. What was she to do? She had only received one letter from Gerrit. She turned to her wardrobe and dug it out where she kept it hidden in its innermost recesses. She unfolded it and reread the contents, which she now knew by heart.

My heart has been true to you all these years…I await the day we will be together again.

Oh, yes, Gerrit, they would be together again. Soon, she promised fervently, hugging the paper to her breast. Nothing would stop them.

A few days later she had a second letter from him. She started when she saw the letter addressed in her friend's handwriting sitting on the salver.

"What is it?" Sky asked her.

"Nothing. Just a letter from my friend, Charlotte. You remember her?"

"Yes. Aren't you going to open the letter?"

"Not just yet," she replied in what she hoped was a casual tone. "I like the anticipation. I shall savor it later in my room. She usually fills me in on all the latest on-dits from London."

He said nothing more but returned to the agricultural digest he had been reading.

Finally, after what seemed hours later but had in fact been only about three-quarters of one, she was able to excuse herself and go to her room.

She undid the wafer and opened the letter. Laying aside her friend's for the moment, she unfolded what she had longed for for so many days.

My dearest love,
These few lines in much haste. We are being shipped over the Channel to Belgium. News of Boney's return to France has all of England in a panic. I don't know if I shall return in one piece. But if and when I do, I shall come to you.
A kiss to seal our pact.
Yours,
Gerrit

She let the letter drop. War again. Her one and only love once again at risk. What if he shouldn't return? It had been a miracle he'd been spared during the Peninsular War. It was a miracle she had seen him again and known he still loved her.

How could fate be so cruel as to separate them again after so many years?

That evening as she sat with Tertius at dinner she ventured, "Charlotte writes that Napoleon has left Elba and landed in France. Do you think we shall again be at war?"

"I daresay. But I can't think Napoleon would be able to

muster the kind of troops he had before. I've heard Wellington is leaving for Belgium and marshalling quite a force. Doubtless he counts on Blücher coming from Austria. What remains to be seen is how many French will still be loyal to Napoleon."

She itched to ask him about their return to London. But he hadn't said anything yet, and pride forbade her to stoop to requesting the information from him. She had promised him she would be patient until he was ready to return.

She eyed him surreptitiously over their meal. He certainly seemed fitter than she'd ever known him. His face had filled out and taken on a healthy color. He looked much better than he had even on his return from the Indies when she'd first met him. In other circumstances she would venture to say he was even handsome. His dark hair and eyes and dusky skin tone would cause many a woman to linger, picturing him as the corsair in Byron's poem.

The women in London would undoubtedly go wild about him, the way his face always broke out in a smile these days. He had become a man of laughter and joy. He was forever praising God for the smallest thing, from the sight of the first violets amidst the grass to the rain falling against the windowpane. And that little Bible—he carried it everywhere and was always flipping it open whenever they sat to rest.

Thankfully, he hadn't taken to quoting it to her yet. She shuddered inwardly, wondering what the London ton would make of the new Lord Skylar.

She hoped the war would be brief enough, and her captain would return unharmed and she would not have to be in London long enough to be known as the wife of the evangelical Lord Skylar.

A villa in Italy, she mused, picturing an old palace covered in sweet-smelling vines, orange groves perfuming the surrounding air, a community of artists and writers nearby.

More than one couple had fled a loveless marriage and run to Italy to make a life for themselves.

She would write to Gerrit immediately and give him Godspeed. If she hurried, she could go down to the village and post the letter. Perhaps Gerrit would even receive it before he left England.

Whatever confusion she was now feeling would end as soon as she returned to London.

Tertius went looking for Gillian to invite her to ride with him to a nearby farm, where he knew some lambs had been born. He didn't find her in the sitting room. Her maid was not to be found either. Perhaps the two had gone to the village together.

Finally he stopped outside her bedroom door and knocked, on the chance she might have lain down for a nap. There was no answer.

As he turned to leave, he paused. Slowly, not really thinking what he was about, he turned the knob and pushed open the door.

He swallowed the sense of disappointment he felt when he saw the room was empty. What had he hoped? To find her sleeping and giving him the chance to gaze upon her for a few moments unseen?

He'd never entered her room, he thought with an odd pang. Here he was, her husband, and he'd never had a glimpse of her private world.

How he longed for intimacy with his wife, to wake up seeing her sleeping face, her hair rumpled by sleep, to watch her at her dressing table…

He stepped inside and shut the door behind him. The room was neatly made up, just another room furnished in the heavy Jacobean style of the rest of the manor. No personal effects except for the few toiletries on the dressing table his gaze took in as it roamed around the empty, silent space. His eyes rested on the few books stacked by a night table. The room was dim and somber, the only light coming from the pair of narrow stone embrasures along one wall.

It was no wonder Gillian had contemplated killing herself when she'd first arrived. He was the one who should have been condemned for what he'd subjected her to.

He sighed, prepared to leave the room. He had no right to enter her private quarters. It was the only thing he'd left her. It was as he prepared to retreat that he noticed the folded paper on the floor at his feet.

She must have dropped the letter she'd received from London. He smiled, remembering her anticipation in reading of the news from town.

He stooped to pick it up and replace it on her bedside table.

The paper fell open in his hands, and his eyes fixed on the one word written in a bold black style he wouldn't ascribe to a young woman fresh out of a lady's academy. *Love.*

My dearest love, his eyes took in the surrounding words.

Even as his mind was formulating some explanation—her friend's girlish expression of affection, a letter from an old beau—his eyes were scanning the rest of the letter. The pounding between his temples hardly let him think as he absorbed the contents of the mercifully short letter.

The first emotion that assailed him was rage—the same blind, all-encompassing rage that had engulfed him on their wedding night. He could hardly see past it. The rage he'd thought forever gone from him rose up with violent intensity, mocking his conversion and new self. He wanted to smash everything in the room from the heavy, high-backed chairs to the porcelain figurine gracing the dressing table.

He'd had many women in his past life, but to only one had he given his name, his promise of fidelity....

Even as he remembered his own broken vows, the rage left him and only the hurt remained.

He looked at the letter again and reread it. It sounded as if...no, it was crystal clear that they'd been corresponding more than once.

How long? The question beat mercilessly at him. All his peace and joy evaporated in the knowledge of the fool she'd been playing him for. All the time she'd agreed to docilely let him have his way, fooling himself that he could prove himself a good and attentive husband, she had known she was never going to remain with him!

Oh, God, how could she?

He staggered forward, the note falling from his lifeless hands, until he collapsed onto a bench set by one of the embrasures, his head falling into his hands.

How long? When? How? Why? The questions tortured him. How could he not have known? How could he not have seen the signs?

His thoughts went at last to the afternoon Captain Hawkes had invited him to the fencing match. The man's knowing look as he'd issued the challenge, his amusement and his determination to beat Tertius, as if he'd had something deeper to prove to him than mere swordsmanship ability.

Sky remembered the way his blood had boiled at the man's familiarity when speaking of Gillian.

The captain had been her lover even then. Had Gillian known Captain Hawkes—Gerrit, as he signed his name—since her betrothal to Sky? Hadn't the captain just arrived from the Continent?

Sky strove to remember the details of his first encounter with the captain. Slowly, it came into place…it had been at the Regent's fete. Hadn't Gillian been subdued all of a sudden? He'd found it strange for someone so vivacious and at ease in the social events of London to suddenly admit to being tired. She'd even asked to go home early.

What a poor, solicitous fool he'd been.

A new, sicker suspicion rose in his mind and he almost suffocated with the horror of it. Had the captain been the one to whom Gillian had offered her maidenhood?

Tertius moaned aloud then, his head thrown back against the stone wall.

What a fool…what a fool… The phrase beat against his brain.

What a poor, misguided fool he'd been. Willing to do his duty and obey his father's dictates upon his return from the Indies—bow to the wishes of the man he'd always despised, a man he'd sworn would never again run his life…and yet, what had Tertius done in the Indies but strive to succeed— all so he could return in triumph? And then, what had he done immediately upon his return home but meekly comply with his sire's choice of wife for him?

Tertius had justified his acquiescence with a list of reasons: the girl was comely, it was true he must wed and produce an heir…but oh, how gullibly he'd fallen into his father's plans.

Was he still nothing more than that little boy trying to please a man who only saw his inability to measure up?

A sudden image flashed into his mind—an image he'd thought forgotten.

A maid's giggles in the grape arbor. Sky, a youngster, following the sounds with the curiosity of a seven- or eight-year-old, only to find the girl in his father's embrace. Even at his young age, Sky knew something was wrong with the tableau. His father shouldn't be holding her so, his hands upon her bottom.

The more Sky stood rooted to the spot, the more revolted he grew. The maid's drawstring chemise was loosened and pulled down. His father's hands touched her as their mutual laughter and murmured words reached Sky in the shrubbery.

The buzzing growing inside his head reached a roar, until young Sky had charged out like a mad bull, head down and forward, ready to do battle. He'd rammed into both of them, shouting at them to stop it, for Mama wouldn't like it.

And the result of his boyish defense of his mother's honor?

His father picking him up until his legs dangled in the air.

"What have we here?" he asked with a chuckle. "A little cavalier?"

"Oh, look at how mad he is," the young maid had added. "He'll have a fit, he's so red in the face."

His fists had flailed out, wanting to hurt them both, but his father had only held him at arm's length. "Whoa, there, you young rapscallion. None of that." The look in his eyes was amused. "Now, you run along and don't say a word, or I'll see you have a good whipping."

He let him down then and gave him a good slap on the behind as he shooed his son away. As Tertius ran away, he heard the maid ask, "Do you think he'll say anything?" and again his father laughed.

"No fear. Who would believe the young fellow anyway?"

Would Tertius be fated to live with a spouse constantly untrue to him, just as his dear mother had been forced to put up with his father?

How much he'd loved his poor mother. He hadn't understood until that day why she was such a sad, silent woman. But as he'd grown into a young man, the more clearly he saw how she suffered his father's repeated infidelities in silence, and how his mother's life consisted in living a life retired from London society, poured out into the life of her two sons.

His father had continued on his merry way, living more in town than at home. Edmund and he had been close, but Tertius had done everything he knew as a youth to rebel against the older man, until his father had finally banished him to the Indies, only to call him back the day he'd lost Edmund.

As the full circle of his life closed around him, the tears began to flow. He knelt by the cushioned bench, his head in his hands. Only One could help him through this now.

God, You saved me and gave me a new life. I've tried to show Gillian that I'm not the same man. It isn't enough. I don't think she cares one whit who I am now. Is it Your desire that I keep striving for her?

In the quiet that followed his prayer, he sensed the Lord's words from the night he'd been delivered, *You are to love her as I love you. Haven't I forgiven you?*

The words stunned him, bringing a sudden quiet to his tormented soul.

What if she doesn't want my forgiveness? She has clearly spurned my love. The only thing she wants is to leave me.

He heard nothing more, but the command resonated in his spirit. *You are to love her as I love you.*

It was too much to ask a human being. To love someone who rejected one's love.

I give up, Lord. I can't love her as You command. You must give me that love. I am willing to do whatever You command. You know that. I am willing to die for You, Lord. I want nothing but You, Lord. I would die without Your love. You said that if we love You, we were to obey Your commands. I am willing. But help me, Lord. Give me the grace to love the woman who has betrayed me and scorned my love.

As he prayed, the tears fell anew, but they were no longer tears of despair. The joy he had thought lost, returned, and he was filled with wonder at the joy in the midst of his heartbreak.

He realized he must die to his desires.

Overcome with an overwhelming need to worship God, he began to sing a hymn Althea had taught him.

Sun of my soul, Thou Savior dear/ It is not night if Thou be near/ O may no earthborn cloud arise/ To hide Thee from Thy servant's eyes….

One hymn led to another.

We lift our hearts to Thee, O Daystar from on high…

Some he could only sing snatches of, but the more he sang, the lighter his spirit felt and the higher it arose.

To God—the Father, Son, and Spirit—One in Three, Be glory; as it was, is now, and shall forever be. Amen.

By the time Gillian returned from her walk, her cheeks blooming from the fresh spring air, her eyes bright with the hope of love, Tertius was able to greet her with equanimity.

He excused himself shortly thereafter from her and went to work on the estate books.

When they met again over the dinner table, he asked her, "Did you have a nice outing today?"

"What?" she asked him, clearly lost in her own thoughts. How obvious all the signs he had missed before appeared to him now.

"I was looking for you, and it was apparent you had gone out," he said, watching her closely.

"Oh, just down to the village." Her cheeks flushed prettily as she looked down at her plate. Was it from guilt? She gave a short laugh. "I think Cook has outdone herself tonight. The lamb is quite savory, don't you find?"

"Hmm?" He looked down at the stewed meat on his plate, which he'd hardly been conscious of tasting. "Yes, I suppose."

"Please send my compliments to Cook," she told their new footman with a smile.

They continued eating in silence, Tertius observing her as subtly as possible.

If anyone had been present, they would suppose they supped in the companionableness of a long-married couple.

The same companionableness he'd been fooling himself in the prior weeks signified her growing warmth toward him.

Now, he had no such illusions. Several times he had to fight the bitterness that rose within him and bite down on an acrimonious remark he was tempted to make.

He kept repeating to himself the Lord's words, *My grace is sufficient for thee.*

"Do you think there will be war?" she asked.

He narrowed his eyes at her, remembering the contents of the letter. "It certainly appears likely."

She paled.

"Have you any family in colors?"

"Uh…no."

"Surely one of your many young admirers?"

"There was no one in particular. I…I'm just thinking of our country. We had so many victory celebrations last summer, and now to fear Napoleon again. It's horrible."

"Yes," he agreed, thinking it ironic that his happiness depended on the death of another—a man younger, fitter than he, he thought, remembering his humiliating defeat at swordplay.

"So many young men have died," continued Gillian.

"Yes, it is unfortunate," he said. Suddenly the bitterness rose in him in surprising force and all he wanted to do was confront her. He clenched his glass. *Help me, Lord.*

The peace he'd gained this afternoon was gone.

How dared she sit there and look so saddened by the prospect of losing her lover?

He took a sip and swallowed, the liquid sour on his palate.

"As soon as we return to London, we will be better informed of events on the Continent," he said at last.

At the mention of London, her eyes flew upward, but she didn't say anything.

He could plainly read in those pale green eyes what she wanted to hear—that they would soon return to London. So, he kept silent. Let her stew and worry and fret, as he had to do. Perhaps he would delay his intended trip to London. Physically, he was well enough to return. The thing that kept him here now was the situation down in the mill, as well as estate matters. He needed to gain as much information as possible before going over the changes he wanted to make with his father.

Later that evening, he tried to sit with her as she embroidered. He took up his Bible and attempted to read but found it difficult to concentrate with her so close by. He knew the Lord was trying to speak to him, trying to get him to see, but a part of him didn't want to see. He wanted to nurse his sense of hurt and be justified by it.

He wanted to erase the image of his own filth, which the Lord had washed him clean of, and focus on his wife's guilt. Finally, able to stand it no longer, he rose.

"Good night, Gillian."

She glanced up in surprise. "You're retiring so early?"

"Yes." He held up the Bible. "I want—need—to pray and read."

"Oh, dear, by all means," she said lightly. "You and Althea both."

He made no reply.

In his room, Sky searched the Scriptures, refusing to give up until he felt the Lord's peace once again. As he came to the Sermon on the Mount, he felt on the verge of a discovery and couldn't give up until he knew the truth.

Jesus spoke about loving one's enemy. The Lord's standard was impossibly high, and yet He stated clearly that His followers were to love their enemies. Is that what Gillian had become to him? When he came to the words, *Pray for them which despitefully use you,* he felt the Lord knew exactly what he was going through.

His eyes fell to the next verse, *That ye may be the children of your Father…* and he knew he had arrived at the crux of the matter.

As Sky came to the end of the Beatitudes, he understood what the Lord was requiring of those who chose to be His disciples…of those who wished to be His children.

It was what Sky desired above all else.

He was being made to see the cost. Was he willing to lay down his life, even if it cost him his pride, his honor, his self-respect?

At last, he was able to bow his head and give thanks. He understood how important this victory over himself was. He thanked God for the testing, knowing the Lord wanted to use Him for His greater purposes, but knowing first he needed to defeat his flesh in this most important area. He needed to learn to walk in God's love, cost what it might.

Very well, Lord. I will continue to love my wife…with Your love…regardless of her sentiments for me. Fill me with Your love, Lord. Fill me, Lord.

Katie walked behind Lord and Lady Skylar, along with the rest of the household servants on their way home from church.

She slowed her footsteps, hoping Nigel would follow suit.

The two usually managed to walk together in the general crowd of the Hall's servants and discuss the morning's sermon.

"Do you ever miss your family?" she asked him, curious about this man who was so far from his own home.

"I have no family, Miss Katie."

"Oh, I'm sorry. None at all?"

"Any half-brothers or sisters ended up on other plantations, too far from Lord Skylar's for me to see them. My mother died a few years ago. And my father…well, I have no father."

"You do now," she said with a shy smile.

He returned her smile. "Yes, that be true. I do have a Father now."

Never had she met a man so hungry for God's truth.

Katie stopped and hopped on one foot. When Nigel looked at her, she smiled apologetically. "I have a stone in my shoe." Then, clutching his arm, she lifted one foot and removed her slipper and shook it out.

When she had replaced it, she didn't let go of his arm immediately but looked up at him as she tested her foot against the cobblestones. "That's better."

She let his arm go and they resumed their walk. The rest of the company was far ahead of them now.

"What did you think of that verse from this morning's text: 'there is neither Jew nor Greek, there is neither bond nor free, there is neither male nor female…'?"

"It was interesting. But it doesn't say neither black nor white."

"No, that is true," she admitted. "But don't you think the meaning is the same, that God includes people of all colors in His Son?"

"I don't know. I must study de verse. You will show it to me when we return?"

"Let me show it to you right now," she suggested eagerly. Before he could refuse, she sat down on a stone wall and opened her Bible. Although the church only used prayer books, she was used to carrying her Bible to the Methodist chapel she attended in London.

He sat beside her, and she leaned closer to him as she placed the opened Bible on his lap, her finger pointing to the passage.

He read silently then said aloud, "Galatians three, twenty-eight. I must remember it."

"I'll write it down for you when we return," she promised.

"But no matter what it says," he continued, with a frown that furrowed his smooth brow, "I don't see it in practice here in England, a country that has known de gospel for so many years."

She slumped in discouragement. After a moment she turned to him and said slowly, "Mightn't we—one by one— make a difference?"

His brown-and-yellow flecked green eyes turned to hers in understanding and again he smiled. "Yes, we might."

Sky stood on a rise of land above the moors. Today, he and Gillian had walked to the farthest point they'd ever been. He viewed the long, swaying green grasses on the downward slopes from where he stood. Beyond the meadows were the fields of heather, transformed now to soft pink and green.

The scene was a pattern of light and shadow from the great billowy clouds above them.

He smiled at a lone sheep grazing in the grass below.

The wind blew through his hair and ruffled the surface of the long grasses in waves.

He looked at Gillian beside him. She had a hand up to her bonnet, its ribbons blowing in the breeze.

"I'm ready to go back to London," he announced. "Will you come?"

Her eyes turned slowly from the scene to meet his gaze. He read hope and fear.

She licked her lips. "When will we leave?"

"As soon as we can pack and inform the servants."

She nodded. "Katie and I shall be ready."

"Doubtless we'll find London in a panic over Bonaparte."

"I'm not afraid."

He could find nothing more to say. He had given her what she wanted. It remained to be seen how quickly she took the freedom he was willing to grant her.

Chapter Fifteen

London was deserted when they arrived. Half of society had
sailed to Brussels to be in the thick of war. Gillian felt frustrated at being one of the ones left behind and wished she
could take the next boat across the Channel.

When they arrived at Lord Caulfield's residence, Sky's father was surprisingly in attendance. Sky had written to him
to inform him of their return.

Now, he turned to Gillian with a wide smile lighting
his dissipated features and embraced her. "My dear, at last
I have the pleasure of greeting my daughter-in-law. London has been bereft without your company." She smiled
stiffly, wondering how much he knew of her "banishment." Doubtless more than his cheery countenance was
letting on.

She dreaded the questions society would be asking of her

mysterious absence and now return. For that reason, she was glad so many were caught up in war fever.

Her mother came by soon after.

"Well, it's about time you returned. Rumors were rife when you left. I did my best to scotch them, but of course you were the talk of the town, everything to your husband beating you to your having run away with the footman.

"Thankfully, Byron's engagement to Annabella Millbanke soon filled the gossip columns. And he's given us enough scandal to keep people's minds filled."

Gillian turned away from her mother. What would she say if she knew what her daughter was contemplating? It would serve her mother right to be embroiled in gossip anew. Had she ever come to see Gillian in her exile? Had she ever shown the least understanding of why Gillian had behaved the way she had?

Her mother continued talking, unmindful of Gillian's silence. "If you were enceinte, that would quell all the rumors." She eyed her daughter's waist critically. "You aren't, are you?"

"No, I most certainly am not!" That's all any of them cared about. She could probably carry on as many affairs as she pleased, so long as she gave them all an heir.

"Pity." Her mother sighed. "We shall have to put the best face on things. I know! A ball to welcome the bridal couple home. That should go a ways to show people you and Lord Skylar are perfectly amicable."

Gillian tightened her lips, beginning to feel the cords of family and matrimonial obligations strangle her, and she realized the freedom she had had in Yorkshire. How ironic that what she'd considered her prison now seemed a place where she'd been allowed to be a carefree girl. Lord Skylar had let her do what she pleased. She hadn't been on ceremony with him. Their walks had been impromptu rambles.

He'd never pressed her for anything, but let her be. She compared his behavior to Gerrit's, who'd been demanding when she'd known him, and whom she'd always feared losing. He'd been an Adonis among his fellows, and Gillian knew how easily another woman could have his attention if she didn't satisfy him.

"Well, what do you think of a ball?" her mother asked in annoyance that Gillian wasn't immediately seconding her idea.

"I thought few people were in London," she replied to her mother, not sure she wanted to be put on display to the London ton.

Her mother waved a hand in disdain. "Oh, just about anyone of consequence has gone off to Belgium. Nevertheless, enough remain for a good attendance. Curiosity alone will draw them."

Gillian shuddered. Is that what she'd become, a curiosity? What would it be like if she left her husband? Hadn't she better harden herself to gossip?

Tertius spent his days in the House of Lords, or closeted in the office with his father and business manager. The rest of his time seemed to be spent across town at that Methodist mission run by his sister, but a part of her wished she could join him.

What was she saying? Gillian hugged her arms to herself, aghast at the notion. She should be relieved she didn't see much of Skylar. Isn't that what she'd wanted?

If her husband had any idea of her correspondence with

Gerrit, what would he think of her? If he'd almost killed her on their wedding night, what would he think of her faithlessness now?

Before, she'd kept the secret from her long-ago past out of fear. But now…there was no justification for her behavior now. Tertius would look at her, all warmth vanished from his eyes, and despise her. He would wish her to Jericho if he knew the truth.

A fanciful part of her wondered what it would be like to remain with him. How would that be possible when he and she seemed destined to live such separate lives?

Not that he wouldn't include her if he could, she admitted with a bitter smile. Over dinner, he attempted to tell her of his plans to overhaul their many mills. He told her of the work at the mission. It was she who blocked it out, not wanting to be drawn to that world that demanded sacrifices of one's comforts and the way things had always been.

The night of the ball, Gillian stood with Skylar in the reception line. Despite the dearth of society, more than a hundred people were in attendance.

Gillian had never been so glad of Tertius's presence by her side as on that evening. She saw the speculation in people's eyes. Some were rude enough to speak their conjectures aloud.

"Lady Skylar! How good to see you back. We wondered what had driven you away from London. Where on earth did you disappear to like a thief in the night!" Artificial laughter followed.

In those moments, Sky would deftly take up the response.

"A lover's spat," he answered. "You know how the newly married quarrel." Then he leaned close to her, his hand about her shoulders. "But we have resolved our differences admirably, wouldn't you say, my dear?"

She'd have to turn on her smile to the malicious gossips and reply with a heartfelt, if false, "yes." As the evening wore on, Gillian felt more and more treacherous, and finally convinced herself she was not worthy of such a husband.

The night seemed interminable, not less so because of the incessant talk of troop movements. Everyone was conjecturing on how soon Wellington would face Napoleon in battle. In all the years of campaigning, the former emperor had not yet faced his nemesis, the Iron Duke, on the field.

Lord Caulfield was as gallant as his son. At one point in the evening, he whispered to her, "Steady, my girl. You are holding your own brilliantly. Tomorrow this fete will be in all the papers. Only news from Brussels could eclipse it."

By the time the ball ended, Gillian thoroughly despised herself.

Sky got a rare chance to talk to his father privately the morning after the ball. Life had taken on the rhythm of a whirlwind since his arrival.

He sat with his father in the library.

"I still can't get over how fit you look," Lord Caulfield told him with a shake of his head. "The last time I saw you I thought you were done for, for sure."

"I believe I was. Only one thing could save me then."

His father raised an eyebrow in question. "Oh, what was that? I thought I'd got you the finest medical attention."

"God's mercy."

His father nodded. "Indeed."

"I'd like to tell you how He dragged me from the pit of death to the life you see in me now."

His father eyed him keenly. "I'd certainly like to hear it."

Tertius leaned forward and began to recount his experiences since before leaving the Indies, and culminating in that night of encountering his Lord and Savior.

"My...my..." his father said at last. "Unbelievable, simply unbelievable."

"Yet, nevertheless true."

"Well, all I can say is I'm thankful to have my son and heir alive. Apropos, I'd like to compliment you on your lovely wife. She is positively blooming. No...er...signs yet?" he asked hesitantly.

Tertius merely smiled, not wanting to disappoint his father, who looked so hopeful and had treated Gillian so graciously since her arrival, striving to make her feel welcome and mistress of his house. "You'll be the first we tell," he promised his father, realizing how empty the promise was.

"She is glad to be back in London, I imagine," Lord Caulfield said, hiding any chagrin he felt at their lack of news, as he changed the subject. "Pity so many people are away in Brussels."

"Yes," agreed Sky, thinking of one particular individual he wished would stay away eternally.

A week later the town criers were proclaiming Wellington's victory over Napoleon at Waterloo. The news had just reached Downing Street. Gillian rushed to her window and leaned out in the warm June day, straining to hear the details.

As soon as she could, she fetched Katie, and the two

ventured out into the streets to hear more. Gillian purchased what broadsheets she could find.

Few contained any details of the battle, but were full of news of victory, so she could find nothing of the Coldstream Guards.

Victory on Field of Waterloo! The Iron Duke defeats Boney! His Majesty's Troops Rout the Imperial Army blazed the headlines.

When she arrived home, Sky was already there.

"Hello, Gillian," he greeted her, rising from a sofa in the drawing room. "Out to celebrate the victory?" he asked mildly.

"I was trying to get some news," she replied cautiously, removing her bonnet. "Did you hear anything?"

He handed her some newspapers. "I brought you some of the papers. I know Lord Liverpool received word of Wellington's victory yesterday. It was a bloody battle. There will be many casualties," he said softly. "I believe for that reason celebrations will be muted, compared to last summer, at any rate."

She took the papers from him with trepidation. What would she read? Had Gerrit survived? Suddenly she wished she could run away from everything and not know anything more. What would she do with what she learned?

She scanned the headlines and read of Wellington's retreat from Quatre Bras and of his position at Waterloo the following day. His troops had taken up their stations there through a rainy night and waited nearly half the day before Napoleon gave the order to attack.

Horrific rounds of artillery shells had bombarded them

before the seventy-thousand-man French infantry advanced against the British and Dutch troops.

Gillian knew lists of the wounded and slain officers wouldn't be published for some days. A mention of the Guards caught her eye: Victory at Waterloo Due to Guards' Brave Defense of the Chateau Hougoumont.

She quickly scanned the article.

Colonel Macdonnell's Guards proved their courage at the farmhouse, defending it from overwhelming odds against besieging French troops. At one point, swarms of French stormed through the gates, threatening to take it.

Wellington has said, "The success of the Battle of Waterloo depended on the closing of the gates." Colonel Macdonnell himself with three officers and a sergeant succeeded in closing the gates and keeping the French from taking this English outpost. Light companies of Scots Guards and Coldstream Guards under Scot Colonel Macdonnell were prepared to defend the farthest of Wellington's positions on the edge of the field of Waterloo to the death.

Her heart beat fast, knowing Gerrit belonged to a company of light guards. The article made it sound as if it would have been impossible to live through the siege on the chateau. But clearly there had been some survivors to tell the tale of bravery.

She had to wait several more days before the lists of the wounded and fallen were published. Each day she scanned the page for the heading of Coldstream Guards, then ran her gaze down the list.

The day she spotted his name, her fingers clutched the edges of the paper convulsively, and she looked closer.

Wounded. Captain Gerrit Hawkes, First Company of Light Infantry, Coldstream Guards.

It didn't say how grievous his wounds were. Would he survive? Would he be sent back soon?

She lived in an agony over the next few days, able to find out little. Tertius treated her more gently than usual, which made her fear his coming wrath when he knew the truth of the perfidy of her soul.

For she no longer told herself her actions were justified. Her husband had been all that was noble and good, and Gillian had come to hate what she planned to do.

But it was too late. She felt in a coil that would only come right when she saw Gerrit. She pinned her hopes on seeing his laughing blue eyes again. The two of them would make a fitting pair—both of them wicked and deceitful. She was no longer worthy of being called Lord Skylar's wife. He had been right: she was "used goods."

When had her desire to punish Tertius evaporated, leaving only a sense of unworthiness to be his wife?

The wounded began coming back home while the rest of the troops continued their march toward Paris. One sunny day in early July, the Prince Regent held a review of the troops down the Horse Guards Road.

Tertius took her. They stood at the crowded edge of St. James's Park, watching the glorious parade of uniformed men march or ride past. The band came by first, followed by the drum corps, a group of black men dressed in Turkish style with turbans and feathers. Next came the men by companies in their scarlet coats and buff trousers and black shakos. She scrutinized the uniforms for the Guards' distinctive blue facing along their red coats. When she finally spotted them, she searched for the Coldstream Guards by the red swan's feather in their hats.

She put her hand to her mouth when she saw him, stifling a gasp at the sight of him. Although he marched proudly at the head of his company, his left arm was caught in a white sling.

How could she get word to him? He must think she was still in Yorkshire.

When the parade was over, Tertius made a way for her through the crowd. They strolled through the park, where the crowds were less.

"I told the coachman to wait for us at the entrance to the park. You don't mind the walk?"

"Not at all." In truth, she needed the time to compose herself. It was clear Gerrit was well enough to be out and about. It was only a matter of time before she would see him at some rout or assembly. She didn't want to come upon him in a public place as before. She needed to see him face to face and determine if anything he'd written to her was true. Did he still love her?

She sneaked a peek at Tertius. He hadn't taken her arm. She remembered the night of the ball when for a brief moment he'd put his arm around her. It was the first time he'd touched her like a husband. The feel of his arm around her had been oddly comforting. As soon as old Lady Shaftsbury had moved past them, he had removed his arm and Gillian had felt bereft.

Tertius seemed almost like the older brother she'd never had—there to lean on, to champion her, to defend her honor.

When had Sky's touch gone from disgusting to comforting? When had she stopped hating him and begun hating herself?

Was it since his supposed conversion? She still didn't trust it fully. It was true Sky was proposing radical changes in his father's business holdings and spending all that time reading the Bible.

"Pay laborers twice what they're getting now?" her father-in-law would sputter. "You'll have us all bankrupt before the end of the year."

Sky never raised his voice to his father. Instead he used a more "gentle persuasion," one that was as unrelenting and tenacious as a leech from what Gillian observed.

But still, she didn't trust this new Tertius completely.

He had revealed a side of himself once, a side that had terrified her. What would he do this time when he knew?

In the midst of all his new duties and activities, Tertius began to make discreet inquiries in his different clubs and his old haunts—the taverns and coffeehouses in the seedier parts of town. What he heard he didn't like. He found that the newly returned, much decorated hero, who had been promoted from captain to major for his valorous fighting at the Chateau Hougoumont, was now reaping the rewards of his labors in gambling and drinking in the more popular taverns of the city.

He made inquiries into his background and found that Major Hawkes came of a good if not illustrious family. Their wealth was modest, which caused Sky to wonder what the major's debts at the tables would cost his family. He had several siblings, and he was third or fourth in line, which explained his career in the military. To purchase his colors in the Guards, one of the most elite companies, must have cost his family a pretty penny.

Gillian didn't seem to notice Sky's absences in the evenings. She was busy herself in the London social whirl. After the first questioning looks, their appearance together seemed to satisfy the gossips, and now news of victory distracted the ton.

Tertius called Katie to see him in his office one afternoon.

"I need to ask your help, as your brother in Christ."

The fair-faced young maid looked at him in concern. "What can I do for you, my lord?"

"I would never ask you to betray your mistress, but I need to protect her."

Alarm showed on her face. "Is she in danger?"

"In a manner of speaking. I need to know if she receives any correspondence…or…" This was getting more difficult than he'd imagined. He didn't want to have to expose Gillian, or his own vulnerabilities where she was concerned. "Or, whether she makes any type of…assignation with a…certain officer."

Her eyes grew wide. "Oh, no, my lord, 'tisn't possible she'd do such a thing."

"No, let us hope not. In any case, just keep your eyes open and let me know." Seeing the doubt in her eyes, he added, "Lady Skylar was married very young and not wholly…of her own free will. She still retains many girlhood dreams of a dashing officer in fancy uniform.

"I am your brother in Christ, and I ask you this on that account alone. You can trust me not to hurt your mistress."

The maid nodded slowly. "I'll do anything I can to help the two of you, my lord. You can trust me as your sister in Christ."

"Thank you, Katie."

When she'd been dismissed, Katie walked back upstairs, shaking her head. What was going on with her mistress? Carrying on with a soldier? And with such a wonderful husband.

Of course, Katie wasn't blind. There had been something havey-cavey since the wedding night. Katie had seen the awful disarray in her lady's room the next morning and her mistress's subsequent banishment. Even now, they lived separate lives, and that wasn't natural for a newly married couple, leastways not till a child had been born.

Lady Gillian didn't confide anything in Katie, but of course, she hadn't been her lady's maid long, so that was understandable.

Katie shook her head one last time. She'd better go down on her knees and pray for the mistress and master, as much as keep an eye on her.

Gerrit fumbled with the front door of his rooming house, his other arm draped around a lovely tavern wench named Molly.

"You're soused, you are, Major," the girl told him with a giggle. "Let me have a go."

He relinquished the door to her and she finally managed to unlock it. As they entered the shadowy corridor and headed for the stairs, a door opened halfway down.

"Major Hawkes, is that you?" asked a male voice.

"The very one, my good man," he told the caretaker who worked for the building's owner. "What are you doing up so late, Johnny boy?"

"Waitin' up for you," he replied, emerging into the hallway.

Gerrit squinted at him. "For me? That's a first. I haven't had anyone wait up for me since I was a tyke."

The man came near and handed him a folded paper. "This come for you earlier. Thought it might be important."

Gerrit took the note. "Thank you for your trouble." He fumbled in his pocket. Drat it, his hands seemed two sizes too big. Finally, he extracted a coin. "Here you go. Go buy yourself a pint."

"I'll do so tomorrow. Thank 'ee, Major."

Gerrit finally made it into his rooms, staggering with the effort of walking arm in arm with the buxom maid. The two collapsed onto the couch in a burst of laughter. He extricated himself from her arms and legs. "You hold tight here for me, love, won't you, and I'll light us a lamp."

"I can see all I need to," she answered, tugging at his jacket.

Before she could pull him back down, he managed to step away. "Patience, my love. All in good time, as they say."

He reached a lamp and struck the flint. As the light grew, he glanced down at the note in his hand. The writing looked familiar and the paper was of good quality.

He slit the seal with a fingernail and focused on the writing.

It was short and sweet, and reminded Gerrit of its lovely sender. He hadn't thought of her in a long time, but now the recollection was pleasant. Oh, the delectable Lady Gillian,

Lady Skylar now. There was a morsel. She was probably worth a few hundred thousand by this time, he realized, vaguely remembering her last communication, which informed him she might soon be a widow.

Mayhap he should rethink his aversion to marriage....

Gillian clutched the letter to her breast. At last she'd had word. He was dying to see her. That settled it. She belonged to him. She would be through with all the doubts that had been assailing her since she'd arrived in London.

Your words have filled my heart with longing. I must see you! Each second that ticks by as I await your reply is agony to my soul....

He beseeched her to meet him at Vauxhall Gardens, as the last time. She must think of a way of going there without Skylar. She paced her room, racking her mind until she hit upon a solution. She would need to suggest to some friends to make up a party, and then convince Sky she was going with them. He had been so busy of late that he would scarcely notice if he thought she was being well accompanied. She would make sure Charlotte would go along and a few others Sky knew and trusted.

Vauxhall Gardens was wild that night. People in masquerade, some not. But there was an air of hilarity, whether due to the final victory over Napoleon or just summer madness, Gillian wasn't sure. All she knew was that as soon as she'd arrived, she already felt the doubts well up within her. She immediately tried to quell them, knowing everything would be all right as soon as she saw Gerrit. All she needed to do was see him, she kept repeating to herself.

After wandering the many gas-lit paths with her party for a while, she was finally found by Gerrit. He was bolder this time, coming up beside her in his flowing sultan's robes, his face thinly disguised by a thick mustache. He whisked her away before her companions could notice she'd left them.

He took her to one of the secluded walks and found them an alcove in a Grecian temple.

"My love, at last," he whispered, taking her into his arms.

As soon as his mouth touched hers, she felt how wrong it was.

Instead of satisfying her longing, his kiss filled her with a sudden repugnance and brought back a memory of three years ago, a memory she'd suppressed.

Gently she pushed her face away from his, telling herself she just needed a little time to become accustomed to him, but Gerrit's ardor was strong.

"I have waited months for this," he murmured against her face. "Don't be so cruel to make me wait longer."

"It has been so long since I last saw you," she began, breaking apart from his embrace. "I was so worried about you. Did you get wounded very badly?" she asked in concern, noticing he no longer wore a sling on his arm.

"A mere scratch," he answered with a chuckle. "Many were not so fortunate as I. But I didn't come here to talk of wounds and battle. I came to look upon your beautiful face and persuade myself it's real." His fingers caressed her skin, and soon he drew her back into his embrace.

His whiskers were rough and his breath hot against her. Another wave of distaste swept through her. She remembered how ardent he had been as a youth, always stealing kisses from her in hidden alcoves. At first, it had been pleasant, and such a balm to her loneliness, but soon he'd gone too far, demanding more and more from her.

She tried to push away from him now, but his arms clasped her tightly.

"I don't think we should—" she began when she was able to break away from his lips.

He looked at her with a smile. "You are no little innocent anymore. You have known two men, and I was the first." His eyes glinted in the lamplight, and suddenly they looked feral to her.

"You mustn't speak like that," she said, hurt at his blunt description of her conduct. What she had given to him had been given out of love. "You make me sound like a…a wanton," she protested. "I didn't give myself to you just like that—"

"I'm merely claiming what is mine by rights," he replied, before silencing her with another kiss, gentler this time.

She allowed herself be kissed, telling herself she would begin to feel the passion she had dreamed of. But it didn't come and, taking her passivity for assent, Gerrit became bolder.

He caressed her, and once again, like the seventeen-year-old she'd been, she complied. It seemed easier than fighting him. Before she knew it, he had her bodice half-undone.

"No! No," she pleaded. "Please don't." This was wrong. She could no longer deny the voice of her conscience.

"Why not? You gave it to me before. What scruples are holding you back this time. Aren't you a widow by now?" He touched her garments. "What, no mourning for the grieving widow?" he asked with a low chuckle.

"No!" Realizing his ignorance, she continued more calmly. "Lord Skylar has recovered. He's here in London with me now."

"Ah. The husband lurks in the shadows. Well, it will require more caution, but where there is a will, there is a way," he said, touching her once more.

She pushed his hand away. "I can't, not like this."

As she struggled to explain, he only bent to rain kisses down her neck.

It wasn't supposed to be like this. A man who'd scarcely seen her after such avowals of eternal love in writing, could hardly wait to ravish her. As she felt his hands once more on her, she began to feel like a soiled handkerchief, being passed from man to man as he had implied. She shuddered, disgusted with herself.

"I'm sorry, please stop," she repeated, softly at first, then more firmly, as she strove to evade him.

When he finally saw she was serious, he said with insolence, "You know, they have names for women like you who like to lead a man on with promises and then deliver nothing."

She flinched at the rude words. All her self-reproach died in that instant as she realized the kind of man she'd given her heart to.

Without thinking what she was doing, she brought her hand up and gave him a resounding slap across the cheek.

Instead of becoming angry, he merely smiled. "I suppose I deserved that."

She covered her mouth with her hand, suddenly feeling very sick. "I'm sorry. I shouldn't have done that."

"You should have done that and more," he replied cheerfully. "It is I who shouldn't have heeded the summons of a young lady who doesn't know what she wants. Come, I'll take you back to your companions."

As he spoke he rearranged her bodice, covered her with her cloak, then took her by the elbow and escorted her through the shrouded pathways back toward the center of the park. She walked beside him heedless of where he was taking her. What had she done? How could she have been so foolish? Those two thoughts were the only things running through her mind.

"I shall leave you here." Gerrit touched her lightly on the cheek. "Don't look so forlorn. I was, and am, a thorough blackguard, and I suppose it's good you finally found out."

As she stared at him, finding it hard to accept the calm way he was taking her refusal, he smiled as if reading her mind and said, "As for me, you mustn't worry; I never lack companionship for long." He gave her a small salute. "I wish you well with your new husband."

She stood watching him walk back into the shadows, his parting words confirming what she already knew. He'd behaved at the end with that boyish insouciance she'd once fallen in love with as a girl. Now she felt only sadness that she'd ever given herself to him. It was clear his feelings had never been deep. To him, she'd been just another conquest. His parting wish revealed he harbored no ill feeling, but it also showed how little he'd ever cared.

She couldn't help contrasting it with the blinding rage of her husband. The thought brought her back to the present with a shudder.

Gerrit might be able to coolly walk away, but what of her?

Her night's rendezvous had shown her what a shallow, contemptible woman she was. She could no longer claim the ignorance of youth of her first fall. She was a grown woman now who had willfully blinded herself to everything but her own childish desire for revenge, and now she had destroyed any chance she had for any sort of happiness with her husband.

Where could she go? There was no place far enough to escape from herself.

Tertius sat across from Katie in the dark coach. When the housemaid had first told him of his wife's assignation, it was as if he'd received a mortal blow. Despite all his forebodings, a part of him had never really believed it possible.

But when he'd not found Gillian anywhere, he'd had a moment of panic. The sight of her empty bedroom and sitting room gave him the sudden conviction that she had gone. She had left him.

He searched her drawers and dressing room like a madman, but it looked as if little if anything had been taken. But she had so many things that it was impossible to tell if she'd only taken a few garments. Perhaps she wanted to erase all traces of her former life.

He clutched at one of her gowns and fell onto a chair in her dressing room, breathing in the softly sweet scent of her cologne on it.

He had failed. The overwhelming reality of it hit him. It hadn't mattered how loving and patient he'd behaved toward her in the past weeks. All of his efforts had been in vain.

Why, Lord? Why? Why go through the effort of loving one who couldn't return his love no matter how much he tried?

Is it not Your will to save my marriage? Was it a mistake from the beginning? Maybe You desire to give her a second chance at happiness. Is the man she has loved all along, long before she knew me, the one worthy of her?

Oh, God, he groaned, falling from the chair onto his knees. *Not my will, but Yours, Lord. She's Yours. I've tried all I can and it's not enough.*

I'm not good enough for her. Perhaps this officer is. He has fought bravely on the battlefield. He bested me in our fencing match. Is that it?

In the midst of his surrender, Tertius felt a supernatural peace descend on him and an overwhelming desire to worship God. He realized as he fell on his face that it didn't matter if his wife never came back, the Lord would fill him. The Lord was all he needed, all he would ever need.

In the midst of his tears, the joy began to flow through his spirit, sadness mingled with an overwhelming joy, so that he didn't know where one ended and the other began.

Later, when he left the bedroom, he found Katie waiting for him in the corridor, her face expressing her concern.

"The note says she is to meet this officer, Major Hawkes, at Vauxhall Gardens," he informed her. "I shall go there…to ensure her safety."

"May I…go along with you, my lord?"

He gave the maid a look of understanding. "Of course. Come along."

Chapter Sixteen

As the coach rolled along on the cobblestones southward toward the Thames, Tertius leaned his head back against the leather squabs, wondering what he would do when he arrived at Vauxhall. Most likely, he would not even see Gillian in that immense garden full of tree-lined walkways, groves and hidden temples, nooks and crannies designed for lovers' trysts.

Gillian had mentioned going with Lord and Lady Billingsley and her friend, Charlotte. She had covered her tracks well, Tertius realized with a curious resignation.

"My lord?" Katie's hesitant voice came to him across the shadowy interior of the coach.

"Yes, what is it, Katie?" he asked with a smile. She had proven herself a true ally.

"I'm sorry about the mistress. I'm sure there's some good explanation."

"I'm sure there is," he reassured her. "Thank you for being so faithful."

"Oh, I haven't done anything any good servant wouldn'ta done."

"Yes," he murmured, "what any good servant would have done. That's put very well. That's what we are all called to do, isn't it? Be faithful servants?"

"I hope I can fulfill my duty."

"You have. When…when this is over—" What did that mean? When his wife was gone for good? He cleared his throat and began again. "When this is over, I'd like to do something for you. Is there anything you need, or perhaps your family?"

She was silent a few minutes, her face turned toward the window, so that he thought she might be hesitant in voicing a need.

Finally she answered softly, "Well…there's my mum and dad. They haven't been well. I've tried to help, but it hasn't been much." She bit her lip. "I don't want them to end up in the poorhouse."

He reached across the carriage and patted her hands. "Don't worry. We'll see to them." His heart felt a surge of gladness that he could perhaps help someone else at a time when his own heart was breaking.

"Thank you, my lord," she whispered.

The carriage was going over Vauxhall Bridge. They both turned toward the windows then back to each other.

"We're almost there," she whispered fearfully.

Gillian, too upset to rejoin her party, found them only long enough to plead indisposition. One of the gentlemen immediately offered to see her home in his coach. She accepted the offer gratefully, knowing Vauxhall was no place for a woman alone.

By the time they were able to maneuver the coach out of the long line waiting outside the Gardens, it seemed hours had passed.

When she finally returned home, the house was silent. The servants had all gone to bed except one lone footman, lolling in an armchair in the entryway. She roused him gently, and he sprang up, frightened.

"It's all right. Lord Skylar, is he still out?"

The young man rubbed his eyes. "I believe so, my lady."

"Very well. You run on to bed," she ordered. "We'll leave the lamp here."

He looked more asleep than awake. When he hesitated, she gave him a slight push. "Run along. I shall wait for his lordship."

"Very well, my lady."

When he had left, she checked the lamp, and lighting a branch of candles for herself, she made her way to the library.

Her heart heavy, she went toward the couch. She knew she couldn't stay here any longer. She must confess her sinful behavior to Skylar and let him decide her fate. This time, Yorkshire wouldn't be far enough. Perhaps he had a remote hunting lodge in Scotland, she thought with bitter humor.

As she curled her legs under her on the couch and wrapped herself in her cloak, the self-pity came and, with it, the tears.

What would Sky's God say now? Strike her dead and send her to eternal damnation? That's probably the only thing that would satisfy Tertius.

Oh, God, all she'd ever wanted was to love and be loved. Why was that so wrong? Why was that so much to ask? she cried out to that silent god.

The earlier exhilaration gave way to shame, which now gave way to a weariness, as if the weight of her sin were bowing her down like a bundle of thatch on a farmer's back.

Sky closed and bolted the front door behind him. The entryway was empty, the lamp's wick curled over and black.

He turned to Katie. "Thank you for coming with me."

"I'm sorry we didn't find her."

"Yes, I am, too," he said quietly. "Go, get some sleep. There's no need to arise early in the morning." His mouth twisted. "Your mistress won't be needing you."

With a sad, understanding smile, she turned away and headed toward the back stairs.

He took the main stairs slowly. He must trust that Gillian was safe. Throughout the evening, he'd had to put images of her set upon by robbers or cutthroats out of his mind and pray for her safety. He must trust that if she was with the major—and whom else would she be with?—he would treat her well.

Before he reached his own door, he stopped by hers, his hand on the knob. Perhaps…

He opened it and shone his candle in its interior, but it remained as empty as it had been earlier in the evening.

His shoulders slumped. Part of him had kept hoping it had all been a nightmare.

When he reached his room, Nigel was dozing on a chair. Sky shook his head. He had told the man not to wait up for him. He didn't bother to wake him now, but removed his own coat and boots and replaced them with a dressing gown and slippers. Sky knew it was useless to lie down. He would go downstairs and read. He picked up his Bible and candle and turned back to the corridor.

He entered the library and immediately saw the guttering candles. He entered, curious to its occupant. He didn't see anybody until he reached the back of the sofa.

There, nestled in her cloak, lay Gillian, peacefully asleep, her head resting on an arm.

The waves of relief washing over him were so great, he had to clutch the back of the sofa.

Had she returned to tell him she was leaving definitively? Relief turned to caution. He made his way around the sofa and set his candle down carefully beside the branch of candles. Then he adjusted the cloak around Gillian, thinking he should let her sleep until morning.

Before stepping away from her, he studied her sleeping face a moment. Why did she have to be so beautiful, with her rosy cheeks and innocent mouth? Unable to help himself, he reached up and brushed a cheek with the back of his fingertips. Her eyes opened and gradually they focused on him.

As recognition dawned, she turned her face away, and Tertius felt the power of her repudiation afresh.

Then he noticed the tears forcing their way from between her tightly squeezed lids.

"Oh, Tertius, you can send me away. I'll go away…I won't shame you ever again. This time I'll stay away…I swear it. I'm so ashamed…I feel so dirty…I'll never feel clean again…"

From thinking she was telling him she was leaving him, to a gradual understanding that she was back and telling him in an incoherent way that she was sorry, he saw that something had gone terribly wrong for her.

"Did he hurt you?" he asked softly but tersely.

But she didn't even hear him, so wrapped in her pain.

She turned her face further away from him and deeper into the sofa. "I'll go away, I promise. Only, don't hate me...don't hate me...."

He knelt at the sofa close to her face and asked softly, "Why must you go away?"

"I've done something so f-foolish!" she stammered through her tears. "I don't deserve you."

"You can't have done anything to make me send you away," he argued gently, touching her cheek with his fingertip. "Only you can choose to leave me."

"Oh, no! No! But I can no longer stay."

"What is it?" he asked more sharply. "Did he hurt you?"

His meaning finally penetrated. She opened her eyes and stared at him in horror. "You...know?" Her voice faltered at the enormity of this fact.

"About Major Hawkes? Yes."

Her tear-filled eyes grew rounder. "And you let me continue—"

"I surmised he was your first love."

"Oh, no, no!" She shook her head vehemently against the sofa cushions. "That wasn't love! I was a silly, stupid young girl."

"And now?" he asked her, hope refusing to die within him.

She sniffed and groped for a handkerchief. He handed her his own.

"Now?" she replied after she'd wiped her face. "Now, I'm a foolish woman who has no excuse."

"You're still a young girl to me," he insisted gently.

She sat up and pushed herself into the corner of the sofa. It was then she noticed his position, and she became overwrought once more. "Please don't kneel there. Stand over me. Strike me…anything, but don't kneel before me. I don't deserve it."

Seeing her agitation only grow, he finally rose, but only to sit beside her on the sofa. "Is that better?" he asked mildly. When she said nothing, he tried to help her. "I know you were lonely. I shouldn't have sent you away—"

She shook her head, looking away from him again. "Maybe I thought the only way I could punish you for what you did was to—to—oh, I don't know anymore what I thought." She looked down at the knotted handkerchief in her hands. "I only know that this evening taught me how foolish I was. I don't know what I saw in him before, but this evening opened my eyes. He…he only wanted to use me." She reddened, her fingers working convulsively in the handkerchief.

Tertius clenched his hands but forced himself to remain silent.

"I felt so dirty and disgusted by his manhandling. I could only think, how could I have let myself…how could I have given myself to him before…given him my most precious gift?" Her eyes looked at him in anguish.

And all he felt was the most profound relief, he could only bow his head.

She interpreted his reaction differently. "I'm so sorry, Tertius. I should never have agreed to our betrothal without telling you about that. That I wasn't pure."

He covered her hands with his. "Shh."

She looked at his hand and, with a shudder, removed hers and pressed herself farther against the sofa arm, as if trying to move away from him as much as possible in the confined space.

"I feel so dirty."

"Did he hurt you tonight? Please tell me, Gillian."

She shook her head. "I didn't let him. I pushed him away. I never should have agreed to meet him alone. I don't think anyone saw me with him. I wouldn't want you to be involved in another scandal because of me. That's the last thing you deserve to go through."

He found his voice at last. "I would rather know what it is *you* wish."

She pressed her lips together as if tempted to speak. Still not looking at him, she finally said, "It doesn't matter what I want. It's too late for that."

"It matters to me. For if there is any power in me to give you what you want, I'll move heaven and earth to give it to you."

"Don't say that! I don't merit your pity. You must hate me. You have every right to banish me now. I'll go anywhere you say."

"I don't hate you, Gillian."

She looked at him in disbelief. "How can you not hate me? I lied to you since the day we met. And now, I have deceived you in the worst way a wife can deceive her husband."

"The Lord burned all the hate out of me that night He saved me." He gave her a rueful smile. "I couldn't hate you even if I tried."

He watched the confusion grow in her eyes. "There are a few other things I can't do," he added.

She waited, still, as if not understanding the language he was speaking and yet straining to hear.

"I can't force you to love me. I can't force you to stay with me."

"You knew I was thinking of leaving you?" she asked breathlessly.

He nodded.

"And yet, you still let me correspond with him? Go to him?" she asked in wonder.

"I took away your freedom once. I vowed I wouldn't do so again. I thought tonight you had chosen to leave me. I wasn't going to stop you."

When she said nothing, seeming to be digesting this information, he continued. "I never want you to stay with me against your will." After a moment he added, "There is something you can do, however."

She looked at him fearfully.

"You can hurt me. I thought you might today. I was preparing myself for it." He cracked a smile. "So, you see you are not powerless."

He rested his head against the back of the sofa and closed his eyes as if weary.

Gillian studied his features—the dark, straight hair against the dusky skin, his still-too-thin cheekbones, angular even now in repose. She scarcely knew this man from the one she'd been betrothed to. In one thing he hadn't changed. His manner continued self-deprecating. A sudden wave of tenderness swept over her, and she stretched out her hand and touched a lock of his hair, her own guilt and shame momentarily pushed aside.

He opened his eyes lazily, a question in their dark depths.

When she made no move to withdraw her hand, he reclosed his eyes and turned his face into her palm. Gently, he placed a kiss in it. It was like a courtier's kiss and oddly touching to her. It demanded nothing from her, as Gerrit's hot, hungry kisses had.

It merely communicated his complete acceptance of her.

Still acting on instinct alone, she leaned across the space between them and placed her lips on his. Her heart thudded as she felt his warm lips against hers and an answering wave of warmth swept through her.

It was a light kiss, since he did nothing but stay still under her, and so she lingered, loath to break the contact with him. Slowly, hesitatingly it seemed to her, he responded to the slight pressure of her lips against his.

He drew away a scarce few inches from her along the sofa back and eyed her through half-closed lids. She felt unfulfilled, wanting more.

He stroked her face with long fingers, and she closed her eyes like a kitten for a caress. When he stopped, she reopened her eyes, feeling bereft. "Why did you stop?"

"I don't want to do anything you find repulsive."

The full import of his words hit her. She felt her face grow hot, remembering her odious words to him.

"I…don't find it repulsive," she whispered.

"Would you like to try it again?" he asked softly.

She gave a slight nod.

The next thing she knew he pulled her against himself and kissed her long and deeply, and she found herself responding with an intensity she didn't think she was capable of.

Again he stopped, and when she looked at him questioningly, she realized their wedding night still stood between them, a monstrous chasm dividing them. She understood with sudden discernment that only she had the power to dispel its ugliness.

She looked down at his hand lying idly between them, so close to her, yet not touching her. "I want to be your wife," she articulated slowly, taking a small step over that yawning abyss, "in every sense."

The words he'd longed to hear and despaired of ever hearing. Tertius took her slim, pale hand and touched the wedding band that still graced it. He turned her palm upward and brought it to his lips again. "And so you shall be," he whispered.

He felt her other hand on his bowed head. "How can you ever forgive me, Tertius, and forget all about what I did tonight?"

He lifted his head and smiled sadly. "Perhaps because my sins were much blacker than yours and were forgiven— even blotted out." He sobered. "But before you agree to being my wife, I must confess that I broke our wedding vows after I sent you away. I was so hurt and angry that I went with another woman."

As she listened in silence, he told her of his own sin.

"So, you have more to forgive than I," he ended. "I have done nothing but hurt and abuse you since I wed you. You have a right to leave me if you desire to do so."

"I only wish we could both start over," she told him. "I wish I could come to you pure and innocent." Her voice broke, and she pressed her lips together and swallowed, unable to speak for a moment. "But I can't undo the past."

He touched a finger lightly to her lips, silencing her. "Why don't we both begin anew to promise to love and honor each other and let this be our wedding night?"

Slowly she nodded, and he could read the fear and hope in her eyes.

He rose and held his hand out to her. "Come, my love, come and be my wife."

Tertius awoke early the next morning. He glanced over at his wife's sleeping face, and knew he wouldn't be able to sleep anymore that morning. He felt too full of love and wonder to be able to sleep.

Quietly, resisting the urge to kiss her, he eased out of bed and put on his dressing gown. He slipped out of the room and entered his own, knowing all he wanted to do was kneel before God and give thanks and worship.

He hadn't been there long before Nigel came in softly.

"Good morning, my lord," the valet said. "Are you ready for your coffee?"

"In a bit," he replied, realizing his valet didn't know all that had occurred last night.

Nigel turned and eyed the bed that had clearly not been slept in. He glanced back at Tertius but made no comment, for which Tertius was grateful. Last night was too special to be mentioned casually, even with congratulatory remarks.

He, however, found himself hardly able to keep from whistling or humming a tune as he shaved and dressed.

As he sipped his coffee, he thought about his conversation with Katie early last evening. It had felt good to discover how to help one who had helped him so much. He observed his valet. What could he do to repay all the man had done for him over the years?

"God is good, isn't he, Nigel?" he began, unable to refrain from smiling widely.

"Yes, my lord, that He be."

"You've enjoyed our Bible studies, haven't you?"

"Very much."

"Have you thought how the Lord might some day use you?"

Nigel stopped brushing Sky's coat. "It's funny you should ask that."

"Why?"

"I was recently thinking that some day—" He looked uncomfortable all of a sudden "—that is, when you no longer need me, that mayhap some day I could preach de gospel…back on de island."

Sky nodded thoughtfully. Why hadn't he thought of it? The Lord wouldn't waste the talents of such a powerful man by keeping him a valet for the rest of his days.

"Yes, I think that's a wonderful idea," he told him.

"You don't think it foolish? Could God use a man like me?"

"God looks for a willing heart."

"Even if it be in de skin of a black man?"

"I don't think God regards the color of your skin, except perhaps to mark how handsomely it becomes you."

"You would let me return to de islands?"

Sky nodded, his smile growing. "I would help you establish a church."

Chapter Seventeen

Gillian woke gradually and stretched. Her body felt filled with well-being and gradually she remembered why. As soon as she did, she turned on the pillow to find Tertius but, with a pang, saw the empty space. She noticed the bright light coming in between the curtains.

Groggily she reached for the clock and saw it was nearly noon. Of course, Tertius would be up and long gone.

She sat up in bed and rang for Katie.

"Good morning, my lady," Katie said with a wide smile when she came in. "It's good to see you. Did you have a good sleep?"

The maid seemed inordinately pleased to see her.

"I slept very well, thank you," she murmured, wondering how much the maid knew of her recent behavior. But Katie seemed cheerful enough as she went about her duties.

As Gillian breakfasted and bathed, she wondered how soon she would see her husband. She tingled with anticipation. Where was he? Was he missing her?

She thought maybe he would appear at any moment. As she sat at her dressing table, her gaze fell on her jewelry box.

She reached for it and opened it. There sat her ruby and diamond ring, along with the other jewels Tertius had given her. That last time she had gone to the mill town, determined to pawn them, she had turned back. She hadn't had the courage then and later, when Tertius promised to take her back to London, she'd reasoned she no longer needed the money.

But she knew neither had been the true reason she hadn't parted with his gifts. Even then, love had already begun to awaken in her.

She took the ruby and diamond ring and slipped it on her finger, atop her wedding band.

"That is a pretty ring, my lady," Katie said softly. "It becomes you nicely."

Gillian held out her hand. "Yes, it is beautiful, isn't it?"

She thought of the one who'd given it to her. She felt as if she were walking around in some sort of wonderland since last night.

Tertius had been so tender, so passionate. He'd opened up a heretofore-unimaginable realm for her.

Right before they'd both fallen asleep, he'd even whispered those three words to her, "I love you."

But as the early afternoon wore on and he didn't come to her, Gillian began to doubt whether he'd really meant them.

How many had been Gerrit's avowals of love and had he meant any of them?

Maybe Tertius had reconsidered her conduct in the light of day and decided she was no fit wife for him?

Finally, she could stand it no more and had to see for herself.

She knew Sky usually spent a good part of the day in the office. She went and knocked on its door, but so great was her preoccupation that she was actually startled when she heard his voice telling her to come in.

With a beating heart and a wish that she hadn't ventured forth, she entered the office. Immediately, Tertius and the secretary turned their gazes on her and she felt exposed, as if they could both see her unworthiness to be walking in on them. Tertius smiled and stood. "Gillian!"

She stopped. "I'm sorry, I didn't mean to interrupt...I will come back." She began retreating.

Tertius came around the desk. "No, come in." He turned and dismissed the secretary with a few quiet words.

Gillian and he were alone. She licked her lips, not knowing how to begin.

"Hello, sleepyhead," he said softly. "Did I keep you up last night?"

Blushing, she shook her head, unable to respond to his humor.

He immediately became serious. "What is it, Jilly-girl?"

She looked at him. "You called me that," she said in wonder.

"I'm sorry." His tone was rueful. "It's silly. Would you prefer 'Gillian'?"

"No, I like it. You put it inside my ring." She looked down, fingering her wedding band.

"Yes." He took her hand in his. "You're wearing the other."

"Ye-es," she stammered. "I had…put it away…I'd almost lost it."

"I almost lost you."

She looked into his dark eyes. "But you haven't."

"God be praised." He was looking at her so warmly it emboldened her to continue.

"This morning, when I…woke up…"

"Yes?"

"And you weren't there, I wondered…if it had been…real…" Her voice trailed off in embarrassment.

He bent his head and kissed her, his hands around her shoulders, steadying her. "Does that tell you?" he murmured.

"I never dreamed," she whispered, "I never dreamed…it could be like that…so wonderful…so perfect."

As she spoke, he was tracing her face and neck with a fingertip. "Yes, last night was very real. If I left you early this morning, it was partly because I couldn't sleep anymore, my heart was so full, and I didn't want to disturb you. And partly it was out of fear."

She pulled away from him slightly. "Fear?"

"Perhaps the same fear you had. Was it real? Did you feel the same way I did?"

She reached up her hand and cupped his face. "My dearest, you showed me how beautiful it could be."

He took her hand and kissed the palm. "With my body I thee worship…"

Comprehension dawned in her eyes, and she nodded. Then a shadow clouded her thoughts and she looked downward. "You told me once if I should ever want to tell you about…about how I lost my purity."

"Not anymore if it pains you."

She looked up at him and he could read the apprehension in her eyes.

"I do want to tell you."

When he waited, she finally continued. "I was sixteen when I lost Papa." She pressed her lips together, not wanting to remember that period but needing to have Tertius understand.

"It doesn't excuse what I did, but I was so lonely that year with only Mama. She always said Papa had spoiled me. When he was gone, it was almost as if…as if she delighted in making me face up to things.

"I met—" she lowered her voice to a whisper "—Gerrit at a dancing class I was sent to. He was so handsome and he seemed to pay me particular attention."

Gillian glanced away, not able to bear looking into Tertius's eyes, afraid she would read disappointment in them.

"Gerrit was perfect in every way, and he made me feel special when he singled me out from all the other young ladies.

"I was foolish enough to believe it when he told me he loved me. Then after a while, he was no longer satisfied with sending me little notes during the class or trying to be alone with me for a few moments."

She took a deep breath, determined to tell her husband everything, whatever the consequences. "He began to convince me to meet him in private away from the dance classes. I knew it was wrong, but I couldn't say no. I was so lonely and felt so unloved at home. And I missed Papa so much." She bit her lip to stop its trembling.

"When he obtained his commission, he made me believe I was being selfish in not giving him all…of myself. He would be going to Spain to fight and I might never see him again."

She put a fist up to her mouth and fought the tears of regret. Tertius tried to stop her from saying more, but she insisted on finishing.

"Every time I saw Gerrit, he wore away my resistance a little bit more. I felt I would forever regret it if I denied him this one thing. Finally I agreed to meet him. My maid helped me."

She looked down at her clasped hands. Thankfully, Tertius hadn't interrupted her any more, even though she knew it must be distasteful for him to hear all the details.

She sighed. "Then it was over. Afterward, in the weeks before he left, I began to sense Gerrit wasn't the same. I tried to tell myself it was my imagination, but now I know differently. When he left for the Peninsula, I only received a couple of letters and then nothing more until…until I saw him that night at the Prince Regent's."

"Didn't your mother find out?"

She shook her head. "Later, she found the few notes I'd received from Gerrit and she burned everything. That's when she dismissed my maid and hired Templeton, and made my seasons a misery."

"Oh, Jilly, I'm so sorry," he murmured, taking her in his arms and whispering against her hair.

"When Gerrit came back, and I was so worried about marrying you—that you'd discover my terrible secret on our wedding night—I convinced myself that Gerrit had always loved me. I let myself believe his lies.

"Oh, Tertius, I can't forget what I did." She gently pushed away from him, determined to face his reaction. When she saw only love and tenderness in his eyes, she shook her head. "I can't understand how you can still want me."

"It's because I have been forgiven so much," he answered gently.

"I can't understand that kind of forgiveness." Again, she felt something separated the two of them, and only she had the power to close that divide. "Would you help me understand?" she asked hesitantly.

He nodded. "All you have to do is ask the Father to forgive you and believe that your sins are taken away by the shed blood of His Son, Jesus."

"Will you help me pray?"

"Of course, my love." He took her two hands in his own and closed his eyes, bowing his head.

"Dear Heavenly Father, I come to You by the precious blood of Your Son, Jesus—

"Receive me. Forgive me. Wash me and make me whole again."

Gillian repeated the simple words after her husband, feeling the intolerable burden of guilt and condemnation lift as she prayed.

Tertius hadn't planned on doing anything to Major Hawkes except make sure he didn't upset Gillian in any way.

When Gillian hesitated going out in society, he told her, "We need to be seen in public together to silence any rumors that might arise from your evening at Vauxhall."

"I feel everyone will see my guilt every time they look at me."

"I'll be there at your side." He lifted her chin in his hand. "Courage, my love. You have nothing to fear."

They attended a ball together. Tertius had deliberately chosen a large one in honor of Waterloo. He wanted to see how the major would behave when he met Gillian in public.

It was late in the evening when he finally spotted him in his scarlet uniform. He was with a group of officers, far across the ballroom.

Sky leaned toward Gillian and whispered in her ear. "Hawkes is here."

She turned frightened eyes to him. "I don't want to see him. Can you take me home?"

"I will soon. But we have to stay a bit longer. You understand, don't you? You can't run each time you see him. Let us trust he will behave like a gentleman."

She agreed reluctantly.

Sky stayed by her side as long as he could, but it was difficult in the crowded room. They each had many acquaintances who were eager to greet them. When he turned from talking to a fellow member of the House of Lords on a current bill up for debate, he looked in vain for Gillian.

He went immediately in search of her. It was nearly impossible to find her among so many people and rooms. Thinking she had gone to freshen up, he wandered the corridors, but she was nowhere to be found. He even walked along the terrace, thinking each time he saw a couple hidden in the shadows that perhaps— But no, he was being foolish.

Gillian joined a couple of other ladies when they ascended to one of the rooms set aside for their use. She scarcely listened to their gossip as she followed them, glancing back every now and then to make sure Gerrit was nowhere in the vicinity.

After allowing a maid to rearrange her hair and pat her face dry with a little powder, she descended once again with the ladies.

They were walking along a corridor toward the ballroom when Gillian spotted Gerrit lounging against a doorpost. She quickened her step, hoping to pass unnoticed with the other women.

"The beautiful Lady Skylar," he drawled just as she was passing him.

She started. What would the other ladies think? "G-good evening, Major," she stammered, averting her face.

"Why the hurry? Surely you can spare a few moments for one of the wounded of Waterloo?"

She stopped, afraid he'd say something more. The other ladies, not noticing the interchange, continued on their way, chattering to each other.

"What do you want?" Gillian whispered as soon as they were out of earshot.

"Only to tell you how lovely you look tonight."

She realized he was drunk. His words were spoken slowly, as if he had difficulty putting them together. His eyes looked bloodshot.

Before she could move away, he motioned into the chamber behind him, a small salon. "Come in, m'dear, and let me admire what I've lost."

"Please, I must return." At that moment, she heard voices, male ones this time, further down the corridor.

"Just for a few minutes," Gerrit's voice rose.

Without thinking, she ducked past him into the room, getting out of sight as the men walked by.

Too late, she realized her mistake.

Gerrit followed and now stood before her, a smile on his face.

How could she ever have found him attractive? He was handsome, devastatingly so, but now she saw the lines of dissipation already marring his youthful features.

"Any regrets?" he asked.

She backed away from him, trying to figure out how to sidestep him and reach the door.

Tertius had given up his futile search for Gillian and was wandering back toward the ballroom when he caught a glimpse of a uniform through an open doorway.

He stopped when he heard his wife's voice.

"Please, let me pass."

"Gillian, the ice queen." The major's voice sounded slurred. "You aren't afraid of me, are you?"

Gillian made an attempt to pass by the major, but he laughed and stepped in front of the doorway, but then he stumbled. This only made him laugh harder, and Sky realized how drunk the major was.

Sky took the major by the arm. "I believe you need a little air."

"Wha—" Turning, he recognized Tertius, and his smile broadened. "Why if it isn't the great Lord Skylar himself. The heir presumptive. I believe I should congra—gratulate you. Would that my older siblings would give up the ghost...and leave me with title and wealth...

"I told Gillian I wished her all the best..." His tone

became more slurred. "Better than I could ha' ever given her…tho' I tried…."

Before he could say anything more, Tertius excused himself from Gillian and took Major Hawkes by the arm. He propelled him outside the mansion and didn't let him go until he had seen him safely in a hack with directions to his lodgings.

Then he returned to Gillian. He found her where he'd left her, seated on a couch. Thankfully, she was alone.

As soon as she saw him, she rose and came toward him.

"I didn't come to him. I swear it—" she pleaded.

"Don't fret. I never thought you had," he soothed her, touching her on the shoulder. "Come, sit a moment with me. The major is gone. He won't bother you anymore this evening."

When she'd regained her composure, she told him more quietly, "I had retired with a couple of other ladies to one of the rooms upstairs. When I came down, he was in the corridor, just lounging in the doorway there. He began addressing me.

"I didn't realize he'd had so much to drink, and I didn't want to make a scene, so I merely stepped in, thinking as soon as the corridor was empty, I would leave him."

"I was afraid something like this would happen," Tertius said grimly.

"Oh, Tertius, what am I going to do? I don't want to cause you any scandal. What if I see him again?"

"Don't worry your head about it. I'll take care of things."

She looked even more frightened. "Don't do anything dangerous."

He smiled. "I won't, I promise."

* * *

The following afternoon, Sky headed for the fencing academy. It was as likely a place as any to locate the major. Obviously, he needed to have a few things clarified to him.

He found him standing with a group of men who were watching a match between two of the members.

Sky walked up behind him and said quietly, "Good afternoon, Major Hawkes."

The major turned to him with a smile, which died when he saw who greeted him.

"Ah, the good Lord Skylar. Forgive my condition yesterday evening. I believe I was a little the worse for drink."

"Think nothing it of it. But it is best we keep away from the ladies when we are in such a condition," Sky returned smoothly.

The major eyed him. "My apologies to the lady. I hope I didn't alarm her unduly."

Tertius inclined his head a fraction. "Apology accepted. Let us hope it will not happen again."

"Let us hope."

"I was wondering if you would care to try your hand at another match," Tertius said, indicating the foil he held.

The major's attention had been drawn back to the other fencers and now he looked down at the weapon before meeting Sky's gaze once more.

Hawkes eyed him with a measure of amusement. "Another match?"

"Yes. You remember you had the best of me some months back. I would appreciate the opportunity to have another go."

Hawkes lifted a black eyebrow. "I heard you'd been quite

ill. Are you sure you're up to it?" he asked, only a trace of insolence evident in his dark blue eyes.

"As I heard you were wounded, we shall be evenly matched," Tertius replied, feeling the tip of his foil.

"My wound is not on my sword arm," Hawkes countered. When Skylar said nothing, he answered, "Very well, Lord Skylar. I am prepared to stop anytime you wish."

Sky gave a slight bow of his head. "That is most kind of you."

The two withdrew from the area and found an available room for their own match.

Sky knew he was still not up to form, although he'd been working out almost daily with Nigel. He asked the Lord's grace to see him through without having to forfeit the match. He had no desire to fight the major; he wanted only to defend his wife's honor.

The two men assumed position. As Tertius eyed his opponent, he felt only disdain for the man who would take a young lady's honor and then not do the gentlemanly thing and marry her.

As they moved back and forth across the floor, Sky met each thrust with a parry. But despite his wound the major was fit, and again Sky felt himself tire before he detected any signs of fatigue in his opponent.

He admired the man's stamina. After his weeks in Belgium, a wounded arm, and now a night's excessive drinking, he still fought as if his foil were an extension of his arm.

As Tertius found his own strength slipping, he asked the Lord's help to finish the match.

As he thrust his foil at the major, and took only a split second to wipe the sweat from his brow, the major immediately feinted. Tertius read his intentions correctly and parried where his thrust was intended.

They continued their silent dance back and forth.

It came to Sky, as he attempted a sudden feint and managed to trick the major with his move, that he would win. He didn't know how he was so certain, because the major showed no indication as yet of tiring, but the assurance didn't leave him.

His resolve strengthened, and he continued thrusting and parrying. Fine beads of sweat broke out on the major's wide forehead, and the look of intense concentration began to be replaced by one of desperation.

Finally, the opportunity came and with a final thrust, Sky knocked the major's foil out of his hand.

It went clattering beyond him as the major staggered backwards.

"Touché," Tertius said, his foil pressed gently against the major's heart.

"Yes, indeed," Hawkes agreed with a slight smile.

"I will only say this once," Sky told him softly. "I want you to swear to me that you will stay away from Lady Skylar. You will not address her in any way familiar nor treat her with the slightest disrespect. If not, the next time, it won't be a match fought at Angelo's but at Wimbledon Common at dawn. Is that understood?"

The major's slight smile never wavered. "You have my word as an officer and a gentleman."

Tertius raised an eyebrow. "You have fought bravely on the battlefield, but you have been no gentleman at home."

Blue eyes stared into his for a tense moment. The flash of outrage left as suddenly as it had come, replaced by a look of bleakness that caught Tertius short.

In that instant, Tertius recognized his former self. Clearly, the major was battling some demons of his own.

Tertius remembered the cries of despair that had come to him from the pit of darkness. Compassion replaced the disdain he'd felt for the major. It was a compassion so deep he was tempted to reach out to this man.

But he knew the major wouldn't accept his sympathy. Not yet. He knew better than anyone what it was to need help and not acknowledge it.

"You are right," Major Hawkes said. "I have been no gentleman. My sincerest apologies to the lady I offended." The words were spoken so softly no one but Sky would hear them.

Then the desolate look in his eyes was replaced by the air of nonchalance that had characterized the beginning of their match. Hawkes was once again the careless hero.

Sky felt a conviction to pray for him. The verse came back to him, *pray for those which despitefully use you.* How the Lord had shown him the truth of this command.

Sky withdrew his foil, and the two men stepped apart. The major wiped the sweat from his forehead with his shirtsleeve then bent to retrieve his own foil. They both rolled down their sleeves. Before they parted, Hawkes approached Sky again.

"They say the best man wins. My congratulations to you and Lady Skylar. I wish you both much happiness."

Sky bowed his head in acknowledgment.

When he came home that evening, Tertius greeted Gillian with a kiss.

"How was your day?" she asked him.

He felt a surge of gladness at the warm smile she gave him, a smile that would be there to greet him at each day's end.

"Quite satisfactory. Is anyone coming for dinner this evening?" he asked.

"No one tonight."

"And Father?"

She played with the pin in his neck cloth. "He told me he was dining at White's. He said that he had no business hanging around here with a pair of lovebirds who've scarcely had a chance to be alone together since arriving in London."

"Dear old Father," Tertius said with a chuckle.

"He *is* a dear," she insisted as Tertius took her arm and led her in to dinner.

He had planned on not telling her anything of his match with the major, but found himself saying as they walked toward the dining room, "You won't have to worry about Major Hawkes anymore."

She stopped and looked at him in alarm. "What do you mean?"

"He has apologized and promised not to seek you out again."

She frowned at him. "You fought him, didn't you? You promised me you wouldn't do anything dangerous!"

"Just a friendly sporting match at Angelo's."

"You could have been hurt," she said accusingly.

He smiled. "But I wasn't."

"You should have told me what you planned to do."

"I didn't want to worry you," he said, stopping any further comments with a kiss.

"So," he said when he could speak again, "I think we can

put the major behind us, squarely in the past, along with all the other ghosts which might have troubled us. All right?"

He smiled into her eyes, and she smiled back, telling him she understood.

"I shall never tire of the pretty way you flush when you are pleased," he told her, touching her pink cheek.

"And I shall never tire of telling you that I love you."

The words took him by surprise. "I've waited a long time to hear those words."

Her blush deepened as she admitted shyly, "I couldn't say the words until now. I didn't feel my love could be worth anything, but…since praying that prayer with you, I feel I can offer it to you."

"Oh, my dearest Gillian," he said, drawing her into his embrace, "I shall be forever grateful to God that He has given you to me."

"That He has given us to each other," she corrected. They looked at each other, acknowledging the gift of love, constant and unwavering.

Abiding love. It would endure over their past and future, over pride and petulance and bad temper. Only by loving One greater than themselves could they enjoy this kind of love.

They squeezed hands, too astounded by the miracle, the reality, of love to speak.

There they were, joined not by mutual regard or attraction or need, although those feelings played a part, but by what was stronger: they were joined as two into one by spirit, through the knowledge and partaking of God's Spirit. His Spirit would shape and deepen their love for the coming years and into all eternity.

Questions for Discussion

1) What is revealed about the hero, Lord Skylar, in the first chapter? For example, does Skylar have a good relationship with his father? How would you characterize it? What impressions do you get of Skylar's defense mechanisms?

2) Gillian takes an immediate dislike to Sky, finding him cold and arrogant. His age and recent illness are other strikes against him. What do Lord Skylar and Lady Gillian have in common? What are the advantages to marrying Lord Skylar?

3) Fear is a great motivator in Gillian's actions. What does it propel her to do? What is another motivator in her life?

4) What kind of turning point does the dog-rescue episode mark for Sky and Gillian? Which gesture went further toward softening Gillian toward Sky: the jewels he gave her or the dog collar for Sophie? Why? What did this gift, as well as his agreeing to take Sophie, reveal about his true nature?

5) When do we get hints that Sky might not be the aloof gentleman he reveals to the world, but that there is a toughness and inflexibility within?

6) When Sky's half sister, Althea, comes to nurse Sky, he rejects her love. How are the tables turned on him when Sky offers his love to his estranged wife? What valuable lessons must be learned from this?

7) During his convalescence on their Yorkshire estate, Sky believes nothing he does to Gillian changes her attitude toward him. What is the Lord doing to Gillian in the meantime? How does this involve learning to walk in faith on Sky's part?

8) Why is giving Gillian her freedom (to leave him) so important? How does this reflect God's love for us?

9) What test does Gillian subconsciously demand before she can fully trust the new Sky not to hurt her ever again?

10) What is the meaning of the last paragraph of the story, that Gillian and Sky's love is based on their partaking of God's Spirit, beyond their own mutual like, attraction and need? Why is this former love more abiding than the others?

From the author of
THE ROAD TO HOME

Vanessa Del Fabbro

Sandpiper Drift

When journalist Monica Brunetti visits the town
of Lady Helen, South Africa, she is automatically
drawn to the exquisite beauty of the land and its
people, and begins the journey of a lifetime.

Visit your local bookseller.

Steeple
Hill®

www.SteepleHill.com

SH565TR

NEW FROM AWARD-WINNING AUTHOR
DELIA PARR

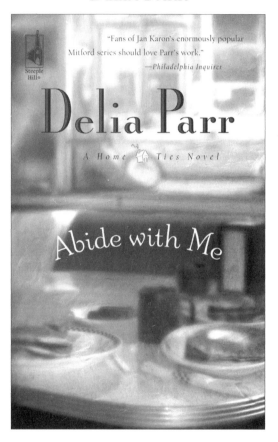

On sale September 2006

When the three Long sisters are faced with sudden critical
challenges in their lives, they must lean on each other and
let their trust and faith see them through.

Visit your local bookseller.

Steeple
Hill®

www.SteepleHill.com

SHDP569TR

Steeple
Hill
Café

New from the author of the
Christian bestseller
THE WHITNEY CHRONICLES

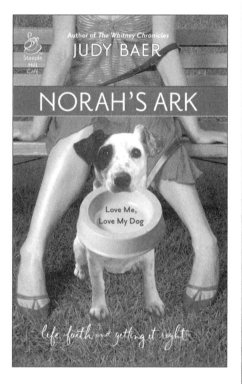

On sale September 2006

Norah won't date anyone who doesn't love her
adorable mutt, Bentley. But what happens when
Mr. Right also happens to be the only guy
terrified of Norah's lovable dog?

Steeple
Hill®

www.SteepleHill.com

Visit your local bookseller.

SHJB566TR